Praise for CHRIS RYAN:

'Gripping from the off'
Sun

'SAS hero Chris Ryan sets a cracking pace'
Lovereading

'Fast-paced action thriller
that hits all the right spots'
The Bookseller

'Chris Ryan proves, once again,
that he is a master of suspense'
Waterstones Books Quarterly

www.**totallyrandombooks**.co.uk

CHRIS RYAN
SAS HERO

- Joined the SAS in 1984, serving in military hot zones across the world.

- Expert in overt and covert operations in war zones, including Northern Ireland, Africa, the Middle East and other classified territories.

- Commander of the Sniper squad within the anti-terrorist team.

- Part of an 8-man patrol on the Bravo Two Zero Gulf War mission in Iraq.

- The mission was compromised. 3 fellow soldiers died, and 4 more were captured as POWs. Ryan was the only person to defy the enemy, evading capture and escaping to Syria on foot over a distance of 300 kilometres.

- His ordeal made history as the longest escape and evasion by an SAS trooper, for which he was awarded the Military Medal.

- His books are dedicated to the men and women who risk their lives fighting for the armed forces.

CHRIS RYAN

AGENT 21 RELOADED

RED FOX

AGENT 21
RELOADED

AGENT 21: RELOADED
A RED FOX BOOK 978 1 849 41008 3

First published in Great Britain by Red Fox,
an imprint of Random House Children's Books
A Random House Group Company
This edition published 2012

1 3 5 7 9 10 8 6 4 2

The Random House Group Limited supports The Forest Stewardship Council
(FSC), the leading international forest certification organisation. Our books
carrying the FSC label are printed on FSC certified paper. FSC is the only forest
certification scheme endorsed by the leading environmental organisations,
including Greenpeace. Our paper procurement policy can be found at
www.randomhouse.co.uk/environment

Set in Adobe Garamond by Falcon Oast Graphic Art Ltd.

Red Fox Books are published by Random House Children's Books,
61–63 Uxbridge Road, London W5 5SA
www.**kids**at**randomhouse**.co.uk
www.**totallyrandombooks**.co.uk

Addresses for companies within The Random House Group Limited
can be found at: www.randomhouse.co.uk/offices.htm

THE RANDOM HOUSE GROUP Limited Reg. No. 954009

A CIP catalogue record for this book is available from the British Library.
Printed and bound by CPI Group (UK) Ltd, Croydon, CR0 4YY

CONTENTS

AGENT 21

Real name: Zak Darke

Known pseudonyms: Harry Gold

Age: 14

Date of birth: March 27

Parents: Al and Janet Darke [DECEASED]

Operational skills: Weapons handling, navigation, excellent facility with languages, excellent computer and technical skills.

Previous operations: Inserted under cover into the compound of Mexican drug magnate Cesar Martinez Toledo. Befriended target's son Cruz. Successfully supplied evidence of target's illegal activities. Successfully guided commando team in to compound. Target eliminated.

AGENT 17

Real name: classified

Known pseudonyms: 'Gabriella', 'Gabs'

Age: 26

Operational skills: Advanced combat and self-defence, surveillance, tracking.

Currently charged with ongoing training of Agent 21 on remote Scottish island of St Peter's Crag.

AGENT 16

Real name: classified

Known pseudonyms: 'Raphael', 'Raf'

Age: 29

Operational skills: Advanced combat and self-defence, sub-aqua, land-vehicle control.

Currently charged with ongoing training of Agent 21 on remote Scottish island of St Peter's Crag.

'MICHAEL'

Real name: classified

Known pseudonyms: 'Mr Bartholomew'

Age: classified

Recruited Agent 21 after death of his
parents. Currently his handler. Has links
with MI5, but represents a classified
government agency.

ADAN RAMIREZ

Also known as: 'Calaca'

Distinguishing features: Right eye missing.
Skin grown over eye socket.

Significant information: Formerly head of
security for Cesar Martinez Toledo.
Currently holds same role for Martinez's
son and heir, Cruz. Highly dangerous.

CRUZ MARTINEZ

Age: 16

Significant information: Has succeeded Cesar
Martinez as head of largest Mexican drug
cartel. Thought to blame Agent 21 for
death of father. Highly intelligent.
Profile has remained low since coming
to power.

1

STRANGER DANGER

Sunday, 16.30 hrs GMT

There are good times and bad times to do almost everything in life. Everything, that is, except visit a grave.

Ellie Lewis always walked away from the church-yard of All Hallows in Camden feeling worse than when she arrived, with tears welling up in her eyes. She had to keep blinking and swallowing hard to keep them at bay. She was fifteen now, and shouldn't be crying in public. But somehow she couldn't stop herself visiting. Once a week – twice, sometimes – she wandered past the sheltered porch at the front of the church, through the tombstones to a quiet corner of the churchyard. Here, under an old oak tree and ten metres from the nearest grave, was a narrow mound of earth, the length of a body. And at the head end, a plain stone with two words engraved upon it: ZAK DARKE.

All the other gravestones in the churchyard contained more information than this. Date of birth and date of death at the very least. And according to their stones, the deceased were sadly missed or always in somebody's hearts. They would rest in peace.

But not Zak Darke's. Ellie remembered the argument well. Her mum and dad had been Zak's guardians after his parents died, but they had never really liked him. Never really wanted him there. When the time had come to decide which words would be carved on his headstone, they'd been stubborn. 'Each letter costs an extra seventeen pounds fifty, Ellie. We're not *made* of money, you know . . .' And so they hadn't even bothered with his full name, Zachary. It was much cheaper to keep it simple.

Her cousin's grave was not well tended. The mound of soil had only really begun to settle about nine months after the burial. Now, little tufts of grass were sprouting from it. In the summer months, Ellie would collect wild flowers and lay them over the grave. But they soon died and now the soil was covered with these withered posies. Ellie didn't have the heart to remove them. Nobody else was going to bring flowers, after all.

It was cold today. Ellie had woken to see a hard frost covering the front lawn of 63 Acacia Drive, and it hadn't disappeared all day. Now it was half-past four and it was almost fully dark as she stomped through the graveyard, her breath steaming and the cold making her fingertips sting. A priest walked out of the church and stood in the porch. As Ellie passed him, she sneezed.

'You should be in the warm, dearie,' the priest said.

Ellie just smiled at him and hurried on. In less than a minute she had made her usual way through the graveyard and was standing at Zak's final resting place.

Ellie still remembered the awful day he had disappeared. The police said he'd disturbed an intruder robbing their house. For weeks, Ellie hadn't believed them. Neither she nor her mum and dad had heard anything that night, for a start. How could all that have happened without one of them being woken? And then there had been the weird thing Zak had said to her just the day before. *Something's about to happen. Don't ask me what. I want you to know I'll be safe.*

She'd kept quiet about that, but for the longest time she'd expected Zak to reappear at any moment and offer a perfectly reasonable excuse for his disappearance. But then they'd found the corpse. A thirteen-year-old boy. Mutilated. Unrecognizable. Lying in muddy water in a ditch in Hertfordshire. Mum and Dad had tried to keep the details from her, but they couldn't stop her reading the papers. The police could only identify the remains by taking a DNA sample. The sample confirmed the body was Zak's.

The thought of it made the tears flood up in Ellie's eyes again. She missed him. *Really* missed him. She turned away from his frosty grave, wrapped her school coat more tightly around herself and stumbled back through the graveyard. Maybe, she thought to herself as she held back the tears, she should come here less often.

Because there are good times and bad times to do almost everything in life. Everything, that is, except visit a grave.

All Hallows Church was situated alongside Camden Road, a busy main street where there was always a lot of traffic. From here to 63 Acacia Drive was about a fifteen-minute walk, but Ellie didn't want to go home. Her mum and dad would be watching TV and she felt like being by herself. So instead, she walked to the centre of Camden and through the doors of Burger King. Katy Perry was playing quietly in the background. Ellie immediately saw several kids from her school gathered around a table along the left-hand wall. They were laughing loudly at something. She pretended not to see them and walked up to the counter. 'Diet Coke, please,' she asked the young man who was serving. 'Regular.'

'Very sensible, if I may say so.'

It wasn't the guy at the counter who had spoken, but somebody behind Ellie. She turned round to see a rather shabby old man. He had grey, shoulder-length hair, piercing green eyes and a stoop to his shoulders. He smelled strongly of tobacco.

'Too much sugar is very bad for you. Rots the teeth.'

'Er, right . . .' Ellie murmured as she removed some change from her purse and handed it over to the young man, who was looking at this old guy like he was some sort of nutter. 'Thanks for the advice.' She took her Coke and looked around for a table.

The raised area on the other side of the restaurant was almost empty. Most of the tables were covered with the debris of other diners' meals, but that didn't matter to Ellie. She just didn't feel like talking to anyone. Couldn't trust her voice not to wobble. There were two used cups on the table she selected, a little puddle of spilled drink – chocolate milkshake, maybe – and an empty cheeseburger wrapper, still greasy. Ellie took a sip of her Diet Coke. She saw with relief that the weird old guy had sat five tables away and wasn't paying her any attention.

Absent-mindedly, Ellie folded the cheeseburger wrapper in half, then half again, and then in half for a third time. She remembered Zak telling her once that you could never fold a piece of paper in half more than seven times, no matter how big it was. He was clever about stuff like that. Ellie was on the fifth fold when she realized a man had approached her table.

What is it with everyone today? she thought to herself. *Why can't they just leave me alone?*

She looked up to see a tall man so skinny that she briefly wondered when he had last eaten. His hair was shaved but his chin wasn't – he had a good three or four days' stubble – and he wore jeans that looked too big for him and a shapeless white T-shirt. The most noticeable thing about him, though, was the patch over his right eye. It was attached to his head by a thin piece of black cord and reminded Ellie of a pirate's outfit she'd had in her dressing-up box when she was very small.

The stranger was staring at her and Ellie felt uncomfortable. She took a slurp of her Diet Coke and stood up, but the stranger wasn't having it. 'Sit down,' he said under his breath. He dug his bony fingertips into Ellie's shoulder and pushed her down into her plastic seat.

'Hey!' Ellie gasped. 'Get off me – that hurt!' She looked over to where her schoolmates were sitting. None of them had noticed what was going on and she almost shouted out to them. But something stopped her. A photograph.

The man with the eye patch had dropped it onto

the table. It landed at an angle to Ellie and one corner blotted up the puddle of spilled milkshake. It wasn't a very good picture. It looked like it had been taken from a distance, then enlarged and cropped. As a result it was grainy and slightly out of focus. It showed a young man with unruly hair and a serious face. He was wearing a hooded top and his face was somehow leaner – somehow *older* – than when Ellie had seen him last.

Which had been just a few hours before he'd disappeared.

The skinny man with the eye patch was sitting opposite her now. His hands were palm down on the dirty table and his good eye managed to look straight through her. It wasn't a nice sensation.

Silence.

Ellie stared at the photograph. The skinny man stared at Ellie.

'You know this boy?'

His accent was foreign. Spanish, maybe? Ellie wasn't very good at languages.

She couldn't stop looking at the photograph. 'Of course I know him,' she said. She dragged her eyes away. 'Who *are* you?'

The man didn't answer immediately. He picked up the photograph and hid it inside his coat before staring at Ellie again.

'Where is he?'

'What do you mean?' Ellie whispered. Was this some kind of horrible joke?

'I don't like it,' the man replied quietly, 'when people pretend they don't understand me.'

'I wasn't—'

'My question was very simple. Where is he?'

For the second time that day, Ellie felt the tears coming and she was angry with herself because of it. Who *was* this man? What *right* did he have to ask her questions like that.

She stood up. 'He's in the same place he's been for the last eighteen months,' she hissed. 'All Hallows Church. And *you* . . . you should be ashamed of yourself.'

But if the stranger did feel any shame, he didn't show it. As Ellie stormed away from the table towards the exit, she looked over her shoulder to see him sitting there, quite calmly, watching her leave. There was something about him that made her flesh prickle. She couldn't wait to get away from him. To get home, where she could lock her bedroom door firmly behind her.

It had started to snow outside. Ellie didn't care. She ran through the wintry night all the way back to number 63 Acacia Drive.

* * *

In Burger King, the man with the eye patch sat quite still, his palms still face down on the table. He was breathing very slowly and the veins on either side of his Adam's apple were pulsing. He didn't look pleased.

'Would you like a French fry? They're a little salty, but quite delicious.'

The man with the patch looked round. Standing a metre behind him he saw a much older man with shoulder-length grey hair, penetrating green eyes and a pronounced stoop. He popped a chip into his mouth, munched it thoughtfully and offered the paper carton containing the remainder.

'Go away, old man.'

But the old man didn't go away. He pointed at the seat Ellie had vacated. 'Do you mind? My legs aren't what they used to be.' He sat down without waiting for permission and smiled broadly.

The smile was not returned.

'Bartholomew's the name. Very pleased to meet you. Sweet girl, that. Be a shame if anything happened to her. A great shame. Are you sure you won't have one?'

No reply. No movement.

'Still,' the older man continued, 'I'm sure that won't happen. That family's had more than its fair share of bad luck.' His smile grew broader. 'I couldn't help noticing that you showed the young lady a

9

photograph.' He popped another chip into his mouth. 'Would you care to share it with me?'

The skinny man stood up rather suddenly. 'You should be careful, Mr Bartholomew, who you interfere with.'

'Oh, you needn't worry about that. I'm a very careful person.'

The one-eyed man turned his back on the newcomer and marched straight for the exit. He stopped at the door and looked back towards the old man, before smiling an unpleasant smile. Very slowly he raised the forefinger of his right hand up to his neck and made a slicing movement. Then he opened the door and walked out into the darkness and the snow.

Mr Bartholomew watched him go. For a full minute after the skinny man had left the restaurant he barely moved, other than to wipe his salty fingers with a paper napkin. Then he too stood up. The stoop in his back had disappeared. If his legs truly weren't as good as they used to be, he must have been quite an athlete in his youth, because now he walked out of Burger King with the gait of a man half his age.

It was half-past two in the morning. Ellie stared at the red glow of her alarm clock as she lay in bed. There was no way she could sleep. Her mind was full of the man with the eye patch and of the picture he had shown her.

Full of questions.

Full of fear.

How had he known to find her in Burger King? She hadn't even planned to go there. Which meant he *must* have been following her. And where did he get that picture of Zak? *When* did he get it? Ellie's cousin looked older than he ever had when he was alive, but that was impossible, wasn't it? She shivered as she lay there, and not just because she was cold.

Five to three. Absolute silence. Ellie crept out of bed and got dressed. Thick socks. Jeans. Two jumpers. Gloves. A woollen hat. A few minutes later she was tiptoeing downstairs, holding her breath and praying that her mum and dad wouldn't wake up.

In the dining room at the bottom of the stairs, she jumped. There was a noise. A mechanical whirring sound. Ellie swallowed hard, then realized what it was. Her parents had bought a cuckoo clock just a couple of weeks ago. They were delighted with it, and cooed with pleasure every time the little bird emerged from its cubbyhole and tweeted the time. 'Look, Ellie!' they kept saying, talking to her like she was a little kid. 'The cuckoo!' They hadn't seemed to notice that she was a bit old to be excited by babyish things like that.

The cuckoo cheeped now. Three times. Three

o'clock. It returned to its cubbyhole with another whirr.

Ellie left the house through the back door because she knew it would make less noise than the front when she opened and closed it. Two minutes later she was stomping to the end of Acacia Drive, her footprints the only ones in the thick layer of snow that had fallen that night.

What on earth was she doing? She didn't even know. She'd never left the house in the middle of the night before. Her mum and dad would go nuts. Somehow, though, her feet knew which way to take her.

It started to blizzard as she walked along Camden Road. There were hardly any cars outside at this time of night. A bus edged down the road, but it moved slower than Ellie because of the snow. On the other side of the road she saw two policemen, the collars of their bright yellow jackets turned up against the cold. Ellie pulled her woollen hat further down over her ears and walked a bit more quickly.

It was ten minutes before she reached All Hallows and by now the snow was falling heavier than ever. Only the inside of the porch remained uncovered. She could barely see ten metres ahead of her and the spire of the church was lost in the snowy darkness. But Ellie could have found her way blindfolded. She walked round the side of the church and into the graveyard at the back.

The tombstones all had ten centimetres of virgin snow settled on the top. There was a muffled silence all around. A rustling to her left and she saw the glinting eyes of an urban fox. It stared bravely at her for a few seconds and quickly scampered away, leaving a trail of tiny footprints. Ellie walked on, her feet crunching as she disturbed the new snow, weaving her way through the tombstones towards the oak tree that she knew so well.

She was fifty metres from the church – about half-way to the oak tree – when she stopped.

All of a sudden, hers were not the only footprints. Ellie bent down to examine the tracks. She could just make out, she thought, three different sets of prints. Human prints, this time. They were all heading in the direction she wanted to go. Towards the oak tree.

Towards Zak.

She kept very still. In the distance, muffled because of the snow, she could hear voices. And was that the flash of a torch?

Ellie squinted up ahead but she could see nothing through the blizzard or the darkness. She wanted to hide, but her tracks in the snow were a dead giveaway. They would lead anyone to her and something told her that would be a very bad thing. She looked around, feeling stuck, and it was only after thirty seconds that the idea came to her.

Walking backwards wasn't easy. She needed to insert her feet exactly into the footprints she'd already made and it was difficult to keep her balance. It took two minutes to get back to the front of the church, where she was able to jump across into the sheltered porch where there was no snow. It was very dark here and there were two deep benches along either side of the porch. She hid underneath the right-hand one, her back against the wall, her right arm and right leg pressed against the cold stone, and waited.

She didn't have to wait long.

Ellie couldn't see the men, but she could hear them as they approached. They spoke in low voices and in a language she couldn't understand, but which immediately put her in mind of the accented man in Burger King. They were right outside the porch now. Any second and they'd be gone—

'Ah-*choo!*' Ellie's sneeze took her by surprise.

'*Shhhh!*' The men fell silent.

Ellie heard the crunching of feet in the snow. The sound of shoes on stone. In the darkness she could only just see a pair of legs walking into the porch. Her eyes followed the legs further up. She saw a hand hanging by the figure's side. And in the hand . . . it looked like a gun.

She lay as still as a statue, holding her breath. *Go away!* she begged silently. *Get away from me!* But the figure didn't go away. There was no movement in the porch for thirty seconds. No sound.

A voice from outside. '*Que es?*'

No reply. The figure turned round but didn't leave. Ellie felt another sneeze coming. Someone had told her once that if you pressed your tongue very hard against the roof of your mouth, you could stop yourself sneezing. She tried it. Seconds later the sensation went away.

And so did the legs, moving slowly away from the porch and out of view.

'*Vamos,*' a voice said. The footsteps crunched away into nothingness.

Ellie barely dared emerge from her hiding place. When, after ten minutes of silence, she finally found the courage, the cold had seeped into her bones. It was hard to move quickly. A little voice told her she should go straight home, but deep down she knew that wasn't happening. She retraced her steps and a minute later the hulking form of the oak tree came into view through the blizzard. And under the oak tree, Zak's grave.

She could tell something was wrong even from a distance. It wasn't just that the snow had been disturbed around the grave. There was now a mound of earth piled up to one side. The blizzard was settling lightly on it, but as Ellie approached she could see that this was fresh soil.

Newly dug.

Her senses screamed at her to run but her limbs refused to obey. She walked towards the grave like she was in a dream, unable to turn back. Ten seconds later she was staring at the full horror of it.

The hole in the ground was more than a metre deep. Ellie couldn't see the bottom because it was too dark. She *could* see, however, a coffin lid, all hacked and splintered. It was lying on the side of the hole opposite the soil and had clearly been prised away. There was a dreadful smell, like meat that had gone past its sell-by date. It made Ellie want to retch but she managed not to. She just stood there and stared into the darkness of the grave, her breath and her body trembling.

And after two minutes of staring, she removed her mobile phone from her pocket.

It was nothing fancy, this phone – an old Nokia that had been cool once, but wasn't any more. A bit like Ellie herself. Weird, the difference a year could make. But the phone would serve its purpose tonight. She pressed a button at random and the screen lit up. Ellie kneeled down, stretched out her arm and held her improvised torch into the grave. Immediately she wished she hadn't.

She'd never seen a dead body before, let alone a corpse that had been mouldering for months. She had never seen the way the lips rotted away to reveal bare teeth, the eyelids to reveal the remains of the eyes in their sockets. She had never seen the paper-thin remnants of skin on the face, or the lazy movement of a fat worm on the forehead, disturbed by the light.

Ellie jumped with fright. And as she jumped, she dropped her phone. It fell into the grave and a couple of seconds later the light went out of its own accord. Ellie wasn't there to see it happen, though. She was already running, back through the graveyard, past the church, up Camden Road and into Acacia Drive, slipping in the snow, sobbing, and with tears burning down her face. The house was still silent as she made her trembling, terrified way back upstairs, undressed and hid beneath the warmth and safety of her duvet.

Even as she warmed up, though, she continued to shake. Who had the three men in the churchyard that night been? Why did one of them have a gun? And why – why on *earth* – had they seen fit to dig up her dead cousin's grave?

2

DEAD MEN CAN'T HURT YOU

Monday, 10.03 hrs GMT

Graves, Zak Darke thought to himself, were scary enough places at the best of times. When they were sixty metres below sea level they were even worse. And as watery graves went, this was one of the biggest.

'HMS *Vanguard*,' his dive buddy Raf had told him the day before as they'd sat eating steak pie for dinner. 'It sank a hundred years ago at Scapa Flow.'

'Scapa Flow?' Zak had asked. The name sounded familiar.

Raf was a serious man with a square face and thick blond hair. They'd first met when he had expertly kidnapped Zak from 63 Acacia Drive. Or perhaps 'kidnapped' wasn't the right word. The orphaned Zak had gone with him willingly, after all. The decision to be plucked from his ordinary life to work for a government agency so secret he didn't even know its name was Zak's alone, even if he had been talked into it by a grey-haired man who sometimes called himself Michael, sometimes Mr Bartholomew – neither of which, Zak knew, was his real name. That night he had stopped being Zak Darke and become Agent 21. Serious and silent, Raf had escorted him here, to the bleak, windswept island of St Peter's Crag – a place that had frightened Zak not because it was so solitary, but because it was impossible to leave.

At first, Zak had felt nothing but anger towards his abductors: they had not been honest with him; they had spirited him away under false pretences. Gradually, though, he had come to realize that their only concern was for his welfare in the dangerous situations Agent 21 would find himself; and that St Peter's Crag itself, far from being an inescapable prison, was for Zak the safest place on earth.

Gradually, the anger he had felt towards his kidnapper had turned into respect. And the respect had turned into a kind of friendship. Zak's life had changed completely in the last eighteen months. For the better? It was difficult to say, but it was certainly a lot more dangerous. He knew that Raf would always look out for him and that was something comforting to hold on to.

'A hundred and twenty square miles of water off Orkney,' Raf explained. 'Natural harbour. The British used it as their naval base during both world wars. HMS *Vanguard* sank at anchor there in 1917.'

'How come?'

'Engine explosion. Eight hundred men on board.'

'That sounds awful.'

'More than awful,' Raf replied. 'If you go on board any modern ship you'll see all sorts of fire precaution measures. The last thing you want is a fire at sea. There's nowhere to hide. The men on board HMS *Vanguard* would have died a nasty death. Hope you're not squeamish because we'll probably bump into some of them tomorrow. What's left of them, anyway.'

'Raf!' Zak's second dinner companion had interrupted. 'Don't fill his head with things like that. Really, sweetie, you mustn't listen to him . . .'

Gabs had white-blond, shoulder-length hair and icy blue eyes. Along with Raf, she was Zak's almost constant companion here on the bleak, solitary island of St Peter's Crag that he now called home. They were his teachers and his friends. His big brother and sister. His Guardian Angels.

Zak – whose muscles burned and who was ravenous after his day's training – swallowed a mouthful of food. 'Dead men can't hurt you,' he replied quietly. And he thought to himself, *It's the living ones you have to worry about.* But he didn't say that out loud. Instead he looked up at Gabs and grinned at her. 'I could take some photos down there if you like.'

Gabs had rolled her eyes dramatically. 'Men!' she said. 'Slugs and snails and puppy-dogs' tails – I don't know why you can't be more like us girls.'

'HMS *Vanguard* is a designated war grave,' Raf had continued as though he hadn't heard any of this. 'Only members of the British armed forces are allowed to dive there.'

'Members of the British armed forces, and us – right?'

'He's getting the hang of this, isn't he?' Gabs said to nobody in particular.

'*Vanguard*'s a good place to practise diving in enclosed spaces,' Raf continued. 'Plenty of . . . unexpected stuff.'

'What do you mean?'

Raf had given him one of his rare smiles. 'If I told you,' he said, 'it wouldn't be unexpected, would it? When you're on ops, you're not likely to be snorkelling in the Caribbean. You need to be confident with difficult sub-aqua environments.' When Raf said difficult, Zak knew he *meant* difficult. His Guardian Angels were meticulously training him in the skills he needed, with little or no respect for his young age. Neither Raf nor Gabs had ever said it, but Zak knew it was true: if he was old enough to die, he was old enough to learn how to avoid death.

Sub-aqua skills would be yet another string to his bow.

That had been yesterday. Now it was just past 10 a.m. Zak and Raf were dressed in black drysuits with neoprene hoods – essential in this cold weather to stop their body temperature dropping too quickly. Over the drysuits they wore inflatable vests. Their fins and dive masks were military grade and they each carried a matt black canister of compressed air on their backs. Both of them had a diver's knife attached to their legs and a powerful torch that lit up the murky underwater world with an eerie glow.

The depth gauge on Zak's Panerai diver's watch told him they were ten metres from the surface. They'd been descending slowly – about a metre every ten seconds – and Zak could feel the pressure building up in his ears. He pinched his nose and blew gently to equalize it, then shone his torch up towards the surface. He could just make out the hull of the vessel from which they'd dived – a rigid inflatable boat with a forty-horsepower outboard motor that had been launched half an hour ago from the sixty-foot *Galileo*, a luxurious yacht that wouldn't have looked out of place moored in Monte Carlo. Only smaller boats were allowed in the vicinity of HMS *Vanguard*. It was good to know that Gabs was waiting for them in that RIB.

A tap on his shoulder. Raf was pointing downwards. Zak nodded at him and they continued to descend.

The water grew colder and darker. He shivered. There was no noise down here. Other than the sound of Zak inhaling compressed air through his breathing apparatus, there was just a thick, icy silence. Zak followed Raf, who was kicking confidently downwards, his torch casting a cone of light towards the sea bed. A school of tiny fish with rainbow scales shot across the beam. There were thousands of them, moving bullet-fast. They changed direction all at the same time. Seconds later they were gone.

More pressure in his ears. Zak equalized again. He continued to descend. The depth gauge read thirty-five metres.

Forty metres.

Forty-five metres.

Something came into view.

It was just a shape at first. A gloomy, ghostly silhouette. Through his dive mask, Zak made out an enormous sharp V with rounded edges. It took a couple of moments for him to realize he was looking at the very tip of a battleship. He followed Raf towards the bow of the ship and as they drew close, he gradually understood how big HMS *Vanguard* was. There was no way he could see the bottom of the hull or the other end of the vessel. It was sitting on the sea bed at a thirty-degree angle like an enormous sleeping monster. Its hull and decks were corroded now, with holes here and there, but Zak could see it must have been an impressive sight when it was above water. They swam along its length – ten metres, twenty metres, thirty metres – and the main body of the ship hulked above them, so vast that Zak's powerful torch could only light up the smallest sections of it at any one time.

Raf headed left and they found themselves floating half a metre above the deck. In front of them was a doorway. The door itself had corroded away from its hinges and was lying on the deck. Zak shone his torch into the opening.

He started when he saw a pair of eyes staring back at him. What was it? What was looking at them? The eyes were ten metres away and coming closer . . .

The fish that emerged from the doorway five seconds later was like nothing Zak had ever seen, even though he'd been studying books on marine life to prepare for this dive. It was at least a couple of metres long and its eyes were the size of grapefruits, and just as bulbous. It swished lazily through the doorway and its tail fin brushed against Zak's arm as it passed him before disappearing into the murky depths. Raf looked over his shoulder and gave him a thumbs-up sign. Zak returned it and together they kicked through the doorway and into the body of the ship, lighting the way with their powerful torches.

They found themselves in a narrow corridor, very cramped. Because of the angle of the vessel, the corridor was tilting downwards. Some kind of seaweed was growing like lichen over the walls. They passed through clouds of plankton that misted their vision for a few seconds at a time, then the corridor turned to the right. They hit a flight of steps going down. Raf and Zak followed this stairwell into the hull of the ship.

They passed through another doorway and finally found themselves in what looked like the engine room. There was debris everywhere – chunks of metal, bits of old machinery – and Zak could tell that the explosion that had sunk HMS *Vanguard* had occurred here. He kicked deeper into the room and the light of his torch fell on something else. At first he thought it was another sea creature, resting on the floor of the ship. It was only when he kicked himself closer that he realized he was looking at the deathly grimace of a skull. Grimly fascinated, he swam nearer.

And his body almost went into shock when he saw the skull move.

Zak immediately kicked away and he felt a bit foolish doing so. He told himself that it was just the underwater currents he and Raf were creating that had caused the skull to move. *Dead men can't hurt you.* Now, though, his attention was elsewhere. He shone his torch up and down, left and right. And everywhere he looked, everywhere he turned, there were skeletons.

There was no way he could count them. The bodies of the dead sailors were still partially covered in the ragged remains of their clothes, but they had been stripped of flesh. Was that because fish had nibbled away at them, or had they rotted away of their own accord? Zak didn't know. His torch lit up the bones of a man lying on his back. His jaw and teeth were fixed in a horrific smile and Zak started as a small silvery fish darted out from behind his ribcage. Bizarrely, he remembered the fish tank his mum and dad had before they died. The little goldfish there had hidden behind ceramic rocks, not human remains.

A tap on his shoulder. Raf was there. He pointed deeper into the cabin. Zak gave him a thumbs-up and together they kicked off.

Suddenly the calmness of that underwater grave disappeared. There was a frenzy of movement. Something had appeared from the murky darkness. Fast, terrifying – several of them, their bodies three metres long, snake-like and muscular. In the split second it took the creatures to approach, Zak was able to identify them. The small eyes, the long dorsal fin, the patterned skin – these were giant moray eels. One of them opened its mouth as it approached. The light from Zak's torch reflected off its sharp teeth; he felt himself shrink away from that horrific sight, and maybe it was this that saved him.

Raf wasn't so lucky.

Zak couldn't tell if the moray eel bit his dive buddy because it was scared or if it thought he was food. It didn't matter either way. It was a vicious attack. The eel bit hard, holding the flesh in its jaws for at least ten seconds and writhing viciously as it did so. Raf's reaction was instantaneous. The mouthpiece of his breathing apparatus shot from his face. Bubbles spurted upwards, and a second stream of bubbles rose from Raf's mouth. There was no sound, but Zak could tell he was shouting in pain.

The eel was still there, still biting. Zak raised his arm and tried to strike at it with his torch, but the water slowed his movements and the blow barely had any effect. When the eel finally swam away, it was on its own terms.

There was blood pumping from the wound, making a dark cloud in the water around Raf's arm. But worse, Raf wasn't moving. His eyes were closed and he was making no attempt to put the breathing apparatus back into his mouth. He was floating helplessly and had dropped his torch, which was now sinking to the bottom of the cabin.

He must have ingested a lungful of water, and he was clearly unconscious. Not breathing. And sixty metres below sea level.

Zak stared through his dive mask in horror. His Guardian Angel was in real trouble. If Zak didn't do something right now, Raf had only minutes to live.

3

GALILEO

Zak moved quickly. He needed to get Raf to the surface. Fast.

He pulled his knife from the scabbard round his right leg and swam up to his mate. Raf's air tank was useless now, so Zak cut it away to reduce his body mass. The tank drifted silently down to the floor of the engine room, along with Raf's torch. It landed on the remains of one of HMS *Vanguard*'s long-dead crew. By now Zak had already moved behind Raf. He put his arms round his waist and pulled him towards the stairwell, still holding the torch in his right hand.

They moved so slowly. Raf was heavy, the water felt like treacle and Zak had to swim backwards up the stairwell. He was only halfway up when he felt his air canister bang against the corner of a metal step. It sent a shock right through him and he dropped his torch.

Zak's only source of light drifted downwards.

Panic. There wasn't time to get it back. Not if Raf

was going to have a chance. He would just have to brave the darkness.

And he had never known darkness like it. By the time he was at the top of the stairwell and pulling Raf into the corridor, he might as well have been blind. He tried not to think about how much water was above him, or about the vicious, sharp-jawed eels that could be anywhere. He just kicked as hard as he could. His muscles burned as he struggled with the dead weight of Raf's heavy body. When the water grew slightly warmer he knew he was passing back through a cloud of plankton. But he'd lost all sense of distance and time. How far had he come? How long had Raf been out? A minute? Two? More? He just didn't know . . .

Zak couldn't tell when he emerged from HMS *Vanguard*. He just knew that one moment there were slimy walls around him, the next there were none. Were they in open sea? Was there anything above them? Which way was up? All these questions tumbled through his mind as he breathed heavily, gulping air in through his breathing system. Trying not to panic, he gripped hold of Raf even harder because he knew that if he let go now, his friend was a goner.

And when he was sure he had a good hold on him, he pulled the rip cord on his own inflatable vest. Compressed air shot sharply into it. One second later they were moving.

Don't let go, Zak told himself. *Don't let go!*

The speed with which they rose to the top was frightening. Like a parachute drop in reverse. Zak felt the water rushing past his ears as he gripped Raf even harder. Water rushed into his nose and he forced himself to breathe out as hard as he could to stop it rushing into his lungs. Seconds later, they crashed through the surface of the water.

After the silence, the noise up here was almost deafening. The wind was screaming and the waves, which were half a metre high, crashed against each other. Zak spat out his mouthpiece and looked around. He was desperately trying to find the RIB, but he couldn't see it at first because of the swell of the sea. When he finally did catch a glimpse of the small black launch bobbing on the horizon it was only for a couple of seconds and it seemed horribly far away – maybe thirty metres. He started shouting. '*Gabs! Gabs! Over here!*' But he wasn't at all sure that he could be heard against the elements.

He had to think about Raf. Think of all the first-aid techniques his Guardian Angels had taught him during his months of training. Raf needed CPR – rescue breaths and possibly chest compressions. He needed to be put into the recovery position so the water could drain from his system. And it needed to happen now, before he sustained brain damage and death. None of this could happen in the water, though. He *had* to get to the boat, but he couldn't see it again. Where was it? *Where was it?*

'*Gabs! Over he—*'

Suddenly she was there. The motor of the RIB caused an extra swell to crash over Zak's head, but then he felt Gabs's strong arms pulling him and Raf towards the boat. 'Help me get him in!' she shouted. Zak did what he could to lift Raf out of the water, but he was suddenly feeling weak and dizzy and Gabs had to take the bulk of the weight. She managed it, though, and five seconds later had Raf in the boat.

'He needs CPR!' Zak shouted, but Gabs was already on it. As Zak scrambled up over the side of the RIB, he saw that she had Raf flat on his back, was pinching his nose and blowing a rescue breath into his mouth. She did this twice, then laid her hands, one on top of the other, over his chest and pressed down sharply thirty times.

'Is he going to be OK?' Zak gasped. He struggled to remove his air canister and felt like the RIB was spinning.

'You need to keep calm, Zak. Tell me what symptoms you get.' Her face was deadly serious as she leaned over and gave Raf another two rescue breaths. *Symptoms? What was she talking about?*

A river of salt water exploded from Raf's mouth

and he started coughing violently. Zak felt a wave of relief. It didn't last long. The dizziness was getting worse. His muscles had started to ache and there was a horrible itchiness all over his skin. 'Er, Gabs,' he said weakly. 'I'm really not feeling great.'

But Gabs was already moving. She'd pushed herself to the rear of the RIB and was knocking the outboard motor into drive. 'What is it?'

'I feel kind of . . .' He realized he was slurring his words.

'You decompressed too quickly,' she shouted. 'We've got to get you to *Galileo*. Now.'

The RIB shot through the water, bouncing up and down on the waves. Zak grabbed hold of one of the row locks on the side and gripped it as hard as he could. Which wasn't that hard. Everything was spinning and it was nothing to do with the violent movement of the boat. When he'd been sixty metres below sea level and needed to get Raf to the surface, he hadn't given decompression a moment's thought. Before he'd arrived on St Peter's Crag, he'd heard about 'the bends' but it had only been when Raf had started teaching him to dive that he'd learned how dangerous decompression sickness was. 'At the bottom of the sea, the gas you breathe is under pressure. Come back to the surface too quickly and the gas forms bubbles in your body.'

'What happens then?'

'Physical pain. Disorientation. Paralysis. Death. Depends how bad you get it.'

And Zak didn't need a doctor on board to know he had it bad. He could feel his joints swelling up; thirty seconds later he realized he couldn't move his arms and legs. He tried to call out to Gabs, but now he found he couldn't speak at all. He collapsed onto the bottom of the RIB, his eyes closed.

The boat bounced up and down, salty spray showering over him. Zak remembered being a little boy – his dad used to play a game that involved bouncing him up and down on his knee. But his dad was dead. His mum too. Killed by a man named Martinez. In a corner of Zak's failing mind, he saw a face. A girl about a year older than himself. Ellie. He wished he could see her one more time, before he died . . .

He knew he was about to join his parents, wherever they were . . .

Noise. Shouting. Zak was too out of it to know whose voices they were or what they were saying. He felt hands on his body – strong hands, pulling him out of the RIB, which was listing against the side of a larger vessel. *Galileo?* It *had* to be. The pain was even worse now. His hand felt like it would burst. He tried to open his eyes but there was no strength left in him. He was limp.

Useless.

Everything was dark.

It was dark when he awoke too. He lay without moving for a few seconds, trying to work out where he was. He was lying on his back, his arms by his side. When he raised his hand, his knuckle rapped against something solid. It was only a few centimetres from his body.

Like a coffin.

Zak panicked. Where was he? How long had he been unconscious? He remembered being in the RIB, wondering if he was about to die.

He started banging on the walls. 'Let me out! *Let me out of here!*' His voice was deadened by the enclosed space, and the banging of his hands against the wall echoed back at him. It was a hollow, metallic sound.

Metallic.

Zak lay still. Nobody, he realized, was buried in a metallic coffin. He felt himself rocking slightly. Like he was still at sea. Seconds later, it dawned on him what his metal coffin actually was – one of two small decompression chambers aboard *Galileo*. Gabs had got him there in time. His thoughts immediately turned to Raf. Was he OK? Had Zak dragged him out of the wreck of HMS *Vanguard* quickly enough? Was he decompressing too?

Time had no meaning in that tiny, cramped space so Zak didn't know how long it was before the top half of the decompression chamber opened up. Light flooded in, half blinding him, and he was aware of two figures standing over him. He blinked and rubbed his eyes.

'Raf?' he asked.

A pause.

'Raf is still decompressing, Agent 21,' said a man's voice. 'When he emerges, I rather think he'll want to shake you by the hand. That was quite something you managed down there.'

Zak pushed himself up into a sitting position. Although he still felt a bit dizzy, his vision was clearing and he could make out the man's features. Shoulder-length grey hair. Green eyes. And the faint aroma of cherry tobacco that always reminded Zak of the first time he'd met this man, back when he was pretending his name was Mr Bartholomew.

'*Michael?*'

They were definitely on the deck of *Galileo*. The decompression chamber in which Zak was sitting was a cylinder about two metres in length and there was a second one alongside it. The sky beyond the deck was as grey and unwelcoming as the sea. He looked around, searching for another vessel or a chopper, because Michael hadn't been on board when they'd started diving. 'How did you get here?'

'I confess,' said Michael evasively, 'that it wasn't entirely straightforward. And you know how I hate to interrupt your training schedule, but I'm afraid I had no choice.' He gave a bland smile. 'It's good to see you looking so well, Zak. When Gabriella told me what happened this morning, I thought you might be feeling a little peaky. And . . . ah . . . please don't take this the wrong way, but it would have been a frightful nuisance if you had been disabled or . . . or anything. Something's come up, you see – and we really don't have any time to lose.'

4

BLACK WOLF

13.25 hrs GMT

Thirty minutes later, Zak was in one of the small cabins below decks. He changed out of his drysuit and into his trademark jeans and hooded top, then went back up onto deck, where he saw Raf, now also out of his decompression chamber. His dive buddy was sitting with his back to the railings, a first-aid box next to him. His face was white and there were dark rings under his eyes. He looked about as well as Zak felt after this morning's scare. He had cut away the right-hand sleeve of his drysuit to reveal a nasty triangular wound in his forearm where the moray eel had bitten him. In his left hand he held a hypodermic needle and was injecting himself just an inch from the wound. He looked up. 'Tetanus booster,' he said shortly, before turning his attention back to the wound.

Zak nodded, suppressing a wave of sickness, before glancing around to see where Michael was.

'Hey, Zak.' Raf was looking at him again and giving him one of his slightly crooked smiles. 'I owe you. You must have moved pretty quick.'

Zak smiled back. 'You're the one who taught me to dive,' he replied.

'Not like that. It takes most people years of training to get to the stage where they can keep a cool head under pressure *and* underwater. I'll be teaching you STARS extractions in high sea states next if you carry on like this.'

'STARS extractions?'

Raf had a little twinkle in his eye. 'Surface-to-air recovery system. We stick a harness on you that has a special inflatable balloon on a cord. The balloon rises up into the air and a Hercules flies along with a clamp at the front, grabs the cord and takes you with it. Not used too often these days because helicopters can normally do the job just as well.' He grinned. 'It's exhilarating, though, if you like that sort of thing.'

Zak grimaced. 'I can think of other words for it.'

'Ah, well,' Raf replied. 'Maybe it's one for another day.'

Zak found Michael back inside, sitting alone at the bridge. It was a comfortable cabin with a large, burnished-wood steering wheel — useless at the moment because the bank of on-board navigation computers were on autopilot, taking *Galileo* back to St Peter's Crag. Michael was staring thoughtfully out to sea.

'I didn't expect to see you today,' Zak said. How the older man had got here, in the middle of the ocean, was anyone's guess.

'It would be a good idea, Zak, if you learned to expect the unexpected. In our line of work, things rarely happen to a fixed schedule.'

Just like Michael to be evasive. He was the one who had recruited Zak in the first place. Plucked him from his ordinary life and dropped him into a world of danger. Turned him from Zak Darke into Agent 21. It was Michael who, just six months before, had sent Zak to Mexico to bring down a notorious drug dealer called Cesar Martinez Toledo by getting close to his son, Cruz. At least, that's what Zak had originally believed, but he had soon found out that Señor Martinez had been responsible for the mass murder that had killed his parents. With Michael, there was always more than met the eye. Raf and Gabs looked up to him and so, Zak supposed, did he. But sometimes he wished the older man could just give him a straight answer.

'You said you wanted to talk to me?'

Michael didn't move. 'Take a seat,' he said. 'Make

yourself comfortable. I want you to take a look at something.'

There was a low cushioned bench along one side of the bridge. Zak sat there as Michael rooted around in his pocket for a moment, like he was searching for loose change. He pulled out something the shape of two pyramids stuck together at their bases. It was opaque, like an ice cube only smaller, but heavier than Zak would have expected when he took hold of it.

'Know what it is?' Michael asked.

'Looks like glass,' Zak replied.

'More valuable than glass, Zak. A lot more valuable. That's an uncut diamond. Value on the open market? About one hundred thousand US dollars.'

A lot of money for such a small thing. But money didn't really mean much to Zak any more.

'That diamond was mined in Angola, West Africa,' Michael continued. 'Angola is the site of some of the world's biggest diamond mines. But it's a war-torn place. Decades of civil war. In most diamond-producing countries, the sale of raw diamonds is strictly regulated. In Angola, things are a little more . . . lax. I'll take that back now, Zak, if you wouldn't mind. I'd be most unpopular if it were to get mislaid.'

Zak handed the diamond back to his handler and waited for Michael to continue.

'Because parts of Angola are so lawless, it's a haven

for terrorist groups. Many of these groups are very rich. Their money, however, comes from highly illegal sources.'

'Like what?' Zak asked.

Michael shrugged. 'Drugs. Gun-running. The usual. Do you understand what money laundering is, Zak?'

'I think so. Is it when criminals take money that they've stolen or whatever, and then put it into proper businesses.'

'Exactly that. They declare it. They pay tax on it. The dirty money becomes clean. The Angolan diamond trade is a very good way of laundering money. Many of the mine owners ask no questions when they sell their raw diamonds. A criminal organization can simply use their dirty money to buy diamonds in Angola, export them to the diamond markets of the West and sell them on. Hey presto! Not only clean money, but also a profit.'

'Clever,' Zak said.

'Oh yes, Zak. That's the thing about terrorists. The good ones, at least. They're very clever. Which means we have to be a little bit cleverer.' He gave Zak a knowing look. 'By "we", of course, what I really mean is "you".'

Zak looked out through the windows of the bridge across the grey, desolate sea. 'Go on,' he said.

'MI6 have been monitoring one particular terrorist

group very closely. They call themselves Black Wolf. Most organizations of this sort commit atrocities to make a point. Sometimes it's religious, sometimes it's political. But there's always a reason behind their actions, Zak. Always an ideology. They say that one man's terrorist is another man's freedom fighter. I wouldn't go that far, but I can tell you this: Black Wolf are different. The only thing they're interested in is money. If another terrorist group wants an atrocity committed in their name, Black Wolf will carry it out for them. If the price is right, of course.'

'Of course,' Zak replied. He felt a bit sick and it wasn't just the after-effects of his decompression.

'Today is Monday. This Thursday, a ship called the MV *Mercantile* is due to make port in Lobambo on the coast of Angola. It's a small village with a natural harbour, normally just used by local fishing vessels. The *Mercantile* is just one of thousands of merchant vessels sailing the oceans at any one time. A very high proportion of them are carrying out illicit activities.'

'How come?'

'The sea is very big, Zak. Ships are very small, relatively speaking. They're impossible to police effectively. You can monitor the ports, of course, but once they're in the open sea . . .' He shrugged, as if to say, *Anything goes*. 'All our intelligence suggests that this particular ship, however, has been chartered by Black Wolf. Its purpose is to collect an extremely large shipment of Angolan raw diamonds, then carry them north-west across the Atlantic to Boston where they'll be sold to a major diamond company. I want you to make sure it never gets that far.'

'Why us?' Zak asked. 'Why . . . why me?'

'There are reasons,' Michael said calmly.

'Ones that you're going to tell me, or ones that you're keeping to yourself?' Zak knew he sounded a bit ungracious, but he remembered how during his last mission Michael had kept to himself the knowledge that Señor Martinez had killed his parents. 'Anyway,' he continued when it was clear Michael wasn't going to follow that line of conversation any further, 'how am I supposed to do that? I thought you said merchant ships were impossible to police.'

Michael smiled. 'Impossible-*ish*,' he said. 'Sometimes we have to . . . how can I put this? Cut corners. You'll need to start off by conducting surveillance on the *Mercantile*. You need to be very sure, Zak, that the traffickers on board are the people we think they are. Positive IDs. Nothing less. I'll supply you with the imagery you need. Secondly, you need to make sure the diamonds are on board. And thirdly, you need to plant an explosive device on the vessel. It will be detonated remotely when the *Mercantile* is in international waters. The loss of their diamond cargo will be a financial disaster for them. It could even put them out of business for ever.'

Zak felt himself frowning. 'What about the *Mercantile*'s crew?'

It took Michael a few seconds to answer. 'Black Wolf are a new organization, Zak. They only came onto MI6's radar about two months ago. All our intelligence suggests they were responsible for an explosion in India that killed thirteen street children and wounded twenty more so badly that they won't walk again. Three weeks ago they targeted a market-place in northern Tunisia. Fifteen dead, including one British national. The *Mercantile*'s crew are, we believe, all members of Black Wolf. There's not a man, woman or child in the world they wouldn't kill if the price was right. I wouldn't waste your sympathy on any of them, Zak. You'll be saving more lives than you'll be ending, in the long run.'

'*They* blow other people up. We blow *them* up. Who's worse? Black Wolf or us?'

'Your attitude does you credit, Zak. It truly does. But believe this: when the enemy stops playing by the rules, sometimes we must do the same. And besides, I'm only asking you to plant the device, not detonate it.'

Zak stood up. Once more he stared out to sea. He

remembered his first op. He remembered his shock when Gabs had shot Martinez. Was Michael turning *him* into a killer? Or was he turning him into someone who stopped people killing others?

'I don't understand,' he said suddenly.

'Have I not been clear?'

'Yeah, you've been clear. But why me? The whole point of having me is so that I can be inserted into places where adult agents would—'

'– where adult agents would stand out. Quite right, Zak. Quite right. Forgive me for not explaining that earlier. The port of Lobambo is a small place. Newcomers stand out. Even if we were to send a special forces team in, it would be almost impossible for them to get close enough to the *Mercantile* to carry out surveillance without being noticed.'

'Well, if *they* can't get close, how can I?'

'A volunteer group has set up camp on the outskirts of Lobambo. They're there to help build a school with foreign aid money. As luck would have it, they've agreed to find space for you to join them.'

Zak gave his handler a cynical look. Luck, he knew, had nothing to do with it. Michael had ways of making things happen. Zak knew there was no point asking him how he'd set this up.

'I've never been to Africa,' he said. *But my parents have*, he thought to himself, *and they died there*.

'I know,' Michael said, in a tone of voice that unnerved Zak.

'But what about Gabs and Raf? They'll be coming with me, right? Like last time? They'll be able to get me out if things go wrong?'

'No,' Michael said quietly. 'Your Guardian Angels won't be able to join you this time.'

'What? Why not?' All of a sudden Zak's stomach was churning.

'They have something else to do. Something rather important.'

'But who can I call if things go wrong?'

A pause. 'Nobody, Zak. And that means you need to be very careful. Angola is a dangerous place. Its citizens have known atrocities like you can't imagine. There are mass graves in that country that are filled with the skeletons of women and children by the thousand. You'll see things there that will shock you. If I understand you as well as I think I do, you'll want to intervene. To help people. To make their lives a little bit better. You must resist that temptation.'

Zak felt a little surge of resentment. Why *shouldn't* he use his skills to help people, if he could. Michael, he had learned, had a strange way of looking at things. 'Either you trust me,' he said, aware that he sounded a bit surly, 'or you don't.'

'Zak!' Michael snapped. There was a fire in his eyes.

'I'm afraid I don't have the leisure to indulge these childish teenage ideals. I'm sending you into an extremely dangerous environment and it's essential that you keep a low profile. That you merge into the background and do nothing to draw attention to yourself. You're there to carry out this op quickly and efficiently, not to right the wrongs of western Africa. Remember, Zak, Black Wolf are pros. They know what they're doing. They'll probably have an agent on the ground liaising with the diamond producers and scouting for suspicious activity, and it'll probably be the last person you expect. Don't get lazy. Because the moment you get lazy is the moment you get dead.'

Silence.

Michael's gaze was flinty.

And then, suddenly, he appeared to relax. He took a cigarette case from his pocket, withdrew a thin black cigarillo and smiled a thin smile. 'Would you mind terribly if I smoked?' he asked, as mildly as if they'd just been chatting about the weather. 'It's a filthy habit, I know, and frowned upon at sea. But somehow I just can't seem to stop.'

5

ANTISOCIAL BEHAVIOUR

Monday, 17.20 hrs GMT

Ellie was standing in the middle of her front room. It totally stank of aftershave. In the adjoining room the cuckoo clock cheeped once. Nobody paid it any attention.

Her mum and dad were next to each other on the sofa. They looked shocked. Sitting in one of the armchairs of the three-piece suite was a policeman. He had introduced himself as DI Andersen but he didn't have a policeman's uniform on. Just a suit. He was probably about fifty years old. The aftershave was his. It was like he'd put half a bottle on that morning. The top of his head was bald, but he'd combed a few strands over from the side, where it was longer. The comb-over was oiled down flat. It made the hair, and the top of his head, very shiny. On his lap was a clear plastic evidence bag.

And in the evidence bag, covered with dirt, was Ellie's mobile.

Ellie's mum broke the silence. 'And this was found in . . .' She sounded like she couldn't bring herself to say it. 'In Zak's *grave*?'

'I'm afraid so, Mrs Lewis,' replied DI Andersen. 'The grave was opened last night and our forensic team tell us the little finger from the right hand is missing.' He gave Ellie a severe look. 'I thought Ellie might like to explain how her phone ended up there.'

Ellie swallowed hard. 'I don't know,' she whispered.

Her mum and dad looked at each other, but DI Andersen didn't stop staring at Ellie. 'Desecrating a grave,' he said, 'is a very serious offence. I've seen children sent into care for much less—'

'I'm not a child,' Ellie snapped.

'Young lady,' the policeman retorted, 'if you weren't a child, we wouldn't be discussing care, we'd be discussing prison.'

'I didn't do anything to Zak's grave.' Ellie felt like crying, but she was determined not to. 'I wouldn't, all right? I just *wouldn't*.'

'I'm sure she's telling the truth, Officer,' her mum said. 'She's a very well-behaved girl. It's true she was very attached to her cousin. I don't know why. One doesn't like to speak ill of the dead but he was an un-remarkable child. Still, I'm sure she wouldn't . . .'

DI Andersen gave her an oily smile. 'Mrs Lewis, when you've been a police officer for as long as me, you soon learn that people can surprise you. Just last week I was interviewing a girl your daughter's age. Her mother swore blind she was as good as gold. Turned out she was stealing from her purse and using the money to—'

'*I didn't do anything to Zak's grave!*'

The grown-ups, clearly surprised by her sudden outburst, turned to look at Ellie as though they'd forgotten she was there.

'There was this guy,' she said. 'He came up to me in Burger King and he had a picture of Zak and this, like, patch over his eye, and he wanted to know where Zak was and he was, like, really mean and he . . .' Her voice trailed off. The grown-ups were looking at her as if she was mad.

DI Andersen stood up. 'We often find, Mr and Mrs Lewis, that young people of an . . .' He looked like he was searching for the right word. 'Young people of an *antisocial* nature benefit from counselling with a—'

Ellie didn't let him finish. She stormed right up to the policeman. 'May I have my phone back now, please?'

The policeman looked surprised that she'd even asked. 'Certainly not,' he replied. 'This is evidence from a crime scene. I won't be charging you today, young lady, but we certainly haven't reached the end of this matter. Mr and Mrs Lewis, this has just been an informal chat. When we next meet, I recommend Ellie has a lawyer with her. I'll show myself out.' He nodded at the grown-ups, gave Ellie a thin-lipped look and left the room.

It was only when they heard the front door shut that Ellie's father spoke. Just like him, she thought, to keep quiet in front of strangers and to give Ellie a hard time when there was just the three of them. '*You* are in a great deal of trouble, Ellie Lewis. Visits from the police? This is such an embarrassment. Your mother and I won't be able to show our faces . . .'

Ellie didn't stick around to hear the rest. She gave her parents a poisonous look and stormed out of the room, slamming the door hard behind her.

Jason Cole. Jay for short. Born 3 September in Kensington, London. Age: 16. Home-schooled by his father James at their house in Notting Hill. Interests include scuba diving and fishing . . .

'Fishing?' Zak looked up from the briefing pack of the identity he was learning. It was amazing how, after months of practice memorizing things, the information planted itself immediately in his head. 'I've never been fishing in my life.' And he thought to himself: *That's for normal people.* Sometimes he wondered whether he'd ever be normal again.

'Never been fishing? Sweetie, you haven't lived!'

Four hours ago, Zak had been on *Galileo* listening to Michael give him the details of his second op. Now, he, Michael, Raf and Gabs were sitting in a large room in St Peter's House with floor-to-ceiling windows that faced out across the windswept island towards the sea. When Zak looked through that window, the ghostly reflection had shown how pale his face still was. Nobody seemed to be making much allowance for the fact that he and Raf had almost died that morning, or that he felt as if twenty-four hours' bed rest was more in order than anything else.

It was in this room that Zak took his lessons, and he'd learned a lot more here than he ever did in school. Now they were standing round a circular wooden table. Lying on the table was a black tube, about a metre long. Next to it was a canvas fishing-tackle bag. Gabs picked up the tube and removed a lid at the end. From inside she pulled three sections of a fishing rod, which she slotted together.

'Er, Gabs,' Zak said. 'Not many fish in here. Probably best till we get outside.'

'Observant, isn't he?' Gabs murmured as she opened up the canvas fishing bag and removed a chunky black reel.

'Amazing,' Raf agreed. 'No wonder you picked him out, Michael.'

'It's like sharing a house with Sherlock Holmes . . .'

'Or James Bond . . .'

'All right,' Michael said like a stern schoolmaster. 'That'll do. We haven't got much time. The *Mercantile* docks in Angola in three days' time. Zak needs to be in-country by then. He's booked on a flight from Heathrow tomorrow.'

Gabs fitted the reel to the rod and handed it to Zak.

'I guess someone will *eventually* get round to telling me why we're putting a fishing rod together,' he said.

Gabs's face grew more serious. 'Check out the reel,' she said. Zak examined it a bit more closely. At first glance it looked quite ordinary: a spindle, transparent fishing twine. It only took him a few seconds, though, to locate a small switch on the underside. Zak flicked it. There was a whirring sound and the front and back ends of the reel's barrel opened up like a camera shutter.

'Hidden scope,' Gabs said. 'In-built camera. Night-sight capability.' She pointed at the canvas fishing bag. 'There's a selection of telescopic lenses in there. You'll be able to conduct surveillance discreetly using this.' She sighed. 'Michael, *really*, it wouldn't be difficult for Raf and me to be inserted along with Zak. We can easily come up with a cover story.'

But Michael shook his head. 'I need you somewhere else.'

Zak removed the reel from the rod and walked over to the window. He didn't like the idea that Raf and Gabs wouldn't be with him, but he didn't want it to show in his face. He held the sight up to his right eye.

'Adjust the focus by turning the spool.' Gabs's voice was soft and just behind him. Zak did so and a distant portion of sea became sharp and clear.

'Neat,' he murmured. 'Does it catch fish too?'

'Course it does. We like to think of everything, you know. But I get the feeling you won't have much time for that.'

'Come on,' Michael said a bit impatiently. 'We need to go down to the basement. There's a lot to get through.'

The basement of St Peter's House was given over to an indoor firing range. It was here that Zak had learned the difference between an Uzi and an MP5, between a Browning semi-automatic and a 1911 45, between an AK-47 and an M16. And it was here that he'd spent more hours than he could count learning to fire them. Today, though, Raf had a new firearm to add to the list. It was a very strange-looking weapon. It had five barrels, each the same length as a normal handgun but a lot more bulky. The handle was about twice the size of an ordinary gun.

'Heckler and Koch P11,' Raf explained once they were standing by the firing range. 'Underwater pistol. Ordinary rounds are no good underwater. Not accurate. Short range. This fires ten-centimetre steel darts instead – five of them, one in each barrel. Effective underwater range about fifteen metres. Effective range above water, double that.'

Zak took the weapon. It was heavy – more than a kilo, he reckoned. He aimed it down the firing range and squeezed the trigger. The dart that shot from the weapon looked like a miniature rocket, with fins and a sharp, pointed end. At the end of the firing range was the silhouette of a man. The dart entered the shape in the centre of its forehead. When he lowered his arm and turned back to the others, he could see that Michael was faintly amused. 'Yes, well . . .' the older man murmured. 'Hopefully it won't come to that. But if it does . . .'

Zak handed the gun back to Raf.

'The port of Lobambo has a long pier,' Michael explained. 'There'll be one of these weapons fixed to the underside, along with other equipment you might need.'

'Such as?'

'A Draeger rebreather and a swim board.'

'What are they?'

'Specialized diving equipment,' said Raf. 'The kind of stuff the SBS use all the time.'

'SBS?' Zak asked.

'Special Boat Service.'

'Their motto,' Michael interrupted, 'is "Not by Strength, by Guile". Something for us all to remember, I would say.' He looked sharply at Zak, who felt like he'd just been told something important, but he didn't know what.

Raf coughed a bit uncomfortably. 'The rebreather allows you to swim close to the surface of the water without any air bubbles appearing,' he explained after a few seconds. 'If you want to approach a vessel without being seen, that's what you use. The swim board has an illuminated compass. It means you can keep an accurate direction when you're underwater.'

'You'll also find the explosive device that you need to plant on the vessel once you've ID'd the Black Wolf personnel,' Michael continued. 'It'll be housed in a waterproof flight case.'

'Hope nobody finds this stuff,' Zak said.

'It'll be well camouflaged. Nobody will find it unless they're looking for it. Which they won't be. Your briefing pack contains pictures of the Black Wolf members. You need to memorize them before you leave the country, along with Jason Cole's personal details, of course. Do you have your phone?'

Zak nodded and pulled his iPhone from his back pocket. Michael had given him this at the beginning of his first operation. He had used it to capture and upload evidence. Since then he'd hardly used it. It wasn't like he had a whole bunch of people he could phone up for a chat.

'You'll find schematics of the *Mercantile* already uploaded onto it,' Michael said. 'Our intelligence says there's only a very small crew on board, so staying hidden should be straightforward. Use the schematics to guide yourself towards the engine room. That's where you need to plant the device.'

Zak thought back to the devastation of HMS *Vanguard*. Michael was right: if you wanted to cause some damage, the engine room was the place to start.

Michael looked at his watch. 'Fourteen hundred hours,' he said. 'A helicopter will be here in twenty minutes to take us to the mainland. Do you have any questions, Zak?'

Did he have any questions? Of course he did. Like, wasn't this all happening too quickly? What was so important that Raf and Gabs couldn't be on standby to help him like last time? Why hadn't they given him more time to prepare? And wasn't it madness anyway, sending someone like him into a hostile part of the world to carry out such a sensitive operation?

But these were questions there was no point asking. This was his life now. This was what he had chosen. And besides, what was the point of all this training if he never had a chance to put it into action?

'No,' he replied. 'No questions.'

Michael nodded. 'I'll continue your briefing on the chopper,' he said. 'Let's get ready to go.'

6

IN-COUNTRY

'British Airways departure BA912 to Luanda, now boarding at Gate Three.'

Luanda. Capital of Angola. It seemed a million miles from where he was now.

Zak stood outside Boots on the ground floor of Heathrow Terminal Five. The chopper from St Peter's Crag had touched down at the London heliport near Battersea at six the previous evening. Zak had shaken Michael and Raf by the hand and given Gabs – who was clearly very anxious – a hug. Then, his hair still blowing in the downdraught of the chopper's rotary blades, he'd climbed into a waiting Mercedes, fishing gear in hand. The windows were tinted black and the driver didn't say a word as he drove him to the Holiday Inn on the outskirts of the airport.

Zak's bags were packed and ready for him in his

room. He had no idea who had prepared the single rucksack, but he remembered Michael's words on the chopper. *You'll find clothes, Angolan currency and a passport in Jason Cole's name.* Sure enough, he found all three. Jay had been around. His dog-eared passport had stamps from the United States, Sweden, Italy – though none from any African country. But Zak already knew this information from the briefing pack Michael had given him. He'd only 'met' Jay the previous day, but already he felt he knew him well. He'd chucked the passport onto the rucksack, then lain on the bed and looked through his briefing documents once more, paying special attention to two photographs.

One of these photographs had showed a swarthy-looking man with thick black eyebrows that met in the middle of his forehead. His neck had the thickness of someone who was used to bodybuilding. *Name, Antonio Acosta*, Michael had told him. *Born and raised in the favelas of Rio de Janeiro. There's a rumour that he murdered his own brother when he was thirteen. We now believe he's a Black Wolf general. Formerly a gun for hire guarding drug boats against piracy in international waters. Not a job for the faint-hearted, if you take my meaning.*

Acosta was a distinctive-looking man. Easy to recognize. Zak had put the photo to one side and pulled out the second. This showed a man with a shaved head and a line of piercings along his left eyebrow. They made it look swollen and sore. *Surname, Karlovic. First name unknown. Georgian national. Understood to have links with a terrorist group who call themselves the Patriots of Georgia. Recruited to Black Wolf for his prowess with car bombs and other IEDs.*

Nice couple, Zak thought. Just about deserve each other.

We can't be sure who else will be on board the Mercantile, *but a positive ID of these two men will be enough. Put it this way: if Antonio Acosta and Karlovic are on board, the rest of the crew aren't very likely to be sweet old pensioners.*

Zak walked away from Boots and followed the sign to the gate, half expecting a tap on the shoulder from airport security, even though his fake documentation had got him this far without so much as a raised eyebrow. Thirty minutes later, however, flight BA912 was taking off. It juddered and rattled through the cloud cover, before settling smoothly into its cruising altitude.

Flight time to Luanda, eight hours twenty-five minutes. Zak took his iPod from his pocket and fitted the earbuds. He was only pretending to listen to music, though. He didn't want to be disturbed by the middle-aged businessman sitting next to him as he cleared his head and thought his way through the details of the mission.

The flight passed quickly. It was nearly five p.m. local time when Zak emerged onto the tarmac at Luanda airport. The heat was intense and it was so humid that his skin was moist within seconds as he walked with the other passengers towards the terminal building. It looked like construction work had been going on here, but it had clearly stalled. There were no work-men on the scaffolding; pallets of building blocks lay abandoned. Half an hour later he had collected his rucksack and fishing gear and was standing in the small but busy arrivals hall. Flight announce-ments in Portuguese echoed from the public address system, but Zak was concentrating on the memory of Michael's briefing. *You'll be collected at the airport by a young man called Marcus. Long hair, black beard, mid-twenties. He's the youth group's team leader in Angola. He'll meet you in-country and escort you to Lobambo. Remember, Zak, he thinks Jason Cole is just another volunteer. Don't do anything to stop him thinking that.*

What? Zak had thought. *Like blowing up a mer-chant vessel in a small fishing village?* But he'd kept quiet.

Marcus was standing in the arrivals hall. He wore pale canvas trousers, a red and white tie-dyed shirt and his hair was tied back in a short ponytail. He held an oblong of cardboard scrawled with the name Jason Cole. Standing next to him was a girl, perhaps three years older than Zak. She had short hair, halfway between red and ginger, and rather small eyes that blinked almost constantly.

'Marcus?' Zak held out his hand once he was standing in front of the young man with the beard.

The young man smiled and shook Zak's hand. 'You must be Jason.'

'Call me Jay,' Zak replied automatically. 'Everyone does.'

'Good to meet you, Jay.' Marcus turned to the girl. 'This is Bea. She's only been with us forty-eight hours. Thought you two new bugs might like to get to know each other.'

'Pleased to meet you, Bea.' Zak offered her his hand.

The girl shook hands briskly. 'Welcome to Angola, Jason. Is that all the luggage you have? Really? Well, I hope you've brought everything you need – it's not like you can just nip out to the shops in Lobambo, you know. Now then, have you put your passport somewhere safe? You *really* don't want to go losing that, do you, and I know what you boys are like. Now it's very hot outside, so I hope you've had plenty of water to drink. And do you need the lavatory? It's a long drive, you know, and Marcus, we really ought to get going, because we *don't* want to be travelling at night . . .' She turned on her heel and started marching towards the exit.

'Forty-eight hours, you say,' Zak observed, suppressing a smile as he watched her go.

'Er, yeah,' said Marcus. 'Forty-eight hours.' He scratched his head and looked a bit apologetic. 'Lovely girl. Bit of a . . . bit of a chatterbox, but I'm sure you'll get on like a . . . like a . . . The truck's just outside.'

Marcus's vehicle was an old Land Rover. It was parked right in front of the terminal building and was by far the fanciest vehicle there. All the other cars, parked up in no particular order by the side of the wide, dusty road, were old saloons covered in rust and dents. Four Angolan kids about Zak's age were hanging around the Land Rover. When they saw the trio approach they all ran up to them, shouting. One of them tried to pull Zak's fishing gear away and carry it to the car. But Zak wasn't letting go of *that* for anyone. The kids soon realized they weren't going to earn any money, and they quickly disappeared.

The Land Rover was khaki in colour, but so covered with dust that the paintwork was almost invisible. Bea immediately took the front passenger seat. 'You'll have more room back there, Jason, and it's probably best if I help Marcus with directions.'

'It's a straight road, Bea,' Marcus said mildly, catching Zak's eye as he spoke. Once more, Zak tried not to smile as he crammed his rucksack onto the seat and sat next to it.

'Is this your first time in Angola, Jay?' Marcus asked as he negotiated his way through the chaotic traffic outside the terminal.

'First time in Africa,' Zak replied. 'Er, why don't we want to travel at night, Bea?'

He heard Bea drawing breath and prepared himself for a long explanation, but Marcus got there first, leaving Bea looking like the carpet had just been pulled from under her feet. 'Angola has had a difficult history, Jay. I'm sure you know that.'

'Civil war,' Zak said.

'Exactly.' Marcus knocked the vehicle into third gear. 'Things aren't as bad now as they were a few years ago, but it's still a dangerous country. Most of the Angolans are very good people who only want peace in their country. But not all of them. There's a risk of bandits on the road, especially at night.'

'Goodness, Marcus. A risk? The roads are very, very dangerous, Jason, and I want you to bear that in mind. You're not to go wandering off. Some of these people will rob you of everything you have and would much rather kill you than leave you to identify them later.'

Zak looked through the window. Already the airport buildings had retreated. They were on a busy main road, but it wasn't exactly the M1. It had no tarmac or markings – just a dusty, pitted surface that made the Land Rover rattle as it went. On either side there was flat, parched earth as far as Zak could see. The occasional bush had managed to sprout and there were a few shacks made out of rotting timber and corrugated iron. They passed the rusting shell of an old car and Zak saw three children, no more than five years old, playing inside it.

He examined the position of the sun. It was ahead to their right. Given the time of day, that meant they were heading south.

Towards the village.

Twenty-four hours ago, Zak had been in the safety of St Peter's Crag. Now he felt anything but safe. He felt like he had been transported to another world.

Journey time from Luanda airport to Lobambo, two hours forty-five minutes. The further south they travelled, the less barren the surroundings became. The parched earth gave way to low brush. The low brush gave way to thicker vegetation. By the time Marcus announced that Lobambo was just a kilometre away, Zak was sweaty and dirty. His skin was caked in dust and he was looking forward to getting out of that rattling Land Rover.

Lobambo was poor. That much was obvious. If there was diamond wealth in the area, the ordinary people had never got their hands on it. There were no streets or pavements – only areas of worn-down earth between the wood and iron shacks that passed as dwellings. Children were playing outside the shacks; women were rolling out bread or breast-feeding infants; men were sitting in groups, chatting. All the adults had the weathered skin of people who'd led a hard life. And some of the kids did too. Everyone stopped what they were doing to watch the Land Rover trundle by.

They passed a building site. Foundations had been dug into the earth and pallets of breeze blocks and timber were lying around. As at the airport, there was no sign of work, though. The only people on the site were four Angolan men. They were loitering lazily, one of them rolling a cigarette, two others playing some kind of dice game. Zak noticed that they all had weapons lying beside them.

More shacks. More stares. 'Everyone looks nervous,' Zak said.

'And so would you, Jay,' replied Marcus, 'if for ten years the arrival of a stranger meant the arrival of somebody who wants to kill you.'

The shacks continued like this for perhaps a kilometre. Occasionally they would pass a more solid structure, built of breeze blocks or concrete. 'Bottle shop,' Bea explained without being asked. Or, 'Doctor's surgery.'

Moments later, the sea came into view. The sun, all orange and pink, was setting on the horizon and the water twinkled in its light. It looked like it was full of jewels.

'It's amazing,' Zak said, and even Bea seemed lost for words as she nodded her head in agreement. But Zak's attention wasn't just on the beauty of nature. He was examining the waterfront intently, comparing it to the mental snapshots he had taken of the satellite imagery Michael had provided. Almost straight ahead of them, Zak saw a pier. It stretched about 100 metres out to sea and was raised ten metres above the level of the water. To its left was a harbour. There was a series of ten much shorter jetties here, but the only boats moored against them were ramshackle fishing vessels.

Zak scanned the beachfront. He counted three palm trees set twenty metres back from the harbour. They were tall and thin and offered nothing in the way of camouflage. A wooden fisherman's hut had once stood just in front of one of those trees, but it had long since collapsed and was now just a mess of timber surrounded by bits of driftwood. There was nowhere, Zak realized, that he could conceal himself in this tiny harbour. Nowhere he could set up a suitable OP.

The Land Rover turned right, away from the harbour and along a golden stretch of beach. It was deserted and very beautiful – the sort of place Zak had only ever seen in holiday brochures. After 500 metres they stopped by a small encampment of sturdy canvas tents. There were ten of them, each one about five metres by five. Washing was hanging from lines between each tent and a small fire was burning ten metres in front of the encampment. Eight people were sitting around the fire. Seven of them had white skin and were about the same age as Bea. The eighth was black and a bit younger. Zak's age, perhaps. It was difficult to tell.

Bea got out of the Land Rover the moment it stopped. She was talking almost before her feet touched the ground. 'Come along, Jason, you must meet the others . . . I'll introduce you . . . Don't worry about your luggage . . .' She walked off, still chatting, without noticing that Zak and Marcus hadn't moved.

'One of the challenges you'll face out here,' Marcus said tactfully, 'is getting used to other people.'

'Does she ever stop talking?' Zak asked.

'Course she does, Jay. The very second she falls asleep. But her heart is in the right place, even if her nose is always stuck into everybody's business.' He winked at him. 'Come on. I think you'll find the others a bit more relaxed.'

Marcus was right. By the time he and Zak had walked up to the camp fire, the others were standing and smiling in their direction, although the younger local-looking boy had now moved away from the group. Marcus started making the introductions. 'Jason, meet your fellow volunteers – Matt, Roger, Alexandra, Tillie, Jacqui, Ade and Christopher. Don't worry, I won't be testing you on their names *just* yet.'

Zak looked at each of them in turn. *Matt, Roger, Alexandra, Tillie, Jacqui, Ade, Christopher*, he repeated silently to himself, reassured somehow by his instant recall.

'Where's Bea?' the guy introduced as Ade asked.

'I thought it was quiet,' someone murmured.

'Over there.' Zak pointed to a space between two of the canvas tents. He'd seen Bea as soon as he'd approached the camp fire. She was standing in the shadows, blinking furiously, but still watching them all. Watching Zak. For some reason it made him a bit nervous.

He turned to the others. 'It's nice of you all to let me join you,' he said. 'I'm looking forward to getting my hands dirty.'

Ade had very tanned skin. He was wearing just a

pair of turquoise knee-length swimming shorts. 'Hands dirty?' he asked, clearly confused.

'Building the school.' He looked around the group. Suddenly things seemed a bit awkward. 'That's what we're here to do, isn't it?'

A pause. 'You didn't tell him?' Ade asked Marcus in surprise.

Marcus didn't answer. He just put one hand on Zak's shoulder. 'I'll show you where you'll be sleeping,' he said quietly. 'We'll have a chat later.'

He led Zak towards the tents, keeping a couple of metres ahead of him. It was almost as if he didn't want to get caught in a conversation. And Zak couldn't help noticing, as he walked away from the camp fire, that Bea was no longer staring at them.

She was no longer standing in the shadows.

She was nowhere to be seen.

7

NIGHT FISHING

19.45 hrs West Africa Time

Zak's tent was simple – a low bed covered with a mosquito net hanging from the ceiling; rush matting on the floor; a clothes rail with a few hangers; a battery-operated lamp. He dumped his stuff and sat quietly on the edge of his bed for a few minutes, gathering his thoughts. He'd only just arrived in Lobambo and already things didn't seem right. Why had everyone gone quiet when he'd asked about the school? And there was something about Bea that didn't quite ring true. What was it? Zak was determined to find out.

But first he had to become one of the group again. To be Jason Cole and not Zak Darke. He cleared his head and prepared to rejoin them. It was fully dark when he walked outside again. The stars were amazing. As he walked towards the camp fire, Zak looked up and quickly identified the Southern Cross. It was his first time in the southern hemisphere, so he had only ever seen this constellation on star charts. He remembered Raf teaching him about astro-navigation, one of the first lessons he'd ever had after being recruited. He wondered where his Guardian Angels were now. What did *they* have to do that was so important?

'Hey, Jay.' The others were all sitting around the fire, chatting quietly. Marcus stood up to welcome him.

'Marcus,' Zak replied with a nod.

'We'll eat soon. Come and meet an important member of our team.' He led Zak round to the far side of the camp fire where the Angolan boy about the same age as Zak was sitting by himself. He had a shaved head and wore a very old Manchester United football top. With his right hand he was drawing shapes in the dusty ground. But it was his left arm to which Zak's eyes were immediately drawn. The boy was missing half the arm. It finished at the elbow in a scarred, knobbly stump. Zak did his best not to stare at it.

'This is Malek,' Marcus said. 'He speaks very good English, which is good, because our Portuguese is rotten. Right, Malek?'

'Right, Marcus,' Malek said with a grin that revealed crooked yellow teeth.

'Malek helps us liaise with the locals. We'd be lost without him. Malek, this is Jay. I'll leave you to get acquainted.' Marcus walked back to the other side of the fire.

'Mind if I sit here?' Zak asked, pointing at the patch of earth next to Malek.

The Angolan boy shook his head. He seemed quite shy.

Zak sat down. Nightfall had brought a chill in the air and he was glad of the warmth of the fire. Unlike Bea, Zak wasn't naturally talkative; he felt a moment of panic as he cast around for a topic of conversation. 'So,' he said after a few awkward seconds and looking at the Man United shirt, 'do you like football?'

'All my friends like football,' Malek replied. He spoke very slowly, with a pronounced African accent. He raised the stump of his left arm. 'But it is difficult for me to play.'

Zak nodded. 'How did that happen?' he asked.

Malek stared towards the orange flames of the fire. 'It was a long time ago,' he said. He paused, and Zak felt a bit guilty for asking. Maybe this was something Malek didn't want to talk about. But then the Angolan boy spoke again. 'There was a war in my country,' he said.

'I heard,' Zak said quietly.

'It was very bad. Nearly thirty years of fighting.

Half a million people were killed. People like me . . .' He looked meaningfully at the remnants of his arm. 'People like me were the lucky ones.'

'I guess we have different ideas of luck, Malek.'

Malek inclined his head. 'Perhaps. Because of the war, there were many land mines in the countryside. I was with my mother. She had me in her arms. When she stepped on a land mine, she was killed immediately.'

Malek spoke without emotion. Zak didn't know what to say.

'It was only because her body took most of the blast that I survived. But a piece of shrapnel entered my arm. It took the townspeople two hours to find me. Any longer and I would have died.'

'It must have been awful,' Zak said.

Malek shrugged. 'I was only three years old. The Red Cross were nearby and they amputated my arm. I have been like this for as long as I can remember.'

'I lost my mother too,' Zak said, before a warning bell in his head cautioned him not to say too much. 'Jason Cole' *had* lost his mother, but his father was still alive. He had to make sure he was keeping fact and fiction separate.

'I'm sorry,' Malek said, and all of a sudden Zak could tell that there was a bond between himself and this quietly spoken African boy.

'Do you remember your mother?' Zak asked.

'Sometimes,' Malek replied. 'Maybe. I have in my mind the picture of a kind face.' He shrugged again. 'But they say your mind can play tricks on you.'

'I'm sure it's her you remember,' Zak told him.

Malek smiled for the first time. A sad smile. 'Thank you, Jay. It is kind of you to say that.'

'What about your father? Is he still alive?'

A dark look crossed Malek's face. 'I don't know who my father was,' he said. Zak could tell this was something he didn't want to talk about.

The two boys sat in silence for a minute. Malek, Zak could tell, was an open, honest young man. And he realized, with a pang of guilt, that he was looking at him not just as a potential friend, but also as a good source of information. 'How's it going with the school?' he asked.

Malek looked at him in surprise. 'They did not tell you?'

Zak shook his head.

'Perhaps they did not want you to be scared.'

'Scared of what?'

'The men with guns.'

'What men with guns?'

Again there was a pause. Malek appeared to be gathering his thoughts. 'Lobambo needs a new school building very badly,' he said. 'The children here want to learn, but without a place for them to go, it is very difficult.'

'In England,' Zak said, 'lots of kids don't even want to go to school.'

Malek didn't seem shocked by that. 'Sometimes,' he said, 'people do not understand what they have until it is gone. And when people *don't* have something, they want it. We want a school in Lobambo very much.'

'So what's happening?'

'The money to build the school,' Malek explained, 'comes from abroad. From charities. There are men in Lobambo who think this money should be given to them. They *say* they will build the school. Everyone knows that if the money goes into their pockets, they will steal it. But they are stubborn. They stand at the building site from dawn until sunset. There are four of them. They have AK-47s. Loaded. They are the only weapons in Lobambo. It makes them very powerful.'

'They wouldn't do anything stupid, would they?'

Malek gave him a serious look. 'In Angola,' he said, 'death is commonplace. Life is cheap. Yes, Jay, I believe they would do it if forced. Your friends here . . .' He pointed at the English volunteers sitting round the fire. 'They have not been to the building site now for two weeks. They are too scared. I do not blame them.'

'Then why are they still here?'

Malek shrugged. 'They think, perhaps, that the gunmen will get bored. That when they realize they are not getting any money they will stop trying.' A dark look crossed his face. 'I do not think they will get bored,' he added. 'One of them – he is called Ntole – is a cousin of mine.' Malek looked as though this was a cause of deep shame. '*He* was violent even as a child. He will not get bored.'

Zak sniffed. 'Sounds to me,' he said, 'like someone needs to do something about it.'

'Of course,' Malek said. 'But what?'

'I don't know,' Zak murmured. 'Stand up to them, I guess.'

'It is difficult to stand up to armed men when you have no guns yourself. It is difficult when they are not our equals.'

Zak looked around the fire. The other volunteers were chatting quietly, but he caught Marcus staring at him. It was almost as if the long-haired volunteer knew what he and Malek were discussing. He looked a bit sheepish.

'Well, maybe we should make ourselves their equals,' Zak said.

An idea was forming. It would have to wait, though, until tomorrow.

* * *

There are different kinds of darkness, Zak thought to himself as he lay in his tent covered with his mosquito nets. When he lived in London, he'd barely ever seen real darkness. There was always the glow of a street lamp, the beam of a car headlight. Never the kind of darkness so thick you thought you could touch it. It was only on the bleak outpost of St Peter's Crag that he had learned what darkness was really like.

It was this kind of darkness that surrounded him now. The only whisper of light came from his diver's watch. The glowing hands told him it was 2.30 a.m.

Darkness, but not silence. All the camp volunteers were in bed. Malik had wandered back up into the town. But there were still noises. The lapping of the sea on the shore. The occasional cry of a wild animal that Zak couldn't place.

He'd got into bed fully clothed after placing his fishing gear by the tent door. That way he could find it without turning on his lamp. He did this now, grabbing the rod and tackle bag and slipping out of the tent.

Zak could see the glowing embers of the camp fire. There was no moon, but the stars were still incredibly bright. Bright enough for the pier to be visible 500 metres south of Zak's position. He set off quietly. The ground underfoot was rocky and hard. For a moment, Zak was back on St Peter's Crag with Raf. *If you don't want to be heard on hard ground you need to step toe first. Make sure you have a firm footing and you're not going to dislodge any stones. Then bring your heel down slowly. Balance on the back foot until the front one can support your body mass.*

It was slow going. Three minutes to reach the camp fire. When he was there, he bent down and picked up a handful of dust. He threw it in the air and watched it fall. A gentle breeze blew it back towards the camp. That meant it would carry the noise of his footsteps too, so he continued tiptoeing until he was 100 metres away. Only then did he pick up his pace.

The area around the pier was deserted. At least, Zak couldn't *see* anybody. The pier itself was a rickety old thing. It stood at a slight slant. His first few steps were nervous. The boards creaked underneath him, but after a few seconds it was clear they would hold his weight so he increased his speed. As Zak ran down it, he crouched low. He didn't want to be lit up against the starlit horizon. Once he reached the end, he sat down quickly with his feet dangling over the edge, opened up his rod case and fitted the three sections of the rod together. He removed the reel from its tackle bag and flicked the switch on its underside. A whirring sound. The front and back edges of the reel opened up. Zak held it up to his eye and looked out to sea.

The night-vision capability of the camouflaged scope bathed everything in a ghostly green glow. He looked up to the stars. Through the NV they were even more spectacular than to the naked eye. Zak could have looked at that sight all night, but he couldn't. There was work to do. In the absence of any suitable camouflage on land, this pier was his best observation post. When the *Mercantile* came into harbour it was from here that he would have to carry out surveillance – just an innocent volunteer passing the time fishing. He turned his head towards the harbour. He could see the ramshackle African fishing boats – five of them – in great detail. He could make out the knotted bundles of fishing net and the big lumps of concrete tied to ropes that clearly acted as anchors. When the *Mercantile* arrived, Zak was confident he'd be able to see everything that happened on deck.

Something flapped in the water. Zak looked down in time to see the shiny arched back of a sea creature. He remembered the moray eels at Scapa Flow, and shuddered.

Zak gently placed the reel down on the boards of the pier. From his tackle bag he removed a thin torch with a red filter. Its beam was only the thickness of a pencil lead but it would give him enough light to work by. And as the filter was red, it wouldn't wreck his ability to see in the dark like white light would. He recalled Michael's words to him in the chopper. *You'll find your gear five boards back from the end of the pier . . .*

He counted the boards, keeping the torch low so it wouldn't be seen from a distance. When he reached board number five he dug his fingertips along its side and pulled. The board didn't lift easily. Zak had to worm his fingertips a little deeper into the gap, but after thirty seconds he managed to lift it up onto its edge. He directed the torch into the cavity.

There was a package there, wrapped in what felt like polythene. It looked red, but that was just the light of the torch. Whatever colour it was, it was definitely opaque. *Don't remove the equipment until you need it*, Michael had said. Zak wasn't so sure. Perhaps he should lift it from its hiding place now. Unpack it. Check everything was there . . .

His decision, though, was made for him. Because just then he heard footsteps.

Quickly he pushed the board back down. It landed crooked, not quite fitting into its proper place. But Zak didn't have time to adjust it. He only had time to hide. But at the end of a pier, where *could* he hide?

His hands were trembling as he packed away the fishing gear. The footsteps were getting nearer, and the closer they came, the more he felt himself panicking. His fingers and thumbs wouldn't do what his brain was telling them. By the time the fishing gear was packed away and the bag slung over his shoulder, he was sweating, and he could see the faint shadow of a person approaching.

Zak kept low. He crawled to the end of the pier and, still trembling, eased his body over the side, grasping the wooden floor with his fingertips. The muscles in his hands and arms burned as he hung there; his knuckles creaked. All he could do was concentrate on not falling, and pray that whoever was coming wouldn't notice his hands gripping the end of the pier.

The footsteps were just metres away when they stopped. Zak held his breath. He could hear the water below lapping against the legs of the pier, and the occasional creaking of the wooden joints; his hands, pinching the end of the pier, shrieked at him; his biceps were on fire and so was his mind. If he was discovered, what then?

He didn't know how much longer he could hold on. His fingers were slipping . . .

Something slammed. From the vibrations on the pier, Zak deduced that whoever was above had kicked the loose board back into place.

And then the footsteps started walking away.

Zak gave it thirty seconds, then slowly, painfully,

started to pull himself back up. It took all his strength to raise his head above the level of the pier, where he could just see the shadow receding. And by the time he had pulled his whole body back, he was drained and breathless. But he couldn't rest. Quickly taking the fishing bag off his shoulder, he pulled out the reel and took a look through the night sight.

There was no mistaking her. Zak recognized Bea's gait, the shape of her hair; her face.

He heard Michael's voice in his head. *Remember, Zak. Black Wolf are pros. They know what they're doing. They'll probably have an agent on the ground and it'll probably be the last person you expect. Don't get lazy.*

The last person you'd expect? Or the first person you meet? Zak waited for Bea to disappear. Then he checked that the board had definitely slotted back, stowed away the NV device and followed her back to the tents.

8

A MIDNIGHT VISIT

Wednesday, 08.40 hrs GMT

Ellie walked slowly to school. She was later than normal. She had waited for her mum and dad to go to work before leaving her bedroom. After that awful policeman, DI Andersen, on Monday and the atmosphere at home all the following day, when they had kept her off school in case the policeman called again and had barely let her out of their sight, she just couldn't face her family.

Now it was twenty to nine. The rush-hour traffic on Camden Road was heavy and the grey sky and exhaust fumes made London look bleak. Ellie knew she should hurry. Her teachers would give her a hard time if she was late. Somehow she didn't care. Her mind was still full of other things.

It was just gone quarter to when she approached the gates of Camden High School. Ellie wasn't the only latecomer. There were nine or ten others approaching; they all looked scruffy and were kicking their heels. Ellie realized that she probably looked the same. On the other side of the road, huddled outside a newsagent's, was a group of four boys she recognized from further up the school. She couldn't see exactly what they were doing, but she knew they were probably sharing out cigarettes. A member of staff would be out soon, but they were the types not to care if they were told off.

Stragglers. Smokers. Ellie wasn't really paying attention to any of them as she walked up to the gates. She'd noticed someone else standing there. Balding head. Comb-over. An unpleasant look of suspicion on his face and a cloud of aftershave pong around him. Ellie could smell it from three metres away.

'Good morning, Miss Lewis,' said DI Andersen. 'I'm quite surprised to see you here.'

Ellie jutted her chin out at him. 'Why? It's my school, isn't it?'

'I just thought you might still be recovering after your late night on Sunday . . .'

'Haven't you got any proper criminals to catch?' She was amazed by her own boldness. She'd *never* normally speak to a police officer like this. Or anyone, for that matter.

DI Andersen's lips thinned. 'You should realize,

young lady,' he said quietly, 'that speaking to me like that is not the way to get yourself out of trouble.'

'I haven't done anything wrong.'

'I'm watching you, Ellie Lewis. Very carefully. My advice to you is to stay at home after school. Because if you put a foot wrong, I'll be there.' He gave an nasty smile. 'And even if you *don't* put a foot wrong, I'll be there. I can tell a troublemaker when I meet one. You might be able to make a fool out of your parents, but you can't make a fool out of me.'

'I suppose that's because,' a new voice, just behind Ellie, said, 'someone's already done it.'

Ellie spun round. The woman standing behind her had approached silently. She was in her mid-twenties, had white-blonde hair, a tanned, pretty face and was wearing all black. Her eyes were an intense blue, her arms were folded and she was looking at DI Andersen like he was a piece of mud on her shoe.

'I'm sorry?' said the police officer. 'Can I help you?'

'Yeah,' the woman replied. 'You can help me by not hounding school kids. Or do I need to discuss this with your Chief Superintendent?'

Andersen frowned. He looked like he was thinking up a reply, but there was something about this strange, blonde woman that seemed to catch him off guard. He looked at Ellie. 'Just remember what I've said, young lady.' He smoothed down the strands of hair combed over the top of his head before walking away. The pungent smell of aftershave, however, lingered.

'You know,' said the newcomer, 'I've never understood why some guys douse themselves in perfume like that. Makes them smell like a department store.' She smiled at Ellie.

But Ellie didn't smile back. She'd been meeting too many weirdos lately – it looked to her like this was just another one to add to the list. She stepped to one side and walked past the blonde-haired woman, heading in through the school gates. The stragglers had all gone in.

'Ellie Lewis?'

She stopped. But she didn't turn round.

'How do you know my name?'

'The same way,' replied the woman, 'that I know you might be having trouble with *this* guy.'

Ellie felt herself shaking. She turned to see the woman holding up an iPhone. On the screen was a photograph. It showed a very thin man. He had only one eye. The skin had grown over the missing eye and it was smooth, with no marks. Ellie recognized him, of course. She'd met him in Burger King on Sunday, only then he had been wearing a patch over the eye that was not.

They stood in silence as Ellie stared at the photograph.

When the woman spoke, her voice was much gentler than before. The voice of a friend. 'I don't blame you if you're scared, Ellie,' she said. 'You should be. He's a dangerous man. The police don't know what they're dealing with. It's out of their league. I'm here to protect you from him, if you'd like me to.'

Ellie swallowed hard. She looked from the photograph to the woman. 'Who are you?' she asked. 'Why should I trust you?'

'Because you haven't got a choice, Ellie. That man is a killer. If he's made contact with you, it puts you in a dangerous position. A *very* dangerous position. Like, potentially fatal. He won't want you to identify him in the future. Do you understand?'

Ellie nodded. She didn't know what to say.

'You'd better get into school,' the woman said. 'He won't try anything there. Too many witnesses. Act normal. If we're going to deal with this, we don't want other people sticking their noses in. Don't tell anybody what's happening. I'll meet you here after school and explain what we're going to do.' She winked. 'I'll even help you with your homework, if you like.'

Ellie was too nervous to smile. She bit her lip instead. 'Is this . . .' She didn't quite know how to ask the question. 'Is this something to do with Zak? The man with the patch – he showed me a photograph and . . .'

'You're going to be late for school, Ellie.'

Ellie looked down. 'Right,' she said. 'I'd better go. I suppose I'll see you later.' She headed towards the school gate again.

'Oh, and Ellie, by the way . . .'

Ellie looked over her shoulder. 'Yeah?'

'You can call me Gabs,' said the newcomer. 'And try not to worry too much, sweetie. I'm pretty good at this sort of thing.'

And with another wink, Gabs walked away, leaving Ellie – confused and more than a little bit scared – to make up a convincing lie to explain to her teachers why she was so late for school.

Zak woke after only a couple of hours: 05.45 hrs. His night might have been disturbed, but he had no intention of staying in bed. This wasn't a holiday, after all.

The sun was only just rising when he stepped out of his tent. There was still a little warmth around the ashes of last night's camp fire but nobody else was up yet. He had a day until the *Mercantile* arrived. A day until he had to pit his wits against the grisly-sounding members of Black Wolf. He knew he should keep a low profile. Avoid drawing attention to himself.

He also knew he'd be doing nothing of the sort.

The road from the beach to the centre of Lobambo

was deserted. Zak walked for 500 metres before seeing anyone. He walked another 100 metres before he realized that the boy coming towards him was Malek.

'You're up early, Jay,' the Angolan said.

'So are you.'

'I prefer it when Lobambo is quiet.' He looked over his shoulder back towards the town. 'Would you like me to show you around?'

'You bet.'

Malek led Zak into the village. Now that he was off the main road, he saw that it was a widespread collection of compounds. These compounds consisted of huts and shacks, grouped around central courtyards and surrounded by wooden fences about a metre high. Some buildings were sturdier than others, and some didn't form part of a compound but stood alone. Malek pointed out the bottle shop where people with money – there weren't many of them, he explained – could buy beer or Coca-Cola. They passed a small breeze-block building no bigger than the tiny corner shop where Zak went to buy sweets when he was much younger. It had no front – just a trestle table running the length of its open side. An incredibly ancient Angolan man was laying hunks of meat out on the table. Hundreds of flies had settled on the meat, but that didn't seem to worry the butcher. He glanced up at Zak and Malek. His eyes lingered on the stump of Malek's arm and he gave an unfriendly glare before continuing his work.

'You get a lot of that if you're seen with us?' Zak asked.

Malek nodded.

Apart from the butcher, they saw very few people as they wandered the dusty roads of the town. A handful of women, colourfully dressed and preparing food outside their houses; a few kids, up early and playing quietly. One of these children – he couldn't have been more than eight years old – was sitting alone, cross-legged, his back up against the low fence of a compound. He wore no shoes and although he was young, Zak saw that the soles of his feet were rough and calloused like an old man's. He was desperately thin and with his forefinger he traced patterns in the dust.

Malek approached him. It was clear the little boy knew him and they spoke together in Portuguese. Malek gestured for Zak to join them. 'This is Bernardo,' he said. 'He says he wants to play a game with you.'

With his forefinger, Bernardo drew a grid on the floor – three squares by three – and drew a cross in the middle. Zak immediately saw that he had been challenged to a game of noughts and crosses. He smiled at Bernardo, bent down and drew a circle in the middle square of the bottom row. Bernardo's second cross went in the bottom right, forcing Zak to put his circle at the top left. And as soon as the Angolan boy made his next move – the middle right-hand side – Zak saw that he couldn't win. Bernardo grinned.

'Bernardo is very clever. But without a school' – Malek looked around – 'he will never leave this place.'

After two more games – one of which Bernardo won, and the other Zak – they continued their tour. Zak saw compounds with thin cattle and scrawny hens wandering in the dust. More people had emerged from their shacks now and everywhere he went his white skin drew silent stares. He was glad he had Malek with him.

Fifteen minutes later they reached the eastern edge of Lobambo. It was here that they came across the building site Zak had seen on his way in. There were four men guarding it, just as there had been last night. There were sitting cross-legged on the ground, like Bernardo. Unlike Bernardo, they didn't look like the types to pass the time playing puzzles. Each of them had a weapon by his side.

'The school?' Zak breathed.

'The school.'

Zak examined the site. It wasn't big for a school –

perhaps twenty metres by twenty. A trench had been dug for the foundations, but that was all it was – a hole in the ground. He checked out the faces of the men on site and compared them with his mental snap-shot of the guys he'd seen when he arrived the previous evening. They were lean and young – all in their twenties, Zak reckoned. They wore grubby jeans and T-shirts. Two of them had shaved heads. One had a nasty scar down the right of his face – it looked pale against his black skin – and a fourth had very blood-shot eyes.

Same people. He was sure of it.

That meant, he reckoned, that these four men were the only troublemakers. If there had been more, they'd be working shifts – the guys on duty last night wouldn't be the guys on duty again this morning.

And then Zak checked out their weapons. He knew he shouldn't be surprised that they were armed with AK-47s. He remembered Raf telling him that they were the commonest rifles in the world. Chances were that they were older than the men themselves, their parts cobbled together from other AKs manufactured in Russia, China or Eastern Europe. Learning about them, though, was one thing; seeing them in the hands of aggressive-looking young men was quite another. Zak suddenly felt very vulnerable.

They didn't notice Zak and Malek immediately.

But as soon as they saw the two boys lingering twenty metres from the building site, their hands felt for their weapons. The man with bloodshot eyes stood up and took a few paces towards them, clutching his AK-47. He shouted something at Malek in Portuguese. Zak didn't understand the words. He *did* understand, though, the man's tone of voice. It wasn't welcoming.

'We should go,' Malek said. He tugged on Zak's sleeve. 'Come on.'

'Which one's your cousin?' Zak breathed.

'It doesn't matter,' replied Malek. '*Come on!*'

The leader of the little group raised his weapon and with a lazy sneer aimed it in Zak's direction. Zak backed nervously away, holding up his hands in an attempt to show that he was harmless.

'Do you know where these guys live?' he asked, keeping his voice low so that only Malek could hear.

'Of course. Jay, we must go.'

Zak nodded. The two boys turned and walked quickly away from the building site. But Zak felt an anxious prickling sensation at the back of his neck. He didn't have to look over his shoulder to know that the man with bloodshot eyes still had him in his sights.

The rest of the day passed slowly. Zak chatted to some of the volunteers, who seemed content to sit around the camp doing not much. Around midday there was a storm. Zak watched the rolling clouds heading towards him from out at sea. He wondered what it must be like on board ship in the middle of such a tempest. When it hit land, he took shelter in his tent and listened as the rain fell like a shower of bullets for at least an hour, all the while going over the details of his mission in his head. When he emerged again, the ground was sodden and full of puddles, the air thick with evaporated rainwater. But the sky was blue again and it only took an hour for the earth to dry.

He saw Tillie, one of the volunteers he'd met when he arrived, emerge from her tent at the same time. She was a petite, pretty girl, with a turquoise Alice band and four small earrings in her right ear. She smiled at Zak and walked over to him.

'We get storms like that quite often,' she said. 'You get used to them.'

'Bit different to London,' Zak agreed, remembering that Jason Cole lived in Notting Hill. *But not so different from St Peter's Crag*, he thought quietly to himself.

'I saw you walking up to the village this morning,' said Tillie.

'Malek was showing me the sights.'

'Poor Malek.' Tillie sighed.

'What do you mean?'

'That arm of his. Kids his own age won't play with

him. The adults in the village treat him like an outcast because he's involved with us. He says he likes to help us so he can improve his English, but I think he just likes that we treat him like a normal person.' She gave Zak a piercing look. 'He's taken a shine to you,' she said.

'We've got a few things in common,' Zak replied. He knew he had to be careful here. Careful to talk about Jason and not himself. 'He lost his mum. So did I.'

Tillie's eyes filled with pity. 'I'm sorry,' she said simply.

Zak shrugged it off with a nonchalance he didn't really feel. 'We went to see the building site,' he said.

Tillie frowned. 'I wish we could do something,' she said. 'I really do.'

'Maybe you can.'

For a moment, she looked like she was going to agree; but then she shook her head. 'It's too dangerous,' she said.

Just then, Marcus, Ade and Alexandra came out of their tents and wandered over to them. The conversation moved on, but Tillie was quiet and looked thoughtful. Her eyes kept flicking in Zak's direction.

By sundown, you'd never have known there had been a storm. Zak ate with the other volunteers – grilled meat cooked on a barbecue. He tried to forget about the flies he'd seen crawling over the butcher's wares. It tasted good, whatever had been on it. Even Bea managed to tuck in – in between henpecking the other volunteers, who looked at her with amused, patient expressions that she didn't seem to notice. After supper, everyone else sat round the camp fire again. Marcus strummed lightly on his guitar and Zak took a seat next to Malek, only half listening to the music and the gentle murmur of chat.

'Tell me about our friends at the building site,' he asked Malek.

Malek thought for a moment. 'The one who spoke to me . . .'

'Bloodshot eyes?'

The Angolan boy nodded his head. 'He is Ntole. The son of my mother's brother. He does not like people to know he is my cousin.'

'Why?'

Malek held up the stump of his amputated arm. 'Because of this,' he said simply. 'Some people in the village are like that. When I was small, he used to tell me that he remembered my mother. He called her . . .' His face darkened. 'I do not want to say what he called her.' Zak could feel himself frowning. 'He was born in Lobambo,' Malek continued, 'but when he came of age he left for five years. They say he went away to fight. That he killed many men.' Malek shrugged.

'I don't know if it's true. But now he thinks he owns the village. He certainly owns the others who guard the site with him. He tells them what to do.'

Zak stared into the fire. 'What if you could get him to stand down from the building site?'

'I have one arm, they have guns. There is nothing I can do.'

'But what if there was?'

'You must be careful of Ntole, Jay. He drinks palm wine every night and sometimes during the day. They all do, but Ntole most of all. You can't tell what mood he will be in from one day to the next. He never goes anywhere without his weapon; it's always loaded and he knows how to use it.'

But Ntole and his men weren't the only people who knew how to fire an AK-47. Zak had received more firearms training in the last eighteen months than that lot put together.

'Listen,' Zak whispered. 'I've got an idea, but I need your help.' He held up one hand to stop Malek objecting. 'All you have to do is show me where they live. Can you do that?'

Malek nodded, but his eyes were still full of doubt.

When ten o'clock arrived and it looked like everybody was going to bed, Zak edged closer to his Angolan friend. 'Meet me at the building site at midnight,' he whispered.

'You're not going to do anything stupid, Jay?'

'Trust me.'

The Angolan boy gave a sigh, as if to say he didn't think this was a good idea, and walked away from the camp fire, disappearing into the darkness as he made his way back up towards the village. Zak said his good-nights and returned to his tent, where he lay on his bed and waited for everything to become silent outside.

Eleven o'clock came and went. Eleven-thirty. There was no noise. No light. Zak crept over to the doorway of his tent where he had left his tackle bag. He removed the reel and silently left the tent. No sign of anyone, just like the previous night. He crept away from the encampment, stopping every twenty metres to look over his shoulder. But he didn't see anyone as he made his way, not to the pier this time, but back up into Lobambo.

It was very quiet in the village. Zak passed the occasional villager – none of whom seemed to be doing anything but sitting outside their shacks enjoying the clear night – but most people were inside.

It was 11.55 precisely when he reached the building site. Malek was already there. 'Jay,' he whispered, looking around, 'what are we doing?' He looked at the reel in Zak's hand. 'Fishing?'

'Yeah,' Zak said. 'Sort of. Just not for fish.'

Malek grabbed his arm. 'You have to be careful with those men, Jay. They are very violent. When they say they will shoot people, they mean it.'

'I know,' Zak breathed. He sounded a lot less nervous than he felt. 'And when I say they can't stop people building that school, I mean it too.' He paused. 'Nobody should call your mother names, Malek. I don't care who they are, or how many guns they've got.'

'I do not want other people to get hurt for my sake, or my mother's.'

'Nobody's going to get hurt, Malek. I promise you. So are you going to show me where they live? Let's start with Ntole.'

'What are you going to do?'

'Just pay him a little visit. You'll see.'

Malek was obviously wrestling with himself. He sighed and nodded, but as he took the lead he was muttering to himself in an African dialect Zak couldn't understand.

The first compound he led Zak to was very close – just fifty metres north of the building site. It consisted of eight shacks around a central courtyard about fifteen metres wide. The moon was so bright that the shacks cast shadows on the ground. Zak could see an old football in the middle of the courtyard, and a motorbike against one of the shacks.

'Which one?'

Malek pointed in the direction of the shack with the motorbike.

'Wait here,' Zak told him. 'Whistle if you see anybody coming.'

'What are you going to do?'

'You'll find out,' Zak told him. Better that he kept his plan to himself, otherwise Malek would try to talk him out of it.

'Jay, I think we should go back . . .'

But Zak was already heading stealthily towards the shack.

When he reached the motorbike, he stopped. He was in shadow now, and it was difficult to see. He flicked the switch on the bottom of his fishing reel and raised it to his eye. The night sight lit the courtyard up brightly. He could see Malek at the entrance to the compound, chewing on the thumbnail of his good hand and looking left and right. Zak turned his attention to the door of the shack. There was no lock on the outside – just a block of wood that acted as a handle. He listened carefully at the door. There was a sound. Regular. Quite loud. Snoring.

The occupant of the shack was asleep.

Slowly, Zak opened the door.

He stepped inside.

The first thing he saw in the hazy green glow of the

night sight was Ntole. The young Angolan man was sprawled in a chair. He wore nothing but a pair of jeans. There were empty bottles littered around his chair, and a further bottle still in his right hand, hanging at an angle. The whole place stank of sweat and alcohol. It made Zak want to retch but Ntole, he could see, wasn't waking up any time soon.

The rest of the shack was a total dump. Clothes, empty food tins – all sorts of junk was littered around. Zak wasn't interested in any of that. He was just interested in the object that was propped up against Ntole's seat: his AK-47.

He lowered the night sight, but didn't switch it off in case the noise woke the slumbering thug. Instead, he stood there, waiting for his own vision to become accustomed to the darkness, listening to the sound of Ntole's snoring. Within two minutes he could see the outline of the sleeping man.

He took a step forward.

And another.

Ntole stirred. He shouted out in his sleep. *He's waking up*, Zak thought. What should he do? Stay still or run? But then the outline of the slumbering man fell still.

Zak could feel his blood pumping. He stepped forward again and five seconds later he had his fingers round the cold metal of Ntole's AK-47.

It felt comfortable in his grip. Zak was well trained and he knew how to handle these weapons, better even than Ntole himself.

He took a deep breath and started his evening's work.

9

A SHOT IN THE DARK

Thursday, 03.00 hrs GMT

Thousands of miles away, in the darkness of 63 Acacia Drive, a mechanical cuckoo burst from the clock in the dining room. It cheeped twice.

Two a.m.

The figure at the bottom of the stairs didn't move.

To look at him, you wouldn't know he was an intruder. He wasn't dressed in black. He didn't wear a balaclava. In order to hide the missing eye that made him so distinctive, he wore a pair of thick-rimmed spectacles with a white swab covering the right-hand lens. It made him look like he'd had medical attention. Other than that, he wore a pair of jeans – a little baggy, because his body was very thin – and a navy jumper that he'd bought earlier that day from Marks & Spencer, along with the rucksack that was now slung over his shoulder. When it was time for him to leave the house, nobody would see anything other than an ordinary man walking down an ordinary street.

They certainly wouldn't know that he'd just carried out a less than ordinary crime.

The weapon in his hand was a Browning semi-automatic. It fired 9mm rounds, enough to kill a man at ten to twenty metres. Or a woman, of course. Or a girl. The barrel of the handgun was longer than normal, because he had fitted a suppresser to the weapon. This would silence the shot. Not completely, but instead of giving a loud retort that would wake up the whole street, the shot would sound like somebody knocking on a door. There was a small risk that it would wake the other occupants of the house. If that happened, the intruder would deal with it. But if everything went according to plan, there would only be one murder tonight. He was experienced enough to realize that leaving more dead bodies behind than necessary was generally a bad idea.

The cuckoo returned to its cubbyhole and the intruder started to climb the stairs. A floorboard creaked underneath his feet. He stopped and listened.

Nothing. The house was still asleep. He continued to creep slowly upstairs, gripping the Browning in his right hand.

The first bedroom he checked was very small. It contained a single bed, but there were no bedclothes on it. The intruder sensed this room hadn't been used for many months. He closed the door and walked past the bathroom to the other end of the landing where there were two more doors. The intruder felt for the door knob of the left-hand door and quietly – *very* quietly – opened it. He peered inside. A double bed. The dark outlines of two people. The sound of gentle snoring.

He closed the door again. There was just one more room to try now.

The door of this final room was slightly ajar. When the intruder pushed it open, it didn't make a sound. He stepped inside. This room was bigger than the first and smaller than the second. The lights were off – he knew that already from staking the house out – but the yellow glow of a street lamp flooded in through the open curtains. There was a dressing table, a mirror on the wall, a cupboard, a chest of drawers and a small pile of clothes that had been dumped on the floor.

And a bed, of course.

And in the bed, huddled under the duvet, the outline of a figure. Not small enough for a child, not big enough for an adult.

The intruder had found his target.

He raised his gun.

He was pleased that the girl was covered by her duvet. It gave him two advantages. The thick padding would absorb a bit more of the sound of his gun. It would, in a way, be doubly silenced. But perhaps more importantly it meant that when he shot her, the blood from the wound would be soaked up. Blood, he knew, was the very devil to get off your skin and out of your clothes. He was glad he'd be able to avoid the spatter.

He pressed the barrel of his Browning against the soft, squashy material.

He fired.

The sound of the shot was quiet, but the impact made the whole bed judder. The figure underneath the duvet shook once and was still. At that range – point blank – the intruder knew it would only take a single shot, so he removed the gun from the duvet, bent over and gently peeled back the covers to check his handiwork.

He took a sharp breath.

There was no blood. There was no blood because there was no wound. And there was no wound because there was no body. All the intruder saw was a pile of pillows. One of them had a bullet hole. In the dim light he could just see the scorch marks around it, and the stuffing that had come loose from inside.

He felt his skin prickle with anger. He'd been outsmarted. By a *girl*. How had she known he was coming for her? *Had* she known it? Perhaps her absence tonight was nothing to do with him. Perhaps she was missing from her bedroom for some other reason . . .

There was no point giving in to his anger. He took his rucksack from his shoulder and hid the Browning away. He removed something else from the bag. It was very small. No different in size from the little chocolate drops he used to give his Alsatian dog when he was a boy. But it wasn't a chocolate drop. He looked around the room again. On the bedside table was a reading lamp. He unscrewed the bulb from the lamp and felt inside the metal shade. The object attached itself to the interior. The intruder screwed the bulb back in. Then he gently drew the duvet back over the pillows, like he was tucking someone in.

As he went downstairs, the same floorboard creaked. He didn't stop this time. He headed straight for the back door, exited the house and locked it again with the picks he had used to let himself in.

And then he walked back up Acacia Drive. There was nobody around to see him go.

'Are you sure there's nobody here?'

Ellie was on edge. Not that this was a surprise. She'd been on edge for days. But watching a serious-faced, fair-haired man breaking into number 62 –

the house directly opposite hers – certainly hadn't been a good way to calm her nerves. 'We come as a pair, sweetie,' Gabs had said. 'Love and marriage, horse and carriage . . .' Apart from telling her that his name was Raf – and what kind of name was that, anyway? – he'd said nothing to her. But it had only taken him a matter of seconds to break into Mr and Mrs Carmichael's house, and only a few seconds more to disable the burglar alarm.

'How does he know the code?' Ellie asked the woman who called herself Gabs.

'It's on file,' Gabs said, 'if you know where to look.'

Ellie could sense that this was the only answer she was likely to receive. 'Are you *sure* there's nobody here?' she repeated.

'Relax, sweetie. I'm sure. Mr and Mrs Carmichael were on a British Airways flight to Lanzarote three days ago. Their return ticket isn't booked for another ten days and Mr Carmichael used his Visa card five hours ago to buy dinner out there. They really aren't going to be walking in on us.'

Ellie stared at Gabs. 'How do you *know* all that stuff?'

'Ways and means, sweetie. Ways and means. You should remember that if you ever need to disappear. If you're not careful, people can track your location very precisely.'

'Why would I want to disappear?' Ellie said quickly. She didn't know why, but the thought of it touched a nerve. Hadn't *everyone* thought of disappearing, even if they didn't mean it?

Gabs appeared to sense her nervousness. 'I don't know, sweetie,' she said. 'Why would you?'

Raf led the way – through the kitchen, up the thickly carpeted stairs and into the front bedroom. The curtains were closed, but Gabs had a torch with a pencil-thin beam which she shone briefly around the room. This was clearly where Mr and Mrs Carmichael slept. There was a double bed and, on the bedside tables, pictures of their three children. They'd all left home now, but Ellie saw them around sometimes and recognized their faces.

'Don't switch the lights on,' Gabs warned as she turned off the torch. Ellie caught herself giving her a cross look in the darkness. Like she was going to do *that*. She lingered by the bed. Raf was carrying a metal case – bigger than the briefcase her dad took to work, but smaller than a suitcase. He laid this on the bed and opened it up. He removed a tripod and set it up just in front of the curtains. Then he removed something that looked like a small telescope with a flat screen, about fifteen centimetres square, at the viewing end. He fixed this to the tripod. With his right hand he drew one of the curtains back just a couple of inches, and with his left he nudged the apparatus towards the window.

'What's that?'

'You don't need to whisper, sweetie,' Gabs said. 'Nobody can hear us. It's a night sight. It means we can zoom in on things in the dark. Things like your bedroom.'

Gabs nodded towards the screen and Ellie approached. Raf had finished fiddling with the sight. It was directed towards Ellie's window. Shrouded in a green haze, she could make out almost every detail of her bedroom. The door. The chest of drawers. And the bed, of course, which on Gabs's instruction she had set up with dummy pillows the moment she knew her mum and dad were asleep, and just before she'd opened her bedroom curtains and sneaked out of the house to meet her and this strange, silent man called Raf.

Ellie stared at it for a moment. It was pretty creepy, like she was looking in on herself while she slept. 'What do we do now?' She was still whispering, despite what Gabs had said.

'We wait. And we watch. And if nothing happens we come back tomorrow night and we wait and watch again. But you know what? I've got a feeling that won't be necessary.'

She was right.

They had been sitting in absolute silence for a good couple of hours. Ellie had started to get cold and, if she was honest, a bit bored. She was staring at her watch, trying to make out the time in the darkness – it was about five to three – when she heard the faint sound of footsteps in the street below.

Gabs and Raf looked at each other. The footsteps stopped. The two adults turned their attention to the screen at the back of the night sight. Ellie did the same. She didn't know what she was waiting for, but she found herself holding her breath in any case.

She shivered. Was it the cold, or something else?

Four minutes past three. Ellie couldn't help gasping as, in the green haze of the screen, she saw her bedroom door open. A man entered. It was difficult to make out his features through the night sight. She could see, though, that he was wearing glasses. One lens was covered up with some kind of dressing. He had a shaved head and was very thin. There was a rucksack on his shoulder.

As he stood by Ellie's bed, looking down on the bulge created by the pillows, she saw something in his right hand. But it was only when he fired silently into the duvet that she realized it was a gun.

Ellie cried out. She felt Gabs's hand on her shoulder. 'It's OK, Ellie . . .'

But it wasn't OK. It wasn't anything *like* OK. The

man was peeling back the duvet to reveal the pillows she'd stuffed down there. She felt herself on the brink of tears. 'He wants to . . . He just tried to . . .' She couldn't bring herself to say the words 'kill me'. 'Why?' she wailed. 'What have I done?'

The ghostly green image showed the man removing something from his rucksack and fiddling with Ellie's bedside light. But suddenly Ellie wasn't concerned with any of that. Another, more sinister, thought had entered her head.

'My mum and dad,' she breathed. 'What's he going to do to my mum and dad?'

She stood up and started to make for the door of Mr and Mrs Carmichael's bedroom. But then she felt Gabs's hands on her again. Firmer than last time. Rougher.

'Get off me!' Ellie hissed. '*Get off me!* I have to go and warn them. I have to go and—'

'Your parents are perfectly safe,' Gabs told her. Even though Ellie continued to wriggle, she didn't let go and she was too strong for the younger girl.

'What do you *mean* they're perfectly safe? There's a murderer in my house with a gun. What are you, stupid? Let me go . . .'

'Stop and think, Ellie,' said Gabs, her voice much more abrupt than it had been up till now. 'Who did he just try to kill?'

'Me, obviously.'

'So if he still wants you dead, why would he kill your parents? The police would be crawling all over this place. He wouldn't be able to get near you.'

Ellie stopped wriggling. She looked over at the screen. The man was just leaving the room, closing Ellie's door behind him.

'Listen carefully,' Gabs breathed.

They stood still. Ellie could hear nothing but the beating of her heart. And then, a minute later, footsteps on the pavement outside again, disappearing up Acacia Drive.

Silence in Mr and Mrs Carmichael's bedroom. Ellie was too shocked, too terrified to speak.

'I think,' said Raf after a few seconds, 'we should find out why our friend was so interested in Ellie's bedside lamp. Ellie, time for you to pop back home.'

Ellie shook her head. 'I can't . . .'

'Yes you can, sweetie,' Gabs told her.

'What if he comes back?'

'He won't come back. Not tonight.'

'But what if he *does*?'

Gabs gave her a bleak smile. She put her hands inside her black leather jacket and pulled out a gun. 'If he does,' she said quietly, 'I'll deal with it. I'll be covering the entrance to your house, Ellie. You'll be fine. Go up into your bedroom, remove the bulb from your lamp and examine it. When – if – you find anything, bring it back here.'

Ellie looked from Gabs to Raf. Their faces, shrouded in the darkness of the room, were very serious. She didn't know if Gabs and her gun made her feel better about all this, or worse.

'Why does he want to kill me?' she asked.

'I don't know. Maybe it's because you can recognize him. He's not the kind of guy who likes to be recognized.'

'Who *is* he?'

'You don't need to know that, Ellie.'

'Yes I do.'

'Trust me, Ellie, it's much better—'

'If you want me to go and check my light, you'd better tell me what's going on, Gabs. Otherwise I'm going to stand in the middle of the street and start screaming for the police.'

Gabs and Raf exchanged another glance, and Ellie saw Raf nod slightly.

'All right, Ellie,' said Gabs, her voice serious. 'His name is Adan Ramirez. His nickname is Calaca, which means *skeleton*. He comes from Mexico and I honestly don't know how many people he's killed.'

'But what's this got to do with me? Why did he show me a picture of Zak? What's it got to do with him? Zak's *dead*, for God's sake . . .'

'Ellie, sweetie, I can't tell you anything else. You've just got to trust us.'

'Trust you? How can I trust you? How can I trust anyone? What happens when you're not here? I'll never get away from him.' She could feel the tears coming again and she didn't care. 'He'll kill me.'

'No he won't, Ellie.'

'How do you know? How can you say that?'

'Because we're here. Me and Raf. And believe me, we're very good at this sort of thing. But you *have* to do as we ask, Ellie. You *have* to go over to your house and check out that lamp. You can do it, sweetie. You really can.'

Ellie took another deep breath and tried to get control of herself.

Raf's voice: 'If you hadn't trusted us up till now, Ellie, Calaca wouldn't have put a bullet into your pillows tonight. He'd have put one in your head.'

There was no way Ellie could argue with that.

Outside Mr and Mrs Carmichael's house, Acacia Drive was silent. A black cat padded across the road, but apart from that there was no movement. 'Can't you come with me?' Ellie asked Gabs. Raf had remained in the house, keeping up surveillance on her room.

Gabs shook her head. She still had the gun in her right hand. 'I need to watch from here,' she said. 'It's safer that way. Go now.'

As the strange woman with white-blonde hair retreated into the shadows cast by Mr and Mrs Carmichael's front porch, Ellie crossed the road. It was only fifteen metres to her house. It felt like fifteen miles. Her head was filled with the terrifying image of the man they called Calaca. They had heard him walking away from number sixty-three, but they hadn't *seen* him. Which meant he could still be here.

And if he was still here . . .

She entered the house by the back door, unlocking it as quietly as she could. Inside the house, all was dark. She heard the cuckoo clock ticking in the dining room. As she walked upstairs, she knew which was the creaking step and she avoided it. Seconds later she was in her room.

She noticed the smell. A faint reek of burning, like someone had lit a match in here. She tiptoed over to her bed and ran the flat of her hand over the duvet. Her fingers brushed against the bullet hole. The edges were crispy and flaked away as she touched them. As she poked her finger into the hole, she couldn't help imagining what that bullet would have done to her skin . . .

Footsteps on the landing. Ellie gasped. She looked towards the window where she knew Raf would be watching her. But before she could make any sign of distress, the footsteps had got closer.

The door was opening.

Ellie spun round.

Light. It hurt her eyes.

A figure in her room.

'Ellie Lewis, what on *earth* do you think you're doing?'

She blinked. Her mum, dressed in a flowery dressing gown and with her hair in a net, was standing in the doorway.

'Why are you dressed? What's going on? What's that smell?'

Ellie looked guiltily at her duvet. Her mum pushed past her and touched her fingers to the hole just like Ellie had done in the darkness.

'What on *earth* is this?' she demanded.

Ellie didn't know what to say. She glanced towards the window again.

'Don't just stand there, young lady. I asked you a question. What is it?'

Ellie bit her lower lip. 'Cigarette burn.' She couldn't believe what she was saying. She'd never touched a cigarette in her life. She *hated* them.

Her mother blinked. 'I beg your pardon?' Her voice was a dangerous whisper.

'Cigarette burn,' Ellie repeated. 'Sorry.'

A second figure appeared in the door. It was her dad. He was wearing nothing but a pair of Y-fronts.

Ellie wished he wouldn't walk about the house like that. His hairy belly wobbled out above the waistband. It made her skin crawl.

'She's been smoking in her room, Godfrey. Look, she's made a cigarette burn in my best linen.'

Ellie's dad gave her a thunderous look. 'You're a very silly little girl, Ellie Lewis. A *very* silly little girl. I don't know what's gone wrong with you lately, but I *won't* have it. Trouble with the police. Now this. You get into bed, young lady, and I don't want to hear another peep from you. We'll discuss this in the morning.'

Seconds later, they were gone.

Ellie was shaking. She switched out the light. It took a minute or two for her eyes to get used to the darkness again. She could hear the murmur of her parents' voices in the room next door and could just guess what they were saying. The voices died down after about ten minutes. In the morning there would be hell to pay. But right now she had work to do.

She fumbled in the darkness for her bedside lamp and very quietly unscrewed the bulb from its fitting. She put her fingertips inside the metal shade and felt around. It didn't take more than a couple of seconds to locate a flat, round object, about the size of a twenty-pence piece. It was stuck to the inside of the shade, but it came away easily. Ellie had no idea what it was. She put it in her pocket and sat on the edge of her bed.

And waited.

She needed to be sure her mum and dad were asleep before she left the house again. It wasn't until she heard the cuckoo clock cheep four a.m. that she dared listen in at their door to hear the steady sound of their breathing. Then she crept downstairs and out of the back door again.

It had turned colder. Ellie shivered as she crossed the road. Gabs was still waiting in the porch of Mr and Mrs Carmichael's house, the gun still in her hand. 'I found something,' Ellie said.

But immediately Gabs put one finger to her lips. She led Ellie back into the house. Before they went upstairs, however, she held out one hand and nodded. Ellie understood what she meant. She put her hand in her pocket, pulled out the object she'd removed from the light shade and gave it to her. Gabs only examined it briefly before laying it on the kitchen table and leading Ellie up to the bedroom. Raf was waiting for them.

'What kept you?'

'My mum and dad woke up.' The words tumbled out of Ellie's mouth. 'I had to tell them the gunshot was a cigarette burn, and . . . and . . .'

'Nice hairnet your mum wears,' Raf said. 'Suits her. Not sure your about your dad's pants, though. You should think about getting him a dressing gown for Christmas. Did you find anything?'

'Listening device,' Gabs said. 'Looks like our friend Calaca wants to keep tabs on Ellie's movements.'

The thought of that made Ellie feel sick. 'I'm going to throw it away,' she said. 'Tread on it or something. Stick it in the bin. I'm not having that man listening in on me.'

But Gabs shook her head. 'No, sweetie,' she said. 'If you do that, he'll know you're on to him. And he'll know you're receiving help. What you're actually going to do is go back home and put the listening device back exactly where you found it. If you want to put an end to all this, that is.'

'*What?* Didn't you see what that man just tried to do to me? Are you crazy or something?'

'No, sweetie. Not crazy. But I do have an idea.' Gabs looked over at Raf. 'You know, Ellie's really got herself in trouble lately. First the police, now smoking in her room. I think it's time she went the whole hog and found herself a boyfriend. Don't you?'

10

RUSSIAN ROULETTE

Thursday, 08.00 hrs West Africa time

Zak was dreaming.

He found, these days, that his sleep was either dreamless, or haunted. Dreamless was good. Haunted was very bad. It was always the same. He was being hunted by a thin figure whose face was the stuff of nightmares even at the best of times. His pursuer only had one eye, and the skin had grown over the socket of the missing eye, smooth and unblemished. No matter where Zak ran, the one-eyed man appeared straight ahead of him. Zak would turn and run in a different direction, but Calaca was always there.

As the dream progressed, a second figure appeared next to him: Cesar Martinez, the drug dealer he had been sent to entrap on his first mission, had a rictus smile and a bloody patch on the front of his shirt. A third figure joined them. His son, Cruz. Zak's former friend.

He tried to run from them, but they kept appearing.

And now, each time they appeared, they were a little closer.

Closer . . .

'Jay! Jay! *Wake up!*'

Zak sat bolt upright. For a moment he couldn't work out where he was. This didn't *look* like St Peter's Crag, the place he'd come to think of as home. Then he saw the mosquito nets surrounding him and everything came flooding back. Lobambo. Black Wolf. The MV *Mercantile*. It was due to arrive today, and the thought made Zak very uneasy. Then he remembered Ntole, drunk and asleep, his weapon by his side. The building site with no building. Bernardo: the schoolboy with no school.

And Malek. Standing outside his tent, calling him. 'Wake up, Jay. It's morning!'

Morning. And Zak had work to do.

He jumped out of bed and shook his head to get rid of the remnants of sleepiness. Moments later he walked out of the tent. Malek looked tired. He also looked worried. He was holding the stump of his bad arm as though it needed protecting. 'Jay, last night – I don't know what you were doing but I think it was a mistake. Ntole is a very bad man. Very dangerous. I don't think we should—'

Zak put one hand on Malek's shoulder. 'It's OK,' he said. 'You'll see. Just trust me.'

The other volunteers were all up. Marcus was stoking the camp fire while the others went about the business of collecting wood and preparing food. Zak walked straight up to Marcus. 'We should go to the site this morning,' he said. 'Put in some work before it gets too hot.'

Marcus looked up from stoking the fire. His friendly, open face was apologetic. 'Jay, mate, it's not as easy as that. We've got this problem with—'

'Yeah, I know. Malek told me. But Ntole and his buddies aren't there this morning.' He looked over at the Angolan boy, who was standing nervously about five metres away. 'Right, Malek?'

Malek looked awkward. 'Right,' he said.

'And anyway,' Zak added, 'if they turn up again, we'll leave.'

Marcus shook his head. 'I don't know, Jay mate. I don't think we should mess with them.'

Zak shrugged his shoulders. 'Then we might as well pack up and go home. We're here to make a difference to Lobambo, not just have a holiday by the beach.'

Marcus stood up straight. 'Jay, we've discussed this – all of us. And we've had a visit from the British Embassy too. They agree with us. Ntole and his men, they'll get bored eventually. They'll realize they're never going to make any money out of keeping us away from the site. And when they understand it's not worth their while, we'll get back to work.'

'How long's that going to be? A month? A year?'

Marcus looked a bit shamefaced. 'Sorry, mate,' he said. 'It's what we've all agreed.'

The other volunteers had gathered round by now. They were clearly happy for Marcus to be their spokesperson. None of them said a word, and as Zak looked at each of them in turn, he noticed that Tillie, in particular, refused to meet his eye.

Zak hadn't expected this to be so difficult. 'All right,' he said. 'I'm going up there by myself.'

'Absolutely not!' Bea had stepped forward and she was talking in her most matronly voice. 'Jason, it's far too dangerous. Those men have guns. *Guns*, Jason! You're not to go anywhere near them. You shouldn't even be going up into the village alone . . .'

'I won't be alone,' Zak told her. 'Malek will come with me, won't you, Malek?'

The Angolan boy looked at him with a pained expression. He nodded his head with a distinct lack of enthusiasm.

Tillie looked around at the others. Her forehead had curled into a frown and she looked torn between two decisions. She swallowed hard. 'Well, if Jay's going, I'm going,' she said.

A murmur from the other volunteers. Marcus turned to look at them. He had the air of someone trying to stop a situation getting out of control. 'If we all go,' he said rather reluctantly, 'I suppose it'll be safer . . .'

'Safer?' Bea's voice had raised at least an octave, and her eyes blinked even more than usual. 'What do you *mean*, safer?'

'Well at least Jay's trying to do *something*,' Alexandra blurted out. She had long dark hair that was tied back with a scrunchie.

Suddenly the mood had changed. Zak sensed he had the others – with the exception of Bea, who was looking at them all with thin lips – on side. 'Look,' he said, 'anyone who doesn't want to come doesn't *have* to come. But I'm going to the building site now.'

'Me too,' said Tille.

'Me too,' said Alexandra.

And one by one the remaining members of the group – all except Bea – said: 'Me too.'

There was a buzz among the little group of seven volunteers, Marcus, Zak and Malek as they set off from the camp. An anxious excitement. As they came to the outskirts of Lobambo, however, their nervous chatter quietened down. They walked in a slow, silent group with Marcus, Zak and Malek in the lead. The villagers gave them curious glances. Zak could see them whispering at each other. Now and then he saw children running ahead of them. By the time they reached the middle of the village, it was clear that the news of their arrival had gone before them. Everyone knew who they were.

And as they drew closer to the building site, Zak noticed mothers hurrying their kids back inside.

The group of volunteers was twenty-five metres away when it became clear that, far from being absent, Ntole and his men were very much in attendance. But the children running ahead to announce their arrival had obviously not been brave enough to carry their news to the gunmen. The Angolans were slouched lazily around the site, marking time. When Zak and the others approached, however, they jumped to their feet and grabbed their AK-47s. Five seconds later they had formed a line between the volunteers and the building site.

The volunteers stopped. 'I thought you said they weren't here,' Marcus breathed.

There was fifteen metres of open ground between them and Ntole's men. Nobody spoke. Somewhere in the distance Zak heard a dog barking. Apart from that, silence.

He took a step forward, but stopped when he heard a voice behind him. 'Jay, no!' It was Tillie. He looked over his shoulder to see her face full of anxiety. The others were shrinking back – all of them except Malek, who looked torn between Zak and the volunteers.

Zak gave Tillie what he hoped was a reassuring smile. Deep down, though, he was far from confident. This had seemed like a good idea back at the safety of the camp, but now that he was faced with four scowling gunmen, he felt a lot less sure of himself. He felt eyes on him too, and he could imagine the look of disapproval on Michael's face at the way he was drawing attention to himself.

But then another part of his mind fought back. Why *shouldn't* he use what he had learned to help the people of Lobambo? As long as he wasn't compromising his real mission . . .

He walked directly up to Ntole. The Angolan's eyes were even more bloodshot than yesterday and he still smelled of alcohol. His hands were trembling, but it was obviously not through fear. Zak stopped five metres away and watched as the Angolan's lip curled.

'What,' he asked, in hesitant, accented English that was no way near as good as Malek's, 'do you want?'

Zak didn't take his eyes from Ntole's. 'To build a school,' he said.

Ntole's face remained expressionless. He looked left and right at his men. Suddenly he started to laugh. The other three gunmen did the same. They looked and sounded like Zak had told them a very good joke. But ten seconds later, as if someone had flicked a switch, Ntole stopped laughing and the others followed suit.

'Go home,' Ntole said, 'if you know what is good for you.' All traces of mirth had left him.

Zak stood his ground. 'I don't think I'll be doing that,' he said.

Ntole raised his weapon. Zak could tell, by the way he dug the butt firmly into his shoulder, that he knew how to use it. His hands had stopped shaking. 'Go home, little boy,' he said.

Zak remained just where he was.

Footsteps behind him. Running. He felt someone tugging on his clothes and turned to see Tillie pulling him away. 'Jay, this is really stupid. Look at him – he's not joking.'

'Let go, please,' Zak said calmly. 'Tillie, please let—'

He was cut off short when one of Ntole's men – the one with the scar down the side of his face – raised his weapon and aimed it towards Tillie. She let go of him and Zak could sense her backing away, rejoining the other volunteers.

He stepped closer to Ntole. He was just a metre away from the barrel of the AK now. 'Get out of my way,' he said.

He could see sweat on Ntole's brow. Now that he was closer, the stench of last night's alcohol was even stronger and he also caught a whiff of stale tobacco.

Ntole spoke very slowly now. 'I *will* shoot you,' he said.

For a moment Zak wanted to run. It took all his courage to keep his feet planted on the floor.

Ntole sneered again. With a flick of his thumb he released the safety catch of the rifle. 'You have three seconds,' he said.

'Jay!' Marcus's voice ten metres behind him. 'Get back from there!'

'One,' said Ntole.

Zak didn't move. A trickle of sweat rolled down the side of his face.

'Two.'

'*Jay! Move!*'

'Three.'

Ntole smiled.

And then he pulled the trigger.

A scream from behind. Zak didn't know who it was. He was more interested in the sound that came from the AK-47. It was not the retort of a round. It was just a thin, metallic click. The stoppage caused a look of annoyance to cross Ntole's forehead. He fired again.

Click.

Zak reached into his pocket. 'Looking for these?' he

asked, and he pulled out a handful of 7.62 rounds.

Rounds that he had removed from Ntole's weapon – and from the weapons of his men – the night before.

Ntole lowered his gun in astonishment and looked, perplexed, at the magazine. Zak took his chance. He grabbed the barrel and with a sharp tug removed the weapon from Ntole's grasp. He heard more clicks – the other gunmen trying unsuccessfully to discharge their rifles. 'You can *try* to shoot us with empty magazines,' Zak said, 'but it might be a bit of a waste of time.' He turned round to look at the volunteers. 'Get their weapons!' he instructed.

The shocked volunteers didn't move immediately. They were staring at Zak like he was insane. Marcus was the first to step forward. He was soon followed by the others, who surrounded the remaining three gunmen, but then looked at each other, apparently unsure what to do. Their decision, though, was made for them. The gunmen dropped their useless weapons on the floor and edged nervously backwards. The bullies looked a lot less brash now they were unarmed and outnumbered. Once the volunteers had collected all the weapons, they turned to Zak. But they didn't look pleased. Their expressions of shock had turned to anger.

'Me and Malek will throw the weapons off the pier,' Zak said. 'I guess the rest of you can stay here and start work.' He turned to Ntole. 'You and your men should probably go now. I think your little game of soldiers is over.'

Ntole's face was a picture of hatred. He'd been out-smarted. Humiliated. He clearly didn't like it. He looked like he wanted to pounce on Zak, to do some him damage. But he could also see that he and his men were beaten.

He turned to the other gunmen and nodded at them. And then, with a final, malevolent glare at Zak, he led them away and they disappeared from sight.

The volunteers were silent as they watched Ntole go. Marcus turned to Zak. 'Jay, that was *incredibly* . . .' He looked like he couldn't find the right word.

'Stupid?'

They all turned to see Bea standing about ten metres apart. For once, however, she seemed lost for further words.

'You could have been *killed*,' Tillie said. 'How . . . how *dare* you not tell us what you were planning.'

'I thought you wanted to get rid of Ntole . . .'

'In our own way. We're not idiots, Jay.'

'Tillie's right,' said Marcus. 'This isn't a game, you know. Ntole and his men are dangerous.' He nodded at the weapons. 'And so are those. Mate, I think you'd better go back to the camp. We need to have people we can trust around us. And Malek, I'd have expected better of you . . .'

Malek looked like he didn't know where to put himself.

Zak looked at each of the volunteers in turn. Their faces were serious. They clearly agreed with Marcus's suggestion. He felt his own face flushing red with embarrassment. When he'd disarmed Ntole, he'd felt so clever. Now he felt totally stupid. Worse than that, he had a sudden vision of his Guardian Angels, a look of disappointment on their faces. It was that imagined look that stung more than anything. He turned to Malek. 'Come on,' he said quietly. 'Let's get rid of these AKs.'

Malek could only carry a single weapon on account of his arm. It was up to Zak to carry the remaining three. He strapped one over each shoulder and held the third with both hands. The villagers drew back nervously as they passed. Zak could tell Malek felt very uncomfortable carrying a weapon. He held it with his arm slightly stretched out, like it was a snake. And it was a full five minutes before he even spoke.

'They're right,' he said as they walked down the long, dusty path between the village and the pier. 'You could have been killed.'

'Calculated risk,' Zak replied, trying to sound casual. 'Sometimes you've got to—'

'*No!*' Malek's eyes were ablaze. 'You don't understand. Bea was right too. It was *very* stupid.'

'Malek, I—'

'If I'd known that was what you were up to, I would
never have taken part. You think we want to see *more*
bloodshed in Angola? What would it have meant if an
English boy had been shot by an Angolan thug? You
think you were just risking your own life? Wars have
been started for smaller things than that, Jay. Perhaps
if you had seen babies slaughtered by enemy troops,
you would not have risked your childish game of
Russian Roulette.'

They walked on in silence.

'I'm sorry,' Zak said finally. 'I didn't think.'

But Malek didn't reply.

When they reached the pier, Zak saw three fishing
boats drifting out to sea from the harbour area to the
left. Some children were at the water's edge, splashing
and waving the fishermen off. When they saw Zak,
Malek and the guns, they too grew quiet. They stood
ankle deep in sea water and watched them walk down
to the end of the pier.

Malek threw his weapon in first, flinging it out as far
as he could with his one good arm. He didn't stop to see
how quickly the AK-47 sank. With a final dark look at
Zak, he stormed back towards the shore. Zak watched
him go. He had the feeling he'd just lost a friend.

'Idiot,' he whispered. But he was talking to himself, not Malek. He hurled the rifles, one after another, out to sea, followed by the ammo. The guns spun like boomerangs, but they were never coming back. The moment they hit the water, they sank and disappeared.

Zak sat at the end of the pier. Foiling Ntole and his men had seemed like such a good idea. Malek was right, though. Zak hadn't thought it through properly. He remembered Michael's words of a few days ago. *You're there to carry out this op quickly and efficiently, not to right the wrongs of western Africa.* It was one thing undergoing training on St Peter's Crag; it was quite another putting that training into action. It meant nothing, he realized, that he was proficient with every weapon known to the modern military. It meant nothing that he was as highly trained as any special forces operative. It was no use having skills if you didn't know the right time to use them.

He thought back to his first operation, and the thin, serious face of Cruz Martinez, the son of South America's most wanted drug dealer, came into his head. In the few days that he'd known him, Cruz and Zak had bonded. Though they came from opposite sides of the world and from backgrounds as different as could be, they'd become close. Zak had helped Cruz stand up for himself, and Cruz had trusted him. He would never forget the look on the young man's face when Gabs delivered a fatal bullet to his father's skull. The look of betrayal. Of hatred. The way he'd vowed to take his revenge.

Losing friends, Zak realized, was something he would have to get used to.

He wished Raf and Gabs were here. He suddenly felt very alone, stuck in this strange, threatening place, thousands of miles from home. Wherever home was. He found himself thinking of Ellie. He wondered what she was doing now. If she was still mourning him. Half of him hoped she was. The other half hoped she'd moved on.

Zak stared out to sea.

And he stared.

He'd been sitting there for twenty minutes when he suddenly realized what he was looking at.

The vessel on the horizon appeared gradually. At first it could have been a mirage. As it drew closer, it might have been just another fishing boat. But within fifteen minutes it became clear that this was a bigger ship than any he had seen in Lobambo so far. And it was heading this way.

Zak heard footsteps. He looked over his shoulder to see that the children who had been playing in the water – five of them – were behind him. The look on their faces told him that such a big vessel was unusual here.

Within half an hour it was close enough for Zak to see that it had a black hull and a white body. He could see that there were jets of water pumping from the sides. He didn't know what these were for, and they stopped when the ship was 500 metres away from shore. Zak could just make out two figures talking on deck, but nobody else. And as it slipped into the dock alongside a jetty fifty metres from Zak's position – looking far too big for this small port but not running aground in the deep natural harbour – he saw, quite clearly, the name of the vessel written in large white letters along the side of the hull.

Mercantile.

Agent 21's target had arrived.

11

EL CAPITÁN

11.30 hrs West Africa time

The skipper of the merchant vessel *Mercantile* watched
the shoreline approach.

His name was Antonio Acosta, but the members
of his crew called him *el capitán*. This was not out of
respect, but out of fear. Their *capitán* was a brutal
man. He had swarthy skin and eyebrows that met in
the middle. As he stood at the head of the ship, his
bare chest was wet with sweat and spray. His skin was
as tough as the leather boots he wore. He looked to
port. A bunch of *bambinos* were sitting on a nearby
pier, watching the *Mercantile* make port. Just kids. He
didn't need to worry about them.

He sensed someone behind him.

'What is it?' he demanded in English spoken with a
very heavy Spanish accent. His crew came from all
over the world. English was their common language.

'The men want to know how long we'll be in harbour, *Capitán*. They've been at sea for a long time. They want to get their land legs. Find something to drink . . .'

'Nobody leaves the ship.'

'But, *Capitán* . . .'

The skipper turned. Antonio's first mate, Karlovic, was no weakling. He came from Georgia but was wanted in that country for crimes he never talked about. He had a shaved head and a line of piercings along his left eyebrow. They were almost always weeping and infected. It didn't seem to bother him, and Antonio suspected he kept them like that to make his appearance more threatening.

'Nobody leaves the ship,' he repeated.

He could tell Karlovic didn't like being told what to do. The first mate's face twitched. He was going to argue. It was obvious.

'If they stay on board,' Karlovic asserted, 'they'll fight with each other. Much better if they go ashore. Get nasty with the locals. These Africans, they're used to—'

It was the skipper's habit to carry both a knife and a handgun. The gun was strapped to an ankle holster. It was a .38 snub-nose, very small, its barrel much shorter than that of a normal handgun. It suited him just fine. Out at sea, he didn't need anything bigger.

He'd seen pirates – Somalians mostly, thin and ragged – carrying rocket-propelled grenade launchers and sub-machine guns before now. None of that was necessary. It was easy to kill a man, at close range, when you were surrounded by nothing but sea. Antonio should know. He'd done it enough times.

The snub-nose, however, was only his second favourite weapon. The knife, which was attached to a scabbard hanging from his waist, was made from highly tempered steel. This meant it could be brittle if used carelessly, but it also meant he could make the edge extremely sharp. The blade was fifteen centimetres long. It curved slightly at the end. The other edge had a series of vicious hooks pointing back towards the handle. These hooks would make no difference when the knife entered a human body. When it was pulled out, however, they would bring the innards with them.

The knife was *el capitán*'s favourite because he had learned that people were more scared of it than of a gun. They were scared of the thought of metal slicing flesh. Scared of the exquisite pain it could inflict.

Antonio flicked the knife from its scabbard now and held it up against his first mate's cheek. Karlovic inhaled sharply. A thin edge of scarlet appeared on his face.

'Nobody leaves the ship,' the skipper said yet again. This time there was no argument.

'Yes, *Capitán*,' Karlovic breathed. 'I will tell them.'

He stepped away from the skipper, touched his fingers to the blood and looked at them. He was humiliated. But he knew better than to complain. With a scowl on his angry face, he turned on his heel and walked across the deck, leaving the MV *Mercantile*'s skipper to return to his business of watching the west coast of Africa slowly approach.

Midday.

The sun was high in the sky and it was pushing forty degrees. A crowd of villagers, perhaps fifty of them, had come down to the waterside to stare at the unusual sight of the large merchant vessel in their harbour. But there was no sign of activity on the ship itself. The two figures Zak had seen as the *Mercantile* approached were gone. Hidden below decks, he assumed. Keeping their faces out of sight, their identities a secret. The ship looked far too big for the little jetty it was moored against. Like a hulking, silent giant. Waiting for something.

Zak tried to block out the excited chatter of the children around him. He needed to focus on the vessel. To work out his next move. To sit here in the full glare of the sun, scoping out the *Mercantile*, would just draw attention to himself. But how long would the ship remain docked? He only had a limited window to complete his operation. If she set sail before he'd had a chance to ID the crew and plant the explosive device, he'd have failed. But he couldn't do any of that until nightfall. So it meant waiting.

Zak pushed himself up to his feet and, with a smile at the excited children, walked back along the pier to the shore. He needed to keep eyes on the *Mercantile* even during the daytime, he decided. She was here to collect a shipment of uncut diamonds. Evidence of the diamonds being loaded would be a signal to Zak that the ship was likely to depart soon. If that happened, he'd need a plan B. Until then he just had to watch.

There were no suitable OPs on the waterfront – Zak had already established that. He wandered along the harbour front, behind the crowd that was still ogling the big ship. Now that he was on the other side of the *Mercantile* he was able to scope her out from the opposite direction. He saw a metal ladder fixed to the starboard side of the ship and extending up to the deck. An access point. Good.

He headed towards the nearest of the three palm trees. Here he sat down with his back against the trunk. He hoped he merged into the background. That he looked insignificant. He hadn't done a very good job of it so far, he realized. It was time to up his game.

* * *

The sun started to set. Zak had moved from the palm tree to the water's edge. Most of the Angolans had returned to the village. Only the children remained and even they were getting bored. There had been no sign of movement from the *Mercantile*. Nobody had come out on deck and nobody had approached with any cargo. As far as Zak was concerned this was good news. As soon as it was dark he could set up at the end of the pier and start 'fishing'. With any luck, he could finish the operation tonight and get out of here.

He walked back to the camp. The volunteers had returned from the building site. It was clear that they'd been working hard as their faces were dirty with sweat and dust. They were all drinking deeply from bottles of water. Zak looked around to see if he could find Malek. No sign of him. He walked up to Marcus. 'How did it go at the site?' he asked.

Marcus looked awkward. 'Look, Jay, we've been talking. We all think it's best if you don't stick around here much longer. I can take you back to the airport. It's pretty easy to get a flight back to the UK.'

Zak looked around at the others. Tillie's face was full of regret. So was Alexandra's, and everyone else's – except Bea, who just looked a bit smug.

Zak nodded. 'Right,' he said quietly.

He made his way round the little group of volunteers and into his tent. His stomach was churning.

He felt a mixture of embarrassment and relief. Embarrassment that he'd messed up and was being asked to leave; relief that the *Mercantile* had arrived on time. Another twenty-four hours and the mission would have been compromised.

Zak hunted in his bag for his iPhone. He'd be needing that. Then he gathered up his tackle bag and rod and walked outside again. 'I'm going fishing,' he told the others. 'I'd quite like to be alone.'

And when nobody replied, he wandered off by himself.

It was almost fully dark when he reached the end of the pier. There was still no sign of movement on the *Mercantile*. Zak sat with his legs over the left-hand edge of the pier. This way, he was facing the *Mercantile* and also had a line of sight back towards the shore, so he could see if anyone was approaching him. He removed the fishing rod from its tube, slotted the sections together and laid it across his lap. Then he took the reel from his tackle bag. Five seconds later he was using it to survey the deck of the *Mercantile*.

Everything was still. There were no people around, no lights on deck. It looked like a ghost ship. Zak fitted the reel to his rod and cast out to sea. There was no hook at the end of his line – he didn't want to catch a fish at the wrong moment. The moon was bright enough for him to scan for movement on the

Mercantile's deck with the naked eye. He checked his watch. Eight o'clock. The vessel had been in harbour for eight hours now. Surely something had to happen soon. If this truly was a Black Wolf operation, they weren't here on vacation.

The sea, black beneath him, lapped gently against the legs of the pier. Occasionally there was a splash and Zak imagined a fish flipping above the surface. Every ten minutes he removed the reel and scanned the deck with his night sight. Eight-thirty passed. Nine o'clock. Nine-thirty. It was just past ten when he saw something. It wasn't on deck, but on the shore. Headlamps. Two sets, trundling through the darkness from the direction of Lobambo. Zak watched them without the use of his night sight. They drove along the waterfront and stopped just by the jetty at which the *Mercantile* was moored. The headlamps went out.

Zak reeled in his fishing line and thirty seconds later he was looking through the night sight. He saw four men, two from each car. They looked like native Angolans. They were standing by two four-by-fours. Two of them were carrying heavy suitcases, one was speaking into a mobile phone and the fourth was carrying an assault rifle. He was looking around, clearly checking that nobody was observing them. But Zak was a hundred metres away and it was dark. The gunman couldn't see him.

Zak sensed movement on the *Mercantile*. He panned round. A figure had emerged on deck. He was standing to the port side and he too had a mobile phone to his ear.

Zak zoomed in. This was the first member of the *Mercantile*'s crew he'd seen and Michael's instruction was clear in his mind. *You need to be very sure, Zak, that the traffickers on board are the people we think they are. Positive IDs. Nothing less . . .*

The crew member's face was blurry. Zak adjusted the focus of his night sight. The man's features, still bathed in green haze, grew sharper. He wasn't a looker. His head was shaved and his features severe. It was his left eyebrow that identified him, however. There was a series of piercings along its length and it seemed fat and swollen. Zak instantly recalled the picture in his briefing pack. He'd last looked at it lying on the bed of the Holiday Inn at Heathrow. *Surname, Karlovic. First name unknown . . .*

Positive ID.

He panned back to the Angolans. The gunman stood by the two four-by-fours. The remaining three, however, were heading up the jetty. The man with the mobile took the lead; he was followed by the two carrying suitcases. They stopped halfway along the jetty. Zak examined the hull of the boat. There appeared to be a door there, but it was closed.

Voices.

For a moment Zak thought they were nearby. He looked left down the pier, expecting to see someone approach. But no figures emerged from the darkness and he realized the sound was wafting towards him on the breeze from the deck of the *Mercantile*. He directed his night sight in that direction.

Karlovic was still there, but now he was surrounded by three others. Zak didn't recognize them. The three men were fitting something to the railings of the deck while Karlovic looked on, and Zak could tell from the body language that Karlovic was in charge. He sensed that the three others didn't much like taking their instructions from him.

Another man appeared on deck. Zak focused on him.

He was bare-chested. His torso rippled with muscles. His neck was very thick and his eyebrows, which looked like black smudges in the haze of the night vision, met in the middle of his forehead. Again Zak recalled his briefing pack, and Michael's words. *Name, Antonio Acosta. Born and raised in the favelas of Rio de Janeiro. There's a rumour that he murdered his own brother when he was thirteen. We now believe he's a Black Wolf general . . . .*

Positive ID.

We can't be sure who else will be on board the

Mercantile, *but a positive ID of these two men will be enough. Put it this way, if Antonio Acosta and Karlovic are on board, the rest of the crew aren't very likely to be sweet old pensioners . . .*

Zak looked at the three crew members by the railings. They had attached some sort of pulley system to the vessel and were now lowering a thick rope with a hook at the end down to the jetty. He didn't need to see any more. It was obvious what was going on. The uncut diamonds had arrived. The crew was bringing them on board. It meant that the *Mercantile*'s business here was nearly done.

So Zak couldn't hang around.

He'd identified the Black Wolf personnel. And that meant only one thing.

It was time for him to advance to contact.

12

ADVANCE TO CONTACT

He moved quickly and quietly.

Within thirty seconds he had packed away his fishing rod and secreted the night-vision device back in the tackle bag. He left these on the side of the pier while he located the loose board that hid his equipment cache. He lifted it up and placed it to one side, then looked down the length of the pier to check that nobody was coming. All clear. Zak lifted the polythene-wrapped package from its hiding place. He could see that someone had constructed a wooden frame beneath the pier. It was this that was holding Zak's equipment.

The package was heavy. As Zak unwrapped it, he briefly wondered who had stashed this stuff here in the first place. He'd never find out, of course. That wasn't the sort of intel Michael liked to share. It consisted of four items. The first resembled a large float, the sort of thing he'd used as a kid when his dad used to take him for swimming lessons at the local pool. There were differences, though, between those polystyrene aids and this swim board. It was larger, for a start. Fixed to the top was a circular compass about twenty centimetres in diameter. To one side of the compass was a switch but Zak didn't touch it yet. He knew it would illuminate the compass but if he switched it on here he'd alert the men on the deck of the *Mercantile* to his presence.

The second item was his rebreather. It looked like a heavy black life jacket, with the addition of air tubes, a mouthpiece and a face mask. It had been specially adapted to house two small canisters of compressed air and two waterproof storage pouches. One of these contained a string bag with a magnet at the clasp. A set of military-grade fins were tied to the rebreather, which Zak undid before turning his attention to the third item.

The Heckler & Koch P11 was identical to the one he had fired back at the basement range on St Peter's Crag. Chunky. Heavy. Zak hated to admit it, but he felt a lot better with it stowed, along with his iPhone, in the second waterproof pouch of the rebreather. Especially given the nature of the fourth item he had pulled from the cache.

It was a small metal case, about thirty centimetres by twenty by ten. Zak knew enough about demolitions, however, to realize that a tiny package like this could cause a lot of damage. It weighed about five kilograms and had a rubber seal and heavy metal clasps. On one side of the case were four steel carbine hooks, welded to the metal. As Zak slipped the rebreather over his head, he saw that these hooks clipped easily to a harness across his front. He attached the device, then put his fishing gear and the polythene wrapping back in the hiding place under the pier.

Footsteps.

Zak looked down the pier. Someone was approaching. He couldn't tell who it was in the darkness, but he knew he couldn't be caught like this. He quickly slipped his feet into the fins, grabbed the swim board and the P11, shuffled to the edge of the pier and pushed himself into the water. There was a drop of three metres. And then a splash.

The water was cold and black. Zak had a flashback to the awful minute or so he had spent dragging Raf along the dark corridor of HMS *Vanguard*. He kicked himself back in the direction of what he hoped was the pier, before coming up for breath as quietly as possible.

He found himself just by one of the wooden legs of the pier and he grabbed hold of it. The footsteps were directly above him. They stopped, and the light of a torch shone down through the boards of the pier into the water just a couple of metres from his position. Whoever had the torch was searching for something. Him? It was impossible to say for sure. He clutched the pier leg a bit harder.

As his eyes grew used to the darkness underneath here, he made out the wooden frame beneath the loose board above. And he'd only been looking at it for five seconds when, to his horror, someone lifted the loose board.

He couldn't see the figure who had opened it up. Just the dazzling sight of the torch as they shone the beam through the narrow opening and onto the water. Very slowly he let go of the pier with his arms, clutching onto it with his ankles. He held onto the swim board with his left hand and aimed his P11 towards the opening with his right.

Five seconds passed.

Ten seconds.

He shivered. It wasn't just the cold water. It was a creeping sense of dread and panic. He'd made himself too obvious earlier in the day. *Someone was on to him . . .*

The beam of light disappeared. The loose board was replaced and Zak heard footsteps moving over his position and back towards the shore. And then just the lapping of the sea against the legs of the pier.

He pulled the dive mask over his face. Little

droplets of water covered the inside. He inserted the mouthpiece of the rebreather and took a few breaths. Air flowed into his lungs. Looking in the direction of the *Mercantile*, he switched on the compass light of his swim board. A faint, pale green glow spread out from the board as Zak checked the direction in which he needed to travel. The vessel was south of his position at a bearing of about 179 degrees. He fixed that figure firmly in his mind. Then he let go of the pier leg with his ankles.

The metal flight case acted as a weight to take him below the surface. He estimated that he was a couple of metres down. Hopefully the rebreather was doing its job and stopping any bubbles rising to the top of the water as he breathed out. The sound of the sea disappeared. All he could see was the illuminated compass on the swim board. He adjusted his trajectory so that he was heading at a bearing of 179 degrees, flipped his fins and darted through the water.

Time slowed down. Zak felt himself being buffeted by the underwater currents and he had to use all the strength in his body to keep his bearing correct. There were shadows on the edge of his vision. Sea creatures, he assumed, or maybe just the play of the moon on the waves. *Anything down here will keep its distance*, he told himself. He did his best to forget about the moray eel that had attacked Raf. The last thing he needed right now was memories like that. He concentrated hard on what he was doing. That way, perhaps he could forget that this was just his second mission, and that it didn't matter how much training he'd had; the real thing was a hundred times harder and more dangerous.

The cold water slid past. He suppressed a sense of panic. Surely he'd been swimming too long . . . *Surely* he should have reached the *Mercantile* by now . . .

The hull appeared suddenly, just two metres in front of him, vast and dark. Zak kicked upwards and seconds later emerged into the open air. He looked around. He was underneath the jetty against which the *Mercantile* was moored. Immediately up above, he heard voices. It was the three Angolans, he reckoned. It sounded like they were talking in Portuguese.

Zak moved away, swimming above water now as he was camouflaged by the jetty. The Angolans' voices faded. The water was washing against his dive mask so his vision was divided by sea and air. As he reached the end of the jetty, however, he submerged himself again and followed the line of the *Mercantile*'s hull until he reached the end of the vessel. Here he turned back on himself and started swimming along the far side of the ship.

He was about halfway back down the length of the *Mercantile* when he arrived at the ladder. The bottom rung was about three metres below the water line. Zak came up to the top again and grabbed hold of it.

He needed to ditch his gear. That was where the string bag came in. He removed it from the rebreather pouch and used the magnet to attach it to the metal hull of the ship, then he stowed his swim board and fins in the bag before removing his P11 from its pouch and tucking it into his shorts. He pulled the rebreather over his head. Before stashing the kit away, he removed his iPhone, shoved it into a damp pocket and unclipped the metal flight case. Holding it firmly, and now free of his dive gear, Zak started climbing the ladder.

It was difficult to climb and hold the flight case at the same time, especially with the gentle but un-nerving yaw of the ship. Zak's ascent was slow – a good two minutes before he arrived just below the level of the deck.

He stopped and listened.

Nothing.

Zak was just preparing to climb the final rungs when something stopped him. It was a smell: a waft of cigarette smoke. He froze. Somebody was up there, smoking. Zak might not be able to hear him, but he could sure smell him. He remained where he was, the muscles in his arms burning from holding on so tight.

A minute passed, and so did the smell of cigarette smoke.

Two minutes.

He heard footsteps. They walked directly past his position. Whoever it was up there, all he had to do was look over the railings and he'd see him, pinned against the hull, just a metre or so from deck level. Zak was suddenly very aware of the P11 tucked in his shorts. It wouldn't come to that. Would it?

Nobody did look. The footsteps faded away and Zak knew he had to take his chance.

He pulled himself up the ladder. The deck was in view now. Its floor was made of steel and at the level of his eyes, against the body of the ship, he saw a ring-shaped flotation aid. He checked left and right. Nobody there. Ignoring the fearsome pain in his muscles, he climbed up the final few rungs and pulled himself over the railings onto the deck.

Sea water dripped from his sodden shorts and T-shirt. Zak held the flight case in his left hand. With his right he removed the P11. Now he needed to get the explosive device into the engine room. It meant getting inside the ship.

He headed along the deck in the direction of the shore. He saw nobody. After fifteen metres, he came to a door on his left. He pushed it open. It was heavy. Once he was inside the ship he had to use all his strength to stop it banging shut.

He shivered. The water had leached all the warmth from him – he needed to keep moving. He was in a corridor. On the wall to his left was a laminated poster giving details of the safety regulations of the ship. Up ahead, the corridor stretched for ten metres before ending in another door. To his right was a flight of metal steps.

Zak stashed his weapon back in his shorts, activated his iPhone and swiped to the fourth page of apps. On the bottom row was a red icon with the image of a bicycle and a spanner. If anyone looked at it, they'd just assume it was a bike maintenance app, but when Zak touched the screen it morphed into a green 3D line drawing of the exterior of the *Mercantile*. Using just his forefinger he spun the image round until he was looking at the starboard side. Once he had identified the door he'd just walked through, he zoomed in. The schematics changed with his touch. He knew the engine room was in the bowels of the ship, and thirty seconds later he had identified his route and committed it to memory.

It was difficult to move quietly. His shoes were soaked and he had to take care not to let them slap noisily on the metal steps. Once he reached the bottom, he found himself in a large empty cabin. It was some sort of laundry room – big baskets of dirty linen were stashed in the gap underneath the metal staircase and two enormous, ancient washing machines. They were so covered in dust they looked as if they hadn't been used in years. Clean clothes, he surmised, weren't that high on Black Wolf's list of priorities.

Voices.

They came from beyond a door at the other side of the cabin. Zak's heart jumped and he looked around for a hiding spot. His only option was the linen baskets. He crept behind them and hunkered down, keeping hold of the little flight case and gripping his P11 firmly in his right hand. It wasn't a great hiding place since he was right underneath the stairwell and there was a gap of about thirty centimetres between each step. If anyone climbing the steps was paying attention, they'd see him. No question.

The door opened. The voices were speaking English.

'If you ask me,' a gruff, male voice said, 'Karlovic is getting too big for his boots.'

A spitting sound, and then a second voice, slightly shrill. 'You're worrying about the wrong man, Barker. Karlovic is nothing. It's *el capitán* who calls the shots round here. Karlovic wouldn't go to the toilet without the boss's say-so.'

Both men were obviously English. They had

London accents. The first of them – Barker – laughed. They were halfway across the room, heading for the stairwell. Zak gripped his P11 a little more firmly.

'I still don't see why we're not allowed ashore. I haven't had a drink for weeks.'

Zak could see their feet on the first step. He could smell the tobacco on their clothes.

'Get used to it. We set sail tonight. Moan about it too loudly to Karlovic and you'll be drinking sea water. Straight from the sea, if you know what I mean. He might be *el capitán*'s stooge, but he's got a nasty streak in him. Thinks he's Blackbeard the pirate or something . . .'

They were halfway up the steps. Zak held his breath.

They reached the top.

'It's all wet here,' said Barker. 'It looks like . . . foot-prints.'

A pause.

'The steps are wet too,' he continued. 'What the hell . . .'

'Ah, forget it,' said his mate. 'It's probably nothing. Tell Karlovic and he'll have us searching the ship from top to bottom.'

'Yeah, you're probably right . . .'

Five seconds later they were gone.

Zak stayed where he was for at least a minute. Only

when he was sure all was silent did he venture out from his hiding place. He crept across the laundry room and gingerly opened the door through which the two men had come.

Another corridor, running the length of the ship. There were five doors on either side, spaced about four metres apart. Crew quarters, Zak knew from the plan. At the far end of this corridor was yet another staircase heading down. He hurried towards it, half expecting one of the doors to open at any time. None did. He sensed that Michael's intelligence had been correct: the *Mercantile* had only a skeleton crew.

He found the engine room at the bottom of the second staircase. It stank of diesel and oil. It was nothing like as large as the engine room on HMS *Vanguard*, but it was still the biggest space Zak had seen on the *Mercantile* so far and, according to the schematics on his iPhone, it was one of the largest on the whole ship. But this room was deserted too. There was a metal cylinder lying on its side, about five metres long. Attached to it were six pistons and a perplexing network of pipes and valves. The floor was vibrating and the noise in here was loud enough for Zak to realize he wouldn't hear anybody approaching.

Another reason to move quickly.

He headed round to the far-side cylinder and crouched down. There was a space between it and the floor of about fifteen centimetres. He laid the P11 on the floor next to him, undid the clasps on the metal flight case and opened it up.

Even though Zak knew what he'd been carrying, it was still a shock to see it. The explosive device was very simple. There were eight square cakes of a material that looked like wet clay. Zak recognized it as C4 plastic explosive. The cakes were bound together with thick black tape. On top of the C4 were two very ordinary AAA batteries – the sort of thing you could find in almost any kid's toy. A wire probe led from the battery housing into one of the cakes of C4. There was also a small receiver, the size of a fifty-pence piece. Zak didn't know how or from where Michael intended to activate the remote detonation, but that receiver would detect the signal and send the electric charge into the explosives.

And then . . . *bang*.

Zak gingerly lifted the device out of its flight case. On its underside there was a magnet. He turned the device upside down and attached it to the bottom of the metal cylinder. The magnet stuck to the metal no problem.

Job done . . .

Except suddenly there was a massive noise. Zak started and looked around. There was nobody there, but he realized the cylinder was giving off a churning, grinding sound. The pistons were hissing and the floor was vibrating even more. With horror, he realized the engines had started up. It meant that the ship was preparing to leave . . .

Zak closed the flight case and desperately looked around for somewhere to hide it. He found a detachable panel on the wall just next to him. It was stuffed full of wires – these were vibrating too – but there was enough room to stow the case. Once it was hidden away, he picked up the P11 again and, without wasting another second, headed for the exit.

Zak urgently had to get off the ship. An Atlantic cruise might be some people's cup of tea, but Karlovic and *el capitán* weren't exactly his idea of good shipmates and he didn't much fancy the idea of releasing his dive gear and taking to the water while the ship was moving. He ran up the stairs, past the crew quarters and into the laundry room. Stopping at the bottom of the first flight of stairs, he listened for a few seconds. Nothing, so he ascended and turned left, through the heavy door and out onto deck.

The whole ship was vibrating now, but he couldn't tell if they were moving. He looked towards shore to get a frame of reference. It looked still. They hadn't started off yet, but it was just a matter of time . . .

He turned and ran towards the ladder. It was ten metres away. But suddenly there was a problem.

Shouting!

'*I SAW HIM! HE'S ON BOARD!*'

Zak stopped. A shrill voice was ringing in the air. Female. Young.

'*HE'S UP TO SOMETHING! I SAW HIM! HE'S ON BOARD NOW!*'

Zak couldn't tell which direction the shouting was coming from, but he could certainly recognize the voice.

Bea.

He swore under his breath – what was she *doing*? – and sprinted towards the ladder, trying to block out the sound of Bea's screaming. But the deck wasn't deserted now. He could see figures up ahead. *Two men, running towards him.*

They were going to get to the ladder first . . .

Zak stopped and raised his P11. The two men – they both wore jeans and T-shirts – halted immediately. They eyed the weapon.

'Get back!' Zak shouted. '*Get back now or I'll shoot!*'

The two men stepped backwards. 'OK, kid,' said one of them. 'Take it easy.' How were they to know Zak would never have shot them? Zak edged towards the ladder. If he could just get down to his dive gear before too many others discovered his location . . .

Too late.

Zak felt his hair being clutched tight before he saw

the blade. Someone was behind him. They crooked their right arm around his neck and pressed a sharp blade against his skin.

And then they spoke. A man's voice with a foreign accent.

'Have you ever cut butter with a hot knife?' The voice was no more than a breath.

'I'm not much of a chef,' Zak whispered back. His voice wavered as he spoke, and he immediately regretted sounding cocky.

'What a shame. If you had, you would know how easily this blade will cut through your jugular. I think it's time for you to drop your show-off's weapon, don't you?'

Maybe it was Zak's imagination, or maybe the artery in his neck really was pumping against the wickedly sharp blade of that knife. Either way, he knew he didn't have a choice. He let the P11 fall and it landed with a clatter on the metal floor of the *Mercantile*'s deck.

13

DO NOT ESCAPE

'You're going to turn round very slowly. I'll probably be killing you at *some* point tonight. I don't care if it's now or later. Make any sudden movements, do anything I don't like – it'll be now . . .'

The two men at whom Zak had pointed the P11 were sauntering towards him. Now that they weren't in fear for their lives, they looked arrogant. One of them picked the weapon up off the floor and examined its oversized barrel. He'd clearly never seen such a firearm before and he took great pleasure in turning the tables on Zak. He pointed the P11 at his forehead. 'You heard him, sunshine,' he said in a London accent. Zak realized this was Barker, one of the men who'd almost rumbled him in the laundry room. 'Turn round.'

Zak did as he was told and was confronted by the man wielding the knife. He immediately clocked the piercings along his swollen left eyebrow. Karlovic.

He didn't look much prettier in the flesh than he had through the night sight or in the photograph in Zak's briefing pack. He had a good couple of days' stubble, a nasty curl to his lip and breath like a dog that had gorged on garlic. As well as his knife, he had an MP5 sub-machine gun slung across his front. Easy to use in close-quarters battle and in places where space was restricted. Like ships.

Karlovic gave him a flat-eyed stare and stepped aside.

'Walk,' he said.

A P11 at the back of his head and a knife just inches from his body. It didn't look like Zak had a choice.

He walked slowly to give himself time to think. His dive gear was still stuck to the hull of the boat. If he was fast enough he could jump over the railings of the *Mercantile* and swim towards it. But the rounds from Karlovic's MP5 would penetrate the surface of the water to a depth of three metres, and in any case he'd have to come up for air before he reached his gear. He'd be fish food before he knew it.

And then there was Bea. Was she just a busybody who'd got herself into serious trouble? Or was there more to her than that? It sounded like she was on the ship somewhere. Zak had boarded the *Mercantile* with his eyes open, but if Bea was just an innocent volunteer she couldn't have any idea what she'd just let herself into. She might be totally annoying, but Zak wasn't prepared to leave her to Black Wolf . . .

No. For now, his only option was to go with the flow. See what happened. And when an opportunity presented itself, grab it.

Karlovic, Barker and the third man forced him through the same door he had used to get to the engine room. Instead of heading down the metal steps to the laundry, however, they continued straight along the narrow corridor towards the second door at the end. Zak hadn't even opened it before he heard a voice on the other side.

'Get your hands off me! I said, *Get your hands off me!* What do you think you're doing, you horrible man? What's going on . . .? You know I only came on board to try and find our idiotic volunteer . . .'

'Stupid girl,' said Barker behind Zak.

'Quiet!' Karlovic instructed. He nudged Zak in the small of his back. 'In you go. Now.'

Zak opened the door and stepped into the next room.

It was immediately clear to him that he was on the bridge of the *Mercantile*. It was a lot less plush than that of *Galileo*, the last ship's bridge he'd been on. It measured about ten metres by five and everything – the walls, the floor, the navigation panel – was a dull battleship grey. Zak could tell from its position that the window of the bridge looked out towards Lobambo, but because it was dark outside he saw nothing but blackness. The interior was lit by a flickering strip light on the low ceiling. And in that flickering light Zak saw three people.

The first was Bea. She was on her knees with her hands behind her back. Her pale face, normally so sour, was terrified. Hardly surprising because the second man – whom Zak did not recognize – had the barrel of an assault rifle pressed against the back of her head. The gunman had a wispy beard. It looked like he had grown it to make himself look older than he actually was – probably still a teenager, Zak reckoned. He wore a black and white bandanna on his head. There was a rank stench of body odour in the air, and Zak was pretty sure it came from this guy.

The third man, however, Zak recognized. Antonio Acosta. The man from the Rio favelas who had, according to Michael, murdered his own brother. Zak clocked the dark eyebrows that met in the middle and took note of the enormous strength of his topless upper body.

Acosta waited for the door to shut behind Karlovic and his men before he spoke. His voice was very soft and his English, though heavily accented, seemed good. He inclined his head slightly at Zak.

'You're going to tell me who you are,' he said in a

slightly bored tone of voice. 'And you're going to tell me what you're doing. If you do that, there is a possibility – a *small* possibility – that I will not instruct my men to kill you.'

Silence. Zak desperately tried to work out his next move.

'I'm waiting,' Acosta said. 'But I'm not a very patient man.'

Zak knew he had to sound scared. Not difficult. He *was* scared. 'I . . . I'm sorry,' he stuttered. 'My name's Jason. Jason Cole. I just wanted to look at the ship. I only just got on deck. I've never been on—'

He wasn't expecting the punch. It came out of nowhere. One second Acosta was standing with the same bored look on his face; the next he had swiped the back of his hand against Zak's face. Zak gasped in pain. At first he couldn't work out why it hurt so much. Only when he touched his fingertips to his left cheek and felt that it was bleeding did he look at *el capitán*'s hands. Acosta had a ring on his fourth finger with a sharp, jagged edge. It clearly wasn't there for decoration. It was a weapon.

And talking of weapons . . .

Barker stepped forward and handed the P11 to Acosta.

'What is this?'

'He had it on him, *El Capitán*. And I reckon he's

been on the ship longer than he says. We saw wet foot-prints on the steps down to the laundry room. That was fifteen minutes ago.'

The *Mercantile*'s skipper hardly acknowledged what Barker had said. He was too busy looking at the P11. 'This is quite a toy, Jason Cole,' he said. 'When I was a young man, I did my killing with far less interesting weapons.' He looked at Zak again. 'Do you really expect me to believe that a curious kid would board my ship armed with one of these?'

'It's not mine,' Zak improvised.

Acosta gave him a look of mock surprise. 'Really?' He turned to Karlovic. 'He says it's not his.' His voice was sarcastic and Karlovic's sneer became more pronounced.

Acosta's second swipe was less of a surprise than the first. But it was no less painful. Zak felt blood drip down his face from this second cut. His skin stung.

'Some people,' Acosta said, 'do not like the sight of their own blood. Or indeed of *anybody*'s blood. I am not so squeamish.'

He examined the P11 again and located the safety catch, which he switched off. There was a glint in his eyes now. A sort of fervour. He almost looked like he was enjoying himself. He stretched out his arm and aimed the gun directly at Zak's head.

Nobody spoke. Zak barely dared breathe. Being

threatened by Ntole was one thing; but Ntole's weapon had been empty. The P11 definitely wasn't.

Acosta's movement was sudden. Keeping his arm straight, he swung it round thirty degrees so the weapon was pointing at Barker, who was only standing three metres away.

Then he fired.

The dart from the P11 left the barrel in a perfectly straight line. When it entered Barker's forehead, it made a cracking sound. The sound of a skull splintering. Barker's eyes widened. There was very little blood. A second later, he collapsed. The tip of the dart had clearly pierced his skull and made contact with his brain because his limbs continued to twitch violently, even though he was quite obviously dead.

The other men in the room – Karlovic, Barker's mate and the guy in the bandanna – froze. Acosta looked at each of them in turn.

'*Capitán* . . .' Karlovic breathed.

'If he saw footprints, he should have told me. Do you have a problem with that?'

'No, *Capitán.*'

'Good.' He directed the P11 at Zak. 'What were you doing down there?'

He won't kill me, Zak told himself. *Not so long as he doesn't know why I'm here* . . .

'Nothing. Honestly. The footprints can't have been

mine. I only just came aboard.' He couldn't help staring into the barrel of the gun.

Acosta smiled. 'You're a brave kid. That's not always a good thing.' He turned his attention to Bea. She was still on her knees. Her body was trembling and Zak could see tears of terror welling up in her eyes. The man with the bandanna still had his rifle against her head, but he moved aside when Acosta nodded at him. The skipper aimed his P11 directly at Bea.

'Oh God . . .' she whimpered. Her eyes darted towards Barker's dead body, then up to Acosta and finally at Zak. 'Please . . . tell him what he—'

'You have five seconds,' Acosta interrupted her. 'Five seconds to tell me what you are doing on board my ship. Otherwise I'll be throwing this stupid girl's body out to sea along with Barker's. One.'

Bea collapsed. She held her head in her hands and started sobbing uncontrollably.

'Two.'

Zak looked around the bridge, trying to find something that could act as a weapon. Nothing.

'Three.'

'Four.'

'Wait,' Zak said.

Acosta inclined his head.

'Let her go and I'll tell you.'

Bea looked up. Her face was tear-streaked, her eyes bloodshot.

'I don't negotiate with children,' Acosta said. 'You tell me now or I kill her.'

A moment of silence. Zak knew the game was up. Acosta *would* kill Bea and he wasn't going to let that happen. He had no choice.

'There's an explosive device,' he said. 'It's in the engine room. I planted it there.'

Very slowly, Acosta aimed the gun towards Zak.

'Karlovic, move the ship out of harbour.' The skipper turned to the bearded man with the bandanna. 'Eduardo, take this idiot to the engine room and bring back the device. If he causes you any trouble, just kill him.'

'Yes, *Capitán*,' Eduardo replied. He walked up to Zak – which made the stink of body odour even worse – and prodded him with his rifle. 'Go,' he said.

Zak was halfway down the stairs to the laundry room – not somewhere, he reckoned, that Eduardo spent a whole load of time – when he felt the *Mercantile* shudder into motion. He tried to put a lid on his panic. The further the ship slipped from shore, the more desperate his situation. He needed to keep a clear head. To think his way through this. He needed an explanation for why he'd planted the device – one that didn't reveal his true purpose . . .

The engine room was even noisier than before now that the ship was moving. There was no point pretending the device wasn't there. Under the watchful eye of Eduardo, he removed it from its hiding place under the large metal cylinder. The bearded man kept his distance. As they walked back up to the bridge, Zak noticed that he remained a few metres further behind Zak than he had on the way down. It crossed his mind that he might use Eduardo's fear of the bomb to his advantage. But trying to escape right now wasn't on the agenda. Not with Bea still at Acosta's mercy up on the bridge.

Nothing had changed when they rejoined the others. Bea was still on her knees, sobbing, the blinking of her eyes looking like a nervous tic. Acosta still brandished the P11. Barker's body was motionless on the floor and his mate's eyes were a bit wild. Karlovic still sneered. As Zak walked in, they all stared mutely at the device in his hands.

'Put it on the ground,' Acosta instructed.

Zak did as he was told, then stepped back a couple of paces. The skipper walked towards it and crouched down to examine the device. He stared at it for a full thirty seconds before reaching out his free hand and removing the batteries from their housing.

'Throw it over the side,' he told Eduardo.

'Is it safe, *Capitán*?'

'Throw it over the side, unless you want to take a much-needed bath when I do the same to you.'

Eduardo swallowed hard. He picked up the device – which Zak knew was now completely harmless, even if Eduardo didn't – and left the bridge, holding it at arm's length.

'Who are you working for?' Acosta said.

'Nobody . . .'

'Please,' Bea whispered. 'Please let me go back to shore. This is nothing to do with me.'

'Shut up, girl!' Acosta snapped. 'Who are you working for?'

Zak bit on his lip. 'Don't make me tell you. Please.'

Acosta sighed with impatience. He pointed the P11 at Bea again.

'*Wait!*'

'I'm tired of waiting.'

'There was a man in Lobambo.'

He had Acosta's attention. 'What man?'

'He offered me money to put the device on board. Five thousand pounds. He said it was something to do with diamonds . . .' The best lies, Zak knew, always had a bit of truth in them.

Acosta stared at him. He was obviously trying to decide if Zak was telling the truth.

'Where's the money?'

'Back at camp. Only half of it. He said he'd give me the rest when I did the job.'

'What was this man's name?'

Zak looked down, as if he didn't want to say.

'Kill the girl,' Acosta instructed.

'*Ntole*,' Zak said quickly. 'His name was Ntole. I . . . I know where he lives. If you turn back I can take you to him . . . But you have to let us go then . . . Or at least, let *her* go . . .'

'Quiet! Nobody is leaving this ship.' He walked up to Zak. Just half a metre away. 'Ntole, you say?'

Zak nodded.

A pause. Acosta stared at him, his head at a slight angle. Zak kept perfectly still. He didn't want any hint of deception to show on his face.

'You're lying.'

Bea sobbed again.

'I'm not . . .' said Zak. 'I swear it, I'm not . . .'

'Search him!'

Suddenly Karlovic had grabbed him and was patting him down. It didn't take more than ten seconds to find the only item Zak had on him: his iPhone. Karlovic handed it over to the skipper. Acosta examined it with suspicion on his face. 'I don't trust toys like this,' he said. 'They are too easy to trace. And nobody will be tracing you, my young friend. I can assure you of that.' With a sneer, he dropped the phone to the floor and stamped on it with the heel of his foot. The glass face splintered and cracked. When Acosta stamped on it a second time, the innards of the phone spilled out. It was clearly useless now.

The skipper looked back at Zak, then turned to his men. 'Get me a camera,' he breathed. He didn't have to wait long. Karlovic took his own mobile from his pocket and handed it to Acosta. The skipper prodded the keypad in a rather clumsy way, as if he wasn't used to such toys, as he called them. He knew enough, though, to raise the phone towards Zak and take his photograph. Zak didn't try to stop him. He knew they'd record his image sooner or later, if they wanted to.

Acosta handed the phone back to Karlovic. 'Lock them up,' he said. 'Separate cabins.'

'Please . . .' Bea repeated. '*Please . . .*' Her voice was filled with desperate horror. It did no good. Karlovic grabbed her roughly by her left arm, pulled her to her feet and thrust her in the direction of the door. She stumbled towards it and tripped, falling to the ground again. Zak went to help her up, but she recoiled from him. 'Get away from me . . . *Get away from me . . .*' She scrambled up to her feet and shot him a look of total hatred.

'Move,' Karlovic barked. 'Both of you. *Now!*'

Karlovic had unclipped his MP5 from the sling

round his front. He had it pointed at Zak and Bea as they stumbled in silence out of the bridge and along the corridor. For the third time in the last half-hour, Zak passed through the laundry and along the corridor that led to the engine room.

'Stop,' Karlovic told them. He opened one of the cabin doors. 'You,' he said to Bea, 'in there.'

Bea looked at Zak. 'I hope you're pleased with yourself,' she hissed at him. 'We'll probably die on this ship, you know. I don't understand why you can't just keep your nose out of things that don't concern—'

She was cut off by Karlovic pulling the door shut. Zak casually examined the lock. Yale-type. No need to lock it because it clearly couldn't be opened from inside. If Zak could get the right tools together, it would be straightforward to pick . . .

'You want my advice?' Karlovic said. Zak could see little flecks of pus around the piercings on his eyebrow. 'Tell *el capitán* everything he wants to know. I mean it. *Everything.*'

'There's nothing more to know.'

'Look, you stupid kid. Maybe you don't know who you're dealing with. We're not idiots. You think we haven't dealt with worse pests than you? He'll get the truth out of you somehow. He'll probably kill you in the end, but trust me – push him too far and you'll be begging for death anyway.' He opened the door adjoining Bea's cabin. 'Get in there,' he said, nudging Zak with the MP5. Zak stepped into the dark cabin. The door closed behind him and he heard the sound of a key in the lock.

It was pitch black in here. He stood for a minute, waiting for his eyes to get used to the dark. But there was no light at all – he couldn't see a thing. The floor was vibrating with the movement of the ship as he rotated ninety degrees and stretched out his arms, feeling for the wall. There had to be a light in here somewhere. He just needed to find the switch. Then he could see what was in this cabin. See what he could use to get him and Bea out of here . . .

His fingertips brushed against the wall. At the same time, he heard a knocking sound. Just one of the many noises of a ship at sea, he told himself as he carried on looking for the light. But ten seconds later he stopped.

The knocking sound was still going. It was a repeated pattern and it was coming from the wall adjoining Bea's cabin. Or should he think of it as Bea's cell? He listened carefully. It was a sequence of short and long knocks.

Morse code.

-.. --- -. --- — . ... -.-. .- .--. .

Zak shook his head. It made no sense. Nobody knew who he was. Nobody knew *where* he was. So why was the girl in the next cabin – the girl who had got him into this mess in the first place – tapping a message to him.

And why did the message read: *Do not escape. Repeat, do not escape . . .*

14

IN THE DARK

The knocking stopped.

Zak didn't move. He was totally confused. *What was going on?*

Was it a trap? Was Bea – or someone else – trying to trick him into admitting his true identity? *That's the thing about terrorists,* Michael had said. *The good ones, at least. They're very clever. Which means we have to be a little bit cleverer . . .*

Could Bea be one of Black Wolf's agents? Zak didn't think so. Acosta had been prepared to kill her – he had seen that in his eyes. But then, he had also been prepared to kill Barker. Whatever the truth, there was no way Zak was going to return that message. If this was entrapment, displaying his facility at Morse code was a sure-fire way to make everybody even more suspicious of him. He needed to stick to his story

183

about Ntole. If he could plant enough doubt in Acosta's mind, maybe they stood a chance . . .

It took him a few minutes more to find the light switch. It was lower on the wall than he expected and encased in a waterproof rubber housing. He switched it on and immediately touched his fingers to the wounds Acosta had inflicted across his face. The cuts were still bleeding – Zak needed to put pressure on them to encourage the blood to clot, so he quickly pulled off his T-shirt and pressed it against his face. It was still damp from his swim, and the salt water stung the cuts. He kept it pressed against his cheek for a full two minutes, however, before removing it and gently touching the wounds again. They were dry. His T-shirt, however, was streaked with blood.

Only now did Zak properly look around the room. It was very small. Along the left-hand side was a bunk bed with very narrow mattresses. Its posts were fixed to the floor. He threw his bloodied T-shirt on the bottom mattress. There were threadbare carpet tiles on the floor and a writing desk on the right-hand side. Nothing else. This was not luxury accommodation.

He looked in the desk for anything that might be of use. There were some old biros and a sheaf of blank paper. Apart from that, nothing. On the wall was a laminated safety poster – exactly the same as the one he'd seen earlier. It was set in a steel frame, but was easy to remove. The material was thick and only slightly flexible. That gave him an idea.

He sat on the edge of the bed to get his thoughts together. They must have left the Angolan coast fifteen minutes ago. Even if his dive gear was still attached to the hull he'd be lucky to get at it. But there was only enough gear for one person, and he was too far out to safely make it back to shore in any case. He counted the number of crew members he had seen: Acosta, Karlovic, Eduardo and Barker's mate. Barker, of course, was dead. Four men, but there was no guarantee that was everyone. They were armed; he wasn't. His chances of overcoming them were very small and he had no doubt that Acosta would kill him if he tried.

No. If Zak was going to have a chance, he needed to do something cleverer than that. If he couldn't get himself to safety, safety was going to have to come to him. And to Bea too. Zak couldn't work her out. Maybe she was in league with his abductors, maybe she wasn't. All he knew was that he couldn't just leave her to Black Wolf when there was a chance she might be innocent . . .

Suddenly he felt the ship lurch. It felt like it had risen several metres in the air, then fallen sharply. Instinctively he grabbed the corner post of the bed and he realized now why it was fastened to the floor.

Zak couldn't see outside, of course – there were no windows in this little cabin – but he sensed that the conditions outside were getting rougher. That could make things difficult. He needed to do something to stop the ship. To put it in danger, or at least out of action. If Acosta was forced to issue a Mayday call over the ship's radio, whatever vessel was nearest them would be obliged to respond . . .

Zak stood up. The ship lurched again and he almost lost his footing. But then he headed towards the door. *Do not escape* . . . Bea had tapped on the wall in Morse code. *Yeah*, Zak thought to himself. *Right*.

He stood in front of the safety poster. That, he decided, was his ticket out of this prison. Back on St Peter's Crag, Raf had given him a lesson in lock-picking techniques. Several lessons, actually. Zak knew how to force a lock using nothing but a paper-clip or a hairpin. He knew how to fashion a workable skeleton key. And he knew how to open a locked door with nothing but a credit card. He had none of these at his disposal. But the hard, laminated plastic of the safety poster wasn't far off the flexible strength of a credit card. It was too big, of course – about the size of a piece of A3 paper – but it wouldn't take much to cut it down to size.

Zak slid the poster out of its steel frame and laid it on the floor. It was written in French, and Zak, thanks to his language lessons back at St Peter's Crag, was able to translate it automatically as he read it. Almost without knowing he was doing it, he memorized the positions of the emergency muster stations. He raised a rueful eyebrow at the crudely drawn image of a crew member throwing a life ring out to sea. The only thing Acosta and his Black Wolf buddies would be throwing over the side of the *Mercantile*, he reckoned, would be a body. Barker was probably food for the fishes already. If things didn't go well, Zak would be joining him. The thought made his hands shake.

He folded one side of the laminated poster over so he had a strip a couple of inches wide, and flattened it down to form a crease. Opening it out again, he turned the poster over and bent the strip in the opposite direction. He repeated this several times, and with each fold the crease grew weaker and weaker. A couple of minutes later, Zak was able to tear it carefully so he had a long strip.

He was about to make another crease when the ship lurched again. Worse than before. So badly, in fact, that Zak was thrown against the wall. It took ten seconds for the vessel to settle, but then there was a terrifying rumble from somewhere up above. It took a moment for him to work out what it was: thunder. It felt and sounded like the *Mercantile* was heading straight into the middle of a storm.

The cabin light dimmed momentarily. Zak tried not to imagine what sort of waves would be having this effect on the ship. When the light came on again he turned his attention back to the strip of laminated plastic and repeated the folding process until he was able to tear off a rectangle the size of a credit card.

He looked towards the door. The slip of laminated card in his hand would be enough to get him out of here, but what would he do then? Forcing a Mayday call was all very well, but to disable the ship in the middle of a storm would be madness. He could do nothing unless the gale eased off.

Zak hunkered down in the corner of his cell. The lights failed again. This time they didn't come back on. He crouched in the darkness as the *Mercantile* lurched and swayed. Now and then he heard a massive creaking sound. It was as if the ship was groaning, protesting at the conditions outside. His mouth grew dry with fear. The vessel was being battered. He hoped it was up to the job . . .

He didn't know how long he'd been crouching there when the tapping sounded again. Regular. Monotonous. Almost as if the girl in the cabin next door was trying to taunt him.

Do not escape . . .

Do not escape . . .

Zak clutched his makeshift credit card firmly. He

didn't know what to do for the best. He wished Raf and Gabs were there. They'd be able to help him. They'd tell him the right path to take. He remembered something Gabs had said to him once. *A bit of fear is good. It keeps you alert. Trust me – in our line of work you don't want to get blasé.*

If Gabs was right, Zak reckoned he must be on high alert now.

Do not escape . . .

Do not escape . . .

He felt like beating on the walls with his fists. Yelling at her to shut up. The repeated message of Bea – whoever she was, whichever side she was on – needled him. A repetitive reminder that he didn't fully know what was going on.

That he was in the dark, in more ways than one . . .

Time had no meaning in the total darkness of that little cell. Zak didn't know how many hours he sat there, brooding over the fact that his mission had failed and his chances of escaping were slim. All he knew was that the storm was getting worse, and that the ship's movements were becoming more and more terrifying. As time passed, he grew cold. He felt in the darkness for the T-shirt he'd dumped on the bed. It was still damp – salt water, he now remembered, dried less quickly than fresh water. He put the clammy

T-shirt on anyway. It didn't make him feel much better.

When the door opened and a torch shone from the doorway into the cabin, it hurt Zak's eyes. He sensed two figures coming for him. The room filled with the stench of sweat and salt.

Hands. They gripped the top of his arms and pulled him to his feet, before pushing him violently towards the door. Zak stumbled out into the corridor, where the sway of the ship knocked him to the ground. He looked up, praying they wouldn't notice what he'd done to the laminated poster and half wondering if he could just make a run for it now. But then the men were towering above him. He didn't recognize either of them, which meant he was right about there being more crew members on the *Mercantile* than he knew about. Both of them had MP5s. It crossed Zak's mind that this was Black Wolf's weapon of choice.

'Get to your feet, kid,' one of the men said. He was a pasty-looking man with a large mole on the side of his face. '*El capitán* wants a word with you.'

'I'm honoured,' Zak muttered. He was rewarded for his sarcasm by a sharp kick in the stomach that knocked the wind from him. He gasped and gulped and felt himself being pulled roughly to his feet again.

Acosta was waiting for him on the bridge. It was dark here too, but he could make out the shadow of the skipper's face, thanks to the light from his assailants' torches. Outside it was inky black, but as Zak entered the bridge, a flash of sheet lightning lit up the whole sky. For a couple of seconds, the sea was illuminated. An enormous wave – at least as high as the *Mercantile* itself – rose up just metres from the deck. It was like a nightmare. Everything went dark again, just as the wave crashed over the ship. It made a thunderous noise and it was followed seconds later by *real* thunder that crashed and echoed everywhere around. It took all Zak's strength to keep upright.

If the skipper was alarmed in any way by the raging storm, he didn't show it. He grabbed Zak by the scruff of his T-shirt and pulled him so their faces were only inches apart. He was forced to shout above the dreadful noise.

'Have you ever wondered what it feels like to drown?' he yelled.

Zak shook his head.

'Who are you, and who do you work for?' Acosta's eyes gleamed in the darkness and his face was sweating.

Another great wave crashed against the ship. *If he wanted me dead*, Zak told himself, *he'd have killed me already*.

'I told you!' he shouted back. 'My name's Jason Cole. Ntole made me—'

Acosta swiped him across the side of his face – not with his vicious ring, this time, but the blow made the wound on Zak's face sting anyway.

'They say that drowning is the worst death of all,' Acosta shouted at him. 'Well, you're about to find out, my friend.' He looked at the two men who'd brought him from the cell. 'Grab him!' he instructed.

There was no way Zak could escape. Within seconds each man had taken one of his arms. Acosta was in his face again.

'Do you know what waterboarding is, kid?'

Zak nodded mutely.

'We have our own version on this ship. We'll put a hood over your head. Then we'll tie you to the railings on the deck. You'll feel like you're drowning every time a wave hits you. We'll see how keen you are to talk to me after a few hours of that.' He gave Zak a nasty grin. 'Most people last about ten seconds before they crack.'

'I've told you everything I know,' Zak said. 'Please don't do this. *Please* . . .'

But Acosta had already turned away. He disappeared to a far corner of the deck. When he returned, seconds later, he had an old pillowcase in his hands. He held it up by the corners. 'It's very important,' he said, 'in this day and age, to recycle, don't you think?'

Zak struggled to get away, but the men had him gripped firmly. Acosta advanced, and without another word he pulled the pillowcase over Zak's head. Zak writhed but it was no good. He felt Acosta wrapping a cord around his neck and tying it – not so tight that he couldn't breathe, but tight enough to secure the pillowcase. Within seconds Zak found himself gasping for air, just as his arms were pulled behind his back and tightly bound together.

'Take him outside,' Acosta ordered. 'Let's see how brave he is after a while on deck.'

Zak felt himself being pulled away. 'You're making a mistake,' he shouted. '*You're making a mistake!*' No one replied as he was pushed and pulled, unable to tell which way he was going.

He fell twice before they arrived outside on deck. Each time it was because the ship had lurched, and each time he was pulled roughly back onto his feet and told to move. But when he was out in the open air, all his troubles up till now seemed like nothing.

The first thing that hit him was the noise. He'd heard it inside, of course, but out here it was deafening. The air was cold and filled with spray and hard rain. He hadn't been on deck for more than two seconds before he was soaked through. The pillowcase became saturated and Zak found it even more difficult to breathe as he was pulled along the deck and forced up against the railings, facing out to sea. From beneath his hood he sensed another flash of lightning; ten seconds later there was a boom of thunder that almost shook his bones.

Rope around his ankles. He felt his assailants tying his legs to the railings, before binding his body and his arms. He tried to struggle, to get himself away, but they were too strong for him.

'Let's get inside before we're washed over,' one of the men said once Zak was fixed firmly to the side of the deck.

'Yeah,' the other replied. 'I don't fancy joining Barker.'

'Don't go!' Zak shouted. 'Your skipper's made a mistake . . . I've told him everything I know.'

The two men gave ugly laughs. 'Come sunrise,' one of them said, 'you'll be racking your brains for things you *haven't* told him. You'll be crying like a baby. Oh, hang on, I forgot – you *are* a baby, aren't you. You just thought you could mix it with the big boys.' Another brutish laugh and their voices disappeared.

'Don't go!' Zak repeated. '*Don't go!*'

But it was too late. Zak was all alone. Bound. Hooded. And about to experience everything the ocean could throw at him.

15

WATERBOARD

Zak had undergone torture before, but only as a training exercise. He remembered Michael's words the day after. *Trust me, you'll talk. The only question is how long you'll last . . .* He gritted his teeth. Black Wolf weren't going to beat him that easily. Or so he thought, at first.

Zak didn't know if the first wave was the worst, because it was his introduction to the true horror of the next few hours; or the easiest, because he didn't know what to expect. The force of the water as it crashed over the side of the *Mercantile* was like being slammed into a brick wall. Zak felt his whole body bruising on impact. For a brief, irrational moment he was grateful to the two men who had tied him up. They'd done their work well. If they hadn't, the momentum of the wave would have cast him aside like a feather in a tornado; but the ropes held him firmly to the railings. They strained and burned, but

Zak didn't mind that as long as he wasn't cast into the ocean.

But the pain of the impact and the burning of the ropes was nothing compared to the rest of it.

The wave didn't just crash and disappear. It seemed to surround Zak entirely, as though he'd been thrown into a swimming pool and left to drown. Salt water gushed through the pillowcase, up his nose and into his mouth. He started to choke, but when he breathed in, all he inhaled was more water. His lungs started to burn and his body went into panic.

He needed oxygen.

He needed to breathe.

The wave subsided, but even that didn't bring any relief. The salt water had soaked the pillowcase. Now the hood clung to the front of his face. He tried to breathe in, but the wet material stuck fast to his nose and mouth. It stung the cuts on his cheek too, but that was the least of his worries. His body started to shake from lack of oxygen. Desperately he poked his tongue out against the hood in an attempt to get the wet cloth off his face.

It didn't do any good.

He felt faint.

Dizzy.

He *had* to breathe. If he fell unconscious now, he knew he'd never wake up again. He mustered all his energy and violently shook his head, trying to force the hood away from his face. After several goes, he managed it. He gulped for the air his body so desperately needed and felt it surging into his lungs. But already he could sense the ship dipping in the ocean. He knew another wave was going to hit any second.

Zak shook his head, even though nobody was there to see him. And the storm certainly wasn't going to pay any attention to him. He'd barely taken a second breath when another wave hit.

It was harder than the first. More brutal on impact and longer-lasting. The oxygen starvation was even more agonizing. Zak knew that if Acosta or any of his men were there beside him, he would be begging them to make it stop.

He would be telling them everything.

Anything.

The ship crashed downwards. Zak felt like he was sinking. He panicked that the lashings around his body had come loose. He was surrounded by water. Blind and disorientated, he couldn't even tell which way was up. *He was in the sea . . .* But then the cloth separated from his face and he was able to breathe again.

A brief moment of respite until another wave hit.

Zak hadn't been on deck for more than five minutes. Already nature had thrown everything it had at him – twice. Already he had felt like he had been on the edge of death – twice.

Let's see how brave he is by morning . . .

How much longer till sunrise? How much longer would this storm last? How many more waves would he have to suffer? How many more times would he have to be on the brink of drowning?

Zak didn't know the answer to any of these questions. All he knew was that the next few hours would be among the most difficult of his life.

That he would need every ounce of courage he possessed to make it till morning with his body – and his mind – intact.

It was wet, too, at 63 Acacia Drive. The snow had given way to rain – a freezing, driving rain that could chill you to the bone. A man looked out at it from the rear window of a white Transit van.

The van bore no unusual markings. A bit of rust on the driver's side panel. A sticker on the back that said NO TOOLS ARE KEPT IN THIS VAN OVERNIGHT. The tiny rear windows had a reflective mirror film to stop anybody looking in, and a good thing too. If any nosy parker had peeked through those windows and seen the face staring out, they'd probably have died of fright.

The occupant of the Transit had only one eye. He

was as thin as a skeleton and looked about as friendly as one too. It was for this reason that back home they called him Calaca – although only the bravest did so to his face. Calaca hated this rain and this cold. He wished he could be back in Mexico. Back in the heat. His late employer, Cesar Martinez Toledo, would never have sent him on a fool's mission like this. *Him!* Adan Ramirez. Head of security for the cartel for fifteen years, carrying out a job that should have been given to a subordinate.

But Martinez was dead. And in his place was his son. Cruz Martinez. Just a kid. But a kid with more power and money than the leaders of most countries. A kid who, in the months since he had taken his late father's place, had developed an unusual gift for cruelty – so much so that that even Calaca had grown afraid of him. And Calaca wasn't afraid of *anybody*.

More than anything, though, Cruz Martinez was a kid with just one aim in life. To find the boy he blamed for the death of his father. The boy who had called himself Harry Gold but who Cruz and Calaca now knew was called Zak Darke. He had checked the DNA extracted from the finger he had removed two nights ago from Zak Darke's so-called grave. Proof positive that the kid was still very much alive.

And now he had just one more job to do. To eliminate Darke's cousin. Cruz had been quite determined that she should die. He'd said it was because he didn't want the girl identifying Calaca, but the one-eyed man had his own suspicions. Thanks to Darke, Cruz's father was dead. Killing the boy's cousin didn't fully avenge that death, but it went some of the way . . .

But eliminating her was proving more difficult than he had imagined it would be. A good job, then, that he had decided to carry out this particular killing himself, rather than entrusting it to less skilled minions.

Calaca was a practised assassin. There were few better. Which was why he felt angry that he had failed simply to kill a little girl. She must have had help. He remembered the man calling himself Mr Bartholomew. Calaca didn't know who he was, but he was sure to have something to do with it.

The headphones suddenly burst into life. A voice. It was the girl. Calaca smiled. The listening device he had secreted in her bedroom was doing its job well.

'Hello? Is that you?'

Her voice was quiet. As though she was nervous anyone might hear her talking to someone now, in the small hours of the morning. Calaca listened carefully.

The girl giggled and Calaca wondered what the person she was talking to had said.

'You can't come here. My mum and dad wouldn't have it. Honestly — they'd, I dunno, my dad would

chase you down the street with a gun or something . . .'

Interference. A crackling sound in Calaca's head-phones. He scowled and adjusted a knob on the receiver that lay on the floor of the van. The inter-ference disappeared. The girl was giggling again.

'All right,' she said. *'I'll meet you. But not here. Saturday night. Hampstead Heath. You know the lake – I'll be there at eight o'clock. Don't be late, though. If I'm not back home by nine-thirty, I'll be grounded for a week . . .'*

A slow smile crept over Calaca's face. Hampstead Heath. Eight o'clock. By the lake. How convenient it was, he thought to himself, that his target should choose the time and place of her own execution. He could wait until Saturday for such an easy location.

The phone call continued, but Calaca had stopped paying attention. He had no need to listen to the girlish gabbling of a kid talking to her boyfriend. He had all the information he needed to terminate Ellie Lewis. And when he'd done that, he'd be on the first flight out of London. Back to Mexico City.

Back to where he belonged.

If Zak had the chance, he would have wept with fear and agony. He would have screamed out loud. He would have begged anyone listening to remove the hood, untie the ropes and take him back inside. He'd have spilled any secret. Admitted anything. Told Antonio Acosta, Karlovic – *anyone* – about Agent 21 and about his mission.

But he didn't have the chance.

The hood remained. So did the ropes. The ship continued to lurch and the waves to crash over his head. The wet material stuck to his face each time the water hit and it only seemed to separate from his skin when his lungs were screaming for oxygen. Then he would gasp, trying to get as much air into his body as possible before enduring the dreadful sensation of drowning once more.

Every inch of him felt bruised by the impact of the waves. Never again, he knew, would he think of water as being soft. Each time the waves hit, it was like he had slammed into a sheet of iron. After a while he couldn't even feel the pain any more. Just an icy numbness.

He didn't know how long it lasted. Time meant nothing in the darkness. Gradually, though, he became aware that the waves were perhaps slightly fewer and further between. They still left him breathless and gasping for air, but the moments of relief were longer than the moments of agony. Through the sodden material of his hood, he was aware of it growing lighter.

Morning was coming. The storm was abating.

It stopped suddenly, as though someone had flicked a switch to change the weather. The *Mercantile* no longer lurched and yawed. The roaring of the waves and the wind no longer screamed in his ears. Zak felt sunlight on him, then the hood dried out and grew hot. The skin on his arms and legs crackled with salt. It grew sore and started to burn. He found himself almost glad to be tied to the ship. If he hadn't been, he felt sure he would have collapsed.

The sun became stronger and Zak started to sweat. His mouth was dry and he grew dizzy. All night he had been wishing – praying – for the water to stop. Now all he could think about was quenching his thirst. Getting out of the sun.

His head lolled.

He felt himself on the verge of consciousness as the hours passed . . .

The voices, when he heard them, made no sense. Were they talking a language Zak didn't understand, or was he just too out of it to understand *anything*? They approached, and he felt them untying the ropes that bound his body, their conversation still nothing but a blur. As soon as he was unbound, he collapsed onto the deck, his battered muscles unable to keep him upright. He lay there, his head still hooded, and didn't even have the energy to groan when he felt a boot in his guts.

'Get up.'

Zak was so dizzy he couldn't tell where the voice came from; and he was so weak that he knew he couldn't obey.

'*Get up!*'

Another sharp kick just below his ribs. He gasped for air but still didn't move. He couldn't. And so he felt himself being dragged by his legs across the metal deck, back inside the ship. He tried to keep track of where they were going, but he was too disorientated for that. All he knew was that they dragged him over the threshold of two doorways, each one painful to cross, until finally they came to a halt.

'Take the hood off.'

Zak recognized Acosta's voice. Rough hands removed the hood and he saw the *Mercantile*'s skipper standing above him, before closing his eyes again against the brightness he wasn't used to.

'Who are you working for?'

Zak couldn't have answered even if he had wanted to. His throat was like granite. He had no energy. When the skipper kicked him, he didn't bother with the ribs but booted him in the side of his face.

'*Who are you?*'

Zak's face stung. He could feel the wound Acosta had inflicted with his sharp ring opening up, and blood seeping over his cheek. But somehow, that didn't seem so bad. He forced his eyes open and looked up. The skipper was still standing above him, and despite the bleariness and the pain, Zak saw something in his face. Not panic, exactly, but concern. Doubt. *El capitán*, Zak realized, had thrown everything he had at his prisoner. He had fully expected Zak to be compliant by now. What had Karlovic said? *Push him too far and you'll be begging for death anyway . . .*

Only Zak wasn't begging for death. And whatever Acosta did now, it couldn't be worse than what he'd just endured. Could it?

'*WHO ARE YOU?*' the skipper roared.

'Jason Cole,' he whispered.

He didn't see the fury in *el capitán*'s face. But he felt it. The skipper kicked him in the face twice as hard as before.

Zak wasn't even conscious for long enough to feel the pain. Darkness surrounded him as he passed out on the floor of the bridge.

16

MAYDAY

Saturday, 02.20 hrs West Africa time

Zak's next memories were only of waking, exhausted, and then falling semi-conscious again. And again. Hours and hours for his body to recover from the ordeal. And when he finally woke up, aware of his surroundings, everything was dark. He was lying on his back on a hard floor. Groggily, he reached out his right hand. His fingers brushed up against what felt like the base of a bed. Even then it took him another thirty seconds to realize he had been back in his tiny cell all this time. How long *had* he been there?

It took all his strength just to sit up. He sat motionless in the darkness for a full minute. His skin felt like it had been rubbed with sandpaper. His lungs and muscles ached. The cuts on his face throbbed and his throat was so parched with salt and dehydration that it hurt. In short, he was a mess.

But at least he was still alive. After everything he'd endured since boarding the *Mercantile*, that was something. How long he'd *stay* alive was a different matter. He needed to get help. The volunteer group would surely have declared him and Bea missing by now, but that was scant comfort. As Michael had said, the sea is big and ships are small. Moreover, due to his own actions, the finger of suspicion would be on Ntole, not the *Mercantile*. No, now that the sea had settled and the ship was no longer yawing and lurching, he could try and return to his original plan: to force the skipper to raise a Mayday call.

He winced as he pushed himself to his feet, and he had to stumble against a wall in the darkness just to keep his balance. Breathing deeply, he waited for his nausea to pass. Then he staggered in the direction of the light switch and turned it on. The glow of the bulb burned his retinas. He had to keep his eyes clenched shut for thirty seconds before he could even think of opening them fully.

Sitting on the table was a plate of food. There was also a bottle of water, though this had tumbled onto the floor and rolled to the far end. Zak rushed towards it, unscrewed the top and gulped down half the precious liquid in one. He turned his attention to the food. It was nothing but a few scraps of greasy, fatty, gristly meat and it tasted disgusting, but he knew he had to get some energy from somewhere and he forced the filthy stuff down his throat before finishing the rest of the water.

The room was just as he'd left it. The folded and torn safety poster was still in pieces on the floor. Clearly none of the crew had bothered to look around the room – or if they had, they hadn't worked out why he had cut up this laminated plastic. Zak rooted around under his mattress for the credit-card-sized cut-out and approached the door.

With the fingertips of his left hand, he felt around the frame. The gap between it and the door was very narrow. He gently slipped the short edge of his plastic card into the crevice and slid it down until he could feel the catch. When the plastic was pressed against it, he worked deftly, easing his makeshift key-card against the curved edge of the catch. Within seconds he could feel the catch working away from the frame.

And then, suddenly, the door opened inwards, creaking slightly as it did so.

Zak took a deep breath, then stepped out into the corridor. He examined the door. There was a latch that could be operated from the outside. It meant he could close the door now and be able to return.

It was deserted. Deserted and dark. He realized he had no idea what time it was – or even what *day* it was.

It was impossible to say how long he'd been unconscious for. He shut the door behind him and stood quietly for a moment, listening carefully. All he could hear was the low buzz of the engine room, down the corridor to his right. Other than that, nothing.

He turned towards the room next to his. Bea's room. He pressed his ear against the door. No sound. Her room had a similar latch on the outside. It would have been easy for Zak to enter, but several things stopped him.

He remembered seeing Bea through the night sight from the end of the pier.

Bea had alerted Black Wolf to his presence on the ship.

And then there was the strange Morse code message she had tapped on the wall between their two rooms.

Something wasn't right about her. If she knew he had escaped, could he trust her not to alert his captors? But if she wasn't the enemy, how could he fail to help her, annoying as she was? He decided to creep silently past her door. If he was to go through with his plan to force the skipper to raise a Mayday call, he needed to stay unnoticed; and if it worked, and Bea was innocent, the Mayday would help her too.

A minute later he was out on deck, having moved through the ship without encountering anybody. It was dark again. Zak realized he must have been unconscious for the whole day. There was a wind. It made him shiver and his hair blow around, but he realized it was only caused by the forward motion of the ship. From the hull of the boat, Zak saw powerful jets of water spurting out to sea. He remembered first seeing the *Mercantile* make its way towards Lobambo. It had been shooting out these jets of water then too. Zak still didn't know what they were for.

The moon was out. It was very bright and, beyond where the jets hit the water, it reflected off an almost still ocean. Zak felt like he was a million miles from the storms and terror he had endured the previous night. But he also felt a million miles from safety. He wished he at least had his iPhone, but no: he had no means of communication. He was alone. The sound of the *Mercantile* ploughing through the water was enough to make him shiver. In a corner of his mind he wondered if he'd ever be able to think about the sea again without remembering his horrible ordeal.

For now, though, he had to put the memory out of his head. He had work to do.

Zak kept his back pressed against the body of the ship as he moved towards its stern. Every five metres he stopped and listened. He heard nothing except the ploughing of the ship through the water. He'd been on deck for approximately thirty seconds, however, when something blocked his view of the moon.

He froze and looked up into the sky. The moon reappeared, but Zak was aware of something floating nearby. Something big. He squinted into the darkness and saw a great shadow floating alongside the ship. It was an enormous bird, with wings the size of a dinosaur's. And as it hovered in the air, it emitted a loud, lonely cry that seemed to fill the empty skies all around.

'Albatross,' Zak muttered to himself. He'd never before seen one of these enormous rare birds, of course. But he'd read about them at school. Legend said that it was bad luck to encounter them at sea. Surely his luck couldn't get any worse . . .

He left the albatross to its flight and continued his journey to the stern of the ship. Ten metres along he passed a lifeboat. It was sitting on the deck itself, attached to the main body of the *Mercantile* by an enormous crane-like arm. The arm appeared to be operated by a control panel on deck consisting of a keyhole and a large red button, though Zak assumed that it could also be operated from inside the lifeboat in case of an emergency. At the back of the boat there was a huge outboard motor – much bigger than the one Gabs had operated on the RIB back at Scapa Flow. The boat was covered by a sheet of thick canvas, and there was still a pool of salt water on top of this, which Zak assumed was left over from last night's storm. It crossed Zak's mind that this would be a good escape vessel, but he also knew that to launch himself into the middle of the ocean without any means of navigating back to land would be suicide. Better to trust his luck here in the clutches of Black Wolf than to perish slowly of dehydration, exposure or drowning.

Voices.

Zak spun round. He could vaguely make out two figures at the bow end of the deck. He didn't hesitate. The canvas on top of the lifeboat was tied on by a thin cord, woven through eyeholes about thirty centimetres apart. He headed round to the far side of the boat where anyone passing would be less likely to see that he had loosened the cord, peeled back the canvas and climbed inside the lifeboat, returning the cover to its position from inside the vessel. He heard the puddle of water sloshing above him and waited several excruciating seconds for it to fall still.

It was dark and rather damp inside the lifeboat, despite the canvas. Zak ignored the water seeping into his salt-encrusted clothes again. Another cry from the albatross pierced the air. Five seconds after that, he could hear the voices again.

'I'd like to shoot that stupid bird.' Zak recognized the voice of Barker's friend. He sounded sour and discontented.

'If you do that, you're the stupid one.' The second man was Eduardo, who had taken Zak to the engine room to retrieve the bomb. '*El capitán* is superstitious about things like that. Shoot an albatross, he'll do the same to you.'

'It's only a bird,' the first man muttered. 'I'd like to shoot it down and kill that kid while we're at it. I don't understand why the skipper's keeping him alive.'

'I guess we'll find out soon enough,' Eduardo replied. 'The rendezvous is less than twenty-four hours away now. All we'll have to do then is sit back and watch.'

'Since when did *el capitán* ever sit back and let us do anything? He's got the water cannons on to stop pirates from boarding the ship. Why do we have to keep patrolling the deck? Nobody can board us with those things going . . .'

And with that, the voices faded away.

The rendezvous is tomorrow . . . What rendezvous? Zak had almost forgotten about the diamonds. Was there to be some kind of handover? Perhaps he still had a chance to scupper Black Wolf's plans.

Or perhaps he should just be thinking about his own safety . . .

He waited silently in the darkness of the lifeboat and only emerged after another thirty seconds when his acute sense of hearing told him the coast was clear.

Outside the lifeboat he looked along the deck. Nobody there. Eduardo and company were probably circling the ship. He reckoned that gave him about five minutes before they reappeared at his location again. He continued towards the stern.

Five metres past the lifeboat he saw a white metal chest on the left-hand side. He stopped, checked for crew members again, and opened it up.

Zak couldn't see the contents of this chest very well, so it was up to his fingertips to work out what was inside. It was stuffed full of something soft and dry. Zak felt thin lines of twine attached to each other in a criss-cross pattern. Netting, he realized. A whole bundle of it. Its purpose? Fishing, maybe? Though this was hardly a fisherman's boat. It didn't matter. This tangled mess of twine gave him an idea.

The netting was much heavier than it looked, Zak realized as he plunged his hands into the chest and struggled to pull it out. It spilled out onto the deck – a bundle of about a cubic metre. He had to drag it along behind him. It made a hissing sound on the metal deck that seemed horribly loud to Zak, even though it was in reality little more than a whisper. He kept vigilant as he continued towards the stern, stopping every few metres to check everything was clear before carrying on.

The stern deck of the *Mercantile* was an open area

about fifteen metres wide and ten deep. The churning sound of the vessel moving through the water was louder here. Zak realized this was because the mechanisms that propelled the ship were located at the rear. He stood at the corner of the stern deck, checking for danger, before dragging the netting towards the railings at the very back of the ship.

Zak looked down into the water. He could see the bubbling foam of the ocean as the ship's engines churned it up violently. Then he looked back down at his netting. If he could get this tangled up in the rudder down there, the ship's engines would be disabled. The skipper would have no option but to call for help.

He couldn't just hurl the bundle of netting overboard. The forward momentum of the ship meant that it would fall harmlessly into the ocean behind. No, if his plan was going to work, he needed to keep hold of one edge of the net while the remainder tumbled downwards. It would need all his strength. And after the couple of days he'd had, strength was in pretty short supply. No matter. He gritted his teeth, bent down and rummaged around the bundle of netting looking for a loose edge. It only took him ten seconds to find one. He looped it around the fingers of both hands and grabbed the bulk of the bundle.

He strained to lift it.

And then he felt a tap on his shoulder.

Zak closed his eyes. He felt sick. Cold. He hadn't heard anybody approach, and now his best chance of stopping the ship was gone. Surely they would kill him . . .

He let the netting fall from his hands before standing up straight and turning round to face his captors once more.

But he didn't see *el capitán*. He didn't see Karlovic, or Eduardo or any of the others. He saw a pale-faced girl, just a couple of years older than him, with short red-ginger hair, small eyes that were no longer blinking but keen and alert, and a serious, intense look on her pinched face.

She looked over her shoulder and back to Zak. 'You need to put that netting back where you found it, Agent 21,' she said. 'Otherwise you're going to mess up this whole mission.'

17

SWEETIE

Zak stood very still and stared at Bea.

'Who's Agent 21?' he demanded. 'What are you talking about?'

But Bea barely seemed to be listening. She headed over to the end of the starboard deck, checked it was empty, then did the same for the port deck, which Zak had just crept along. 'It's all clear. We need to return this netting now. If any of them find it here, they'll know we've left our cabins. Come on, I'll help you.'

'What's going on, Bea? Who are you?'

'There's no time to explain. You get one side of the net, I'll get the other—'

'No way,' Zak interrupted. 'I'm stopping this ship now.'

Bea's hand shot out and grabbed his wrist. She was a lot stronger than she looked. 'You need to get back to your cabin,' she hissed. 'We both do. Otherwise the whole thing's going to go wrong.'

If he hadn't been in such a dangerous situation, Zak would have laughed. 'Go wrong? Things started to go wrong when you boarded this ship and told everyone what I was doing. And they *definitely* took a turn for the worse when they tied me to the railings in the middle of that storm . . .'

'What do you want, Agent 21? Sympathy? An easy life?' Bea was looking around again.

'What I want,' Zak replied, turning back round to haul the netting overboard again, 'is to disable this ship and force a Mayday call.'

A pause.

'It's a good idea,' Bea said. 'Well done. Very clever. Now forget about it.'

'No way.'

'In that case, I'll have to tell Mr Bartholomew it was your fault the operation failed.'

Zak stopped. He turned slowly. 'How do *you* know Mr Barth—?'

'Come on, Agent 21,' Bea chided. 'Do you *really* think you're the only person Michael has dealings with?'

Zak blinked. 'You mean you're—'

'Think about it. Who put your diving gear under the pier? And your P11? How did I know you were on board the *Mercantile*? None of the volunteers saw you, nobody in the village – Raf and Gabs taught you stealth if nothing else.'

'You mean, you know—'

'Look, if you're going to stand there staring at me like the class dunce, this could be a very long evening for both of us. Where did you get that net from?'

'A chest on the starboard deck.' Zak was almost in a daze. What was going on? What had happened to the terrified, annoying girl he knew? *What had Michael not told him?*

'You get one side, I'll get the other. Those two guards will complete their circuit any minute. If they see us, they'll do more than tie us to the railings.'

It was much easier to move the net now there were two of them. Zak and Bea were still stuffing it into the chest, however, when Bea hissed like an angry cat. She pointed towards the bow of the ship and Zak saw the outline of two figures approaching.

'Hide in the lifeboat,' Zak breathed. 'Quick.'

'The net!' Bea replied. 'It's not hidden . . .' But there was no time. They scrambled towards the hiding place. Seconds later they were huddled under the canvas cover, barely daring to breathe. There was a moment of silence. Zak used it to get his head together. Bea clearly knew who he was and she clearly knew his Guardian Angels. But was she bluffing? Was she pretending to be on his side? Suddenly nothing was as it seemed. Zak couldn't take anything for granted.

Footsteps by the lifeboat. A foul, greasy stink of BO in the air. Then voices. '*El capitán*'s worse than normal.' Zak recognized Eduardo's voice. He certainly recognized his smell.

'I don't know why he doesn't just kill the kids and be done with it. I don't like having them on board. If customs catch up with us, how's it going to look? Smuggling diamonds is one thing. Smuggling kids – that's another.'

'If you ask me,' said Eduardo, 'he's been told to keep them alive.'

A spitting sound. 'Told?' said the second voice, full of contempt. 'Nobody tells him anything.'

'Don't be so sure. Everybody has a boss. Even *el capitán*. You'll see . . . What's that?'

'What's what?'

'That. Peeking out from the storage chest.'

Zak cursed inwardly.

'It's nothing.'

'It wasn't like that when we passed before.'

'You're paranoid, Eduardo. Who else do you think's been on deck tonight? Mermaids?'

'Very funny,' Eduardo muttered.

'Come on, let's keep walking. I'm getting cold.'

'No way,' said Eduardo. 'I saw what *el capitán* did to Barker for not reporting something suspicious. I'm going to tell him about this. You can come with me, or you can ignore it and carry on patrolling. Up to you. If you think a dart in the skull will improve your looks, stay out here.'

A pause.

'Wait!' called the other man. '*Wait! I'm coming with you!*' His footsteps receded.

Zak and Bea lay dead still for twenty seconds. And then . . .

'*Move!*' whispered Bea.

Zak didn't need any more encouragement. It didn't much matter whose side Bea was on. If he didn't get back to his cell now, all hell would be let loose.

Together, they scrambled back out of the lifeboat and replaced the canvas cover. Zak led the way towards the deck door he'd been using, with Bea following close behind. They entered the ship just in time to see the entrance door to the bridge slamming shut. The two of them hurtled down the stairs, through the laundry room and back into the corridor where their cells were.

'Get inside,' Bea instructed once they were both outside their cells. 'And whatever you do, don't break out again.' She opened the latch of her own door.

'Wait,' Zak said.

'We haven't got time. They'll be here any min-ute . . .'

Now, though, it was Zak's turn to grab her by the

arm. 'I'm not going anywhere until you answer some questions.'

Bea glanced towards the end of the corridor. She looked very nervous. 'We haven't got—'

'Who are you?' Zak demanded. 'You'd better tell me, Bea. I'm not going anywhere until you do.'

Bea's eyes blazed.

'They told me you were good, Agent 21. I haven't seen much sign of it yet.'

'*Who* told you I was good?'

'Michael, among others. He might change his mind when he finds out about your little games with Ntole and the AKs.'

Zak ignored her barbed comment. 'So if you're such good friends with Raf and Gabs, you can tell me what Gabs would call me if she was here.'

'I haven't got time for this . . .'

'Well you'd better *make* time.'

Bea narrowed her eyes at him, and shook her head – like she was a teacher and Zak had been unable to do his homework. 'Haven't you worked it out yet? Haven't you worked out why we can't get caught? Michael *wants* you on this ship. I was sent out here to make sure it happened.'

'*What?*' He felt a crunch of betrayal in the pit of his stomach. '*Why?*'

'Your guess is as good as mine.' Bea glanced along

the corridor again. 'All I know is there's an RV about to happen. I don't know who it's with, but Michael has gone to a *lot* of trouble to arrange it.'

Zak's head was spinning. He didn't understand. 'What about the device? You told them about it – are you saying that after all the trouble I went to, Michael *doesn't* want this ship destroyed?'

The look Bea gave him was sly. 'Don't you worry about that. When the time comes, the MV *Mercantile* is going the way of the *Titanic*.'

'But they threw my device overboard.'

'Of course they did.'

'You're not making any sense, Bea.'

Bea sighed. 'Haven't you ever heard of the double camera trick?' she asked.

'The what?'

She shrugged. 'It's simple. You fix a security camera somewhere obvious, then hide a second one somewhere covert. The person you're spying on will disable the obvious camera and feel very pleased with themselves. They won't twig it was just a decoy.'

'A decoy?' Zak could hardly believe what he was hearing. 'Are you telling me there's *another* device on board?'

'Of course there is,' Bea replied. She sounded just a little bit smug. 'I planted it myself.'

'*Where?*'

But she shook her head. 'They'll be here any second. We *have* to get inside.' She pulled her arm away from Zak. 'You look terrible, Agent 21,' she said. 'You'd better gather your strength. If I'm not mistaken, things are about to get interesting.'

She opened her door and, without looking back at Zak, locked herself in her room once again.

Zak almost went after her. But at that exact moment, he heard something at the other end of the corridor. Voices, maybe? They were drowned out by the hum of the engine room. He quickly opened the door to his own cell and quietly shut it behind him. He switched off the light and groped in the darkness towards his bed.

Zak had only just lain down when the door opened again. He saw two figures standing in the doorway, one of them carrying a torch. The torch-bearer entered the room and strode towards Zak's bunk. He shone the torch directly into Zak's face. Zak winced and squinted, as though his eyes weren't used to the light. Then he groaned. It seemed to satisfy the crew member, whoever it was, because he moved the torch away from Zak's face and walked back towards the door.

'Looks good and messed up,' he said to his mate. 'He's not going anywhere.'

'Good,' said the second man. 'Maybe *el capitán* will give us the rest of the night off.'

'You'll be lucky. Come on, let's get back on patrol before Karlovic finds something else for us to do. He and the skipper seem edgy . . .'

The door closed behind them, leaving Zak in the darkness again.

His body lay very still, but his mind was doing somersaults. So many questions. Why were Acosta and Karlovic on edge? What was the rendezvous the crew was expecting? Was Eduardo right? Had Acosta really been told to keep him alive? If so, why? Why did Michael want him on the *Mercantile* in the first place? Why hadn't he just been straight with him from the beginning?

And what about Bea? Was she on the level? Could he trust her? It hadn't escaped his notice that she'd avoided answering his question about Gabs. Did that mean she was bluffing? Did it mean she'd never met his Guardian Angels, despite what she'd said?

Time passed. Zak lay still.

And then, in the darkness, he heard a noise. A tapping sound, coming from the direction of Bea's room. A rhythmic series of long and short knocks.

Zak listened carefully to the Morse code message coming from the adjoining cell, automatically translating it into letters in his head, almost without knowing he was doing it.

She . . . would . . . call . . . you . . . sweetie . . .

Zak swallowed hard. It meant Bea was telling the truth.

It meant that, for the second time, Michael hadn't told him everything.

And it meant something big was just round the corner.

18

RV

**Saturday, 16.00 hrs West Africa time; approximately
750 miles east of the South American coastline**

'The sea's getting rougher.'

'Tell me about it. We should turn back. It's madness
to carry on.'

'Do you want to tell *him* that?'

A pause.

'No way. I'm not stupid.'

Two men stood on the deck of a vessel that was half
the size of the MV *Mercantile*. It had no name – just
a number: 3182126. They were heading on a bearing
of ninety-three degrees, east into the heart of the
Atlantic. They spoke in Spanish, and they could see
that the clouds up ahead were rolling and black. All
day they'd been listening to the shipping forecast.
All day the radio had been alive with warnings to
avoid the very area to which they were directly headed.

But they had their orders, and their orders were to carry on.

A sudden gust of wind kicked a shower of spray up onto the deck. It would have soaked the two men if they hadn't been wearing their wet-weather gear. As it was, it just knocked them backwards. One man lost his footing. When he scrambled upright again, he looked sourly at his shipmate. 'We should get back inside!' he shouted.

His mate nodded, just as another burst of spray hit them. They struggled back inside, where their gear dripped heavily onto the floor, and made their way to the bridge. Here there were three more men, all grim-faced, all looking like they'd prefer to be anywhere on earth other than here. In the middle of the bridge, a flight of steps led down to the lower deck, at the bottom of which there was a closed door. It had been closed ever since they set sail.

The occupant of the lower deck quarters had the habit of issuing his instructions to the crew over the radio. It was insanity, they all thought, given that he was just metres away from the rest of them. But then, their boss wasn't the type to show his face if he didn't have to. On land he remained incognito, and the same was true at sea.

If it had been anyone else, the crew would have been mutinous. They'd have taken control of the ship and steered it into safer waters. And they'd probably have thrown their skipper to the sharks for good measure. But while the person holed up down below generously rewarded loyalty, he punished betrayal very seriously. They'd seen what happened to people who crossed him. They'd seen the scars on the bodies of the newly dead that told of the terrible agony they had suffered before they were killed. They'd heard of garrotted bodies swinging low from the trees on the outskirts of villages, and of corpses left out in the desert to be consumed by wild animals. They'd heard the stories of how whole families were wiped out because one of their number had offended him. Some of these crew members had sons and daughters, but even those who didn't have children had mothers and fathers, and they all knew how severe the reprisals would be if they so much as entertained a mutinous thought. Their boss did not respect youth, or age. He'd kill anybody if he had to.

No, there would be no arguments on board this vessel. When the instruction came through that they were to maintain their course, even though they were heading into the eye of a storm, they obeyed. Perhaps they were travelling to their deaths. But if they disobeyed their boss, they'd be dead anyway. At least this way they had a chance.

The wind howled around the ship.

The sea grew rougher.

The crew were silent as the vessel continued towards its RV.

In the bowels of the MV *Mercantile*, Zak could also tell that the sea was getting rougher once more. In the gloom of his cell, he kept having flashbacks to the night out on deck. Every time he remembered being strapped to the railings, his skin prickled and he found himself involuntarily gasping for breath. If Acosta decided to repeat the torture, Zak didn't know *what* he'd end up admitting. Not the truth, certainly, because he didn't even know what the truth was. He couldn't trust his abductors, but could he even trust his friends any more?

He had slept after returning to the cabin. A fitful sleep, on and off throughout the long hours of isolation. The cuts on his face were raw with blood and salt; his dreams had been filled with water and the sickening sound of the P11 dart splintering Barker's skull. He saw Michael's face back on St Peter's Crag. *That's the thing about terrorists*, he was saying. *The good ones, at least. They're very clever. Which means we have to be a little bit cleverer . . .*

There was somebody in the room again, but this time he wasn't carrying a torch. Rough hands pulled Zak from the bed, and he saw the piercings along the man's eyebrows glint in the darkness. 'Get moving,' said a harsh voice which Zak recognized as that of Karlovic. The ship was rocking. As Zak staggered sleepily to his feet, he found it difficult to maintain his balance. '*I said, get moving!*' Karlovic hissed, and he pushed Zak out into the corridor.

Bea was waiting for him there. Eduardo stood guard over her. His bandanna was no longer over his head, but round his neck. His black hair was as greasy as his beard. Bea herself was shaking with terror. But Zak had seen her the previous night when she was steely and organized. *Give the girl an Oscar*, he thought to himself. She was clearly a very good actress.

The ship lurched. All four of them stumbled, but Eduardo and Karlovic were the ones with the guns. Zak felt steel against his back. 'Get up on deck,' came the instruction. '*El capitán* wants you.'

'I'm flattered,' Zak said.

'Don't be. He's not in a good mood.'

'Please . . .' Bea whimpered. 'Leave me down here . . .'

'Shut up, you stupid kid. Get up onto deck, both of you.'

Outside, Zak saw the treacherous colour of the sky as evening drew in. Unlike last night, however, when the sea had been still and the sky clear, now the water was a stormy grey colour and the clouds had gathered. The waves weren't as high as when Zak had been tied to the railings, but they were high enough for the walk to the stern deck – where he had tried to throw the netting over – to be treacherous. Even Karlovic and Eduardo seemed more intent on keeping their footing than on pointing their guns in Zak and Bea's direction.

It was raining too. The air was filled with the immense sound of droplets hitting the surface of the ocean, which looked like it was boiling and steaming. Zak noticed that the water cannons had been switched off. Made sense, he thought. Only a fool would try to board in these stormy seas. Acosta was waiting for them. He was no longer bare-chested, but wore a stormproof jacket over his waterproof trousers. His face, though, had lost none of its cruelty. He watched Zak and Bea approach with a sneer on his face that suggested they were the lowest form of life on earth. He had the pillowcase in his hand. The sight of it made Zak feel weak. When the two of them were a metre apart, Zak stopped.

He and Acosta stared at each other, rain dripping through their hair and over their faces.

'I'm going to give you one last chance,' said the skipper. He had to shout against the howling of the wind and the rain. 'Tell me who you are. Tell me who you work for. Then, maybe – *maybe* – I let you live.'

Salt water sprayed through the air, and both Zak and Acosta were forced to shield their eyes. When Zak lowered his hands, however, he saw something. It was only small. Barely there. Just the glimmer of a look in Acosta's face. As the spray subsided, the skipper looked out to sea. He was searching for something and, with a flash of intuition, Zak saw that he was anxious. Whoever it was they were about to meet – *what*ever it was they were about to meet – Antonio Acosta was scared of it. And he was even more scared of arriving at their rendezvous having failed to extract the truth of Zak's identity out of him.

And with that flash of intuition came another. Acosta was never going to kill him. He wasn't going to kill either of them. If that had been his plan, he'd have done it ages ago. He'd been told to find out Zak's identity, and he was terrified of the consequences if he didn't . . .

Zak stood up straight, and when he spoke it was with a confidence he didn't really feel. 'My name is Jason Cole,' he said. 'And to be honest, you might as well give up asking me that question, because it's the only answer you're going to get.' He saw a brief smile of approval on Bea's face.

Acosta's face changed. The hint of anxiety was

replaced by a nasty sneer. 'You think you're a brave kid,' he shouted. 'But we'll soon see how brave you *really* are when you meet someone not as forgiving as me.' As he spoke, he looked over Zak's shoulder and he seemed to notice something far out at sea. Zak turned. Instantly he clocked what Acosta was looking at. It was another vessel, bobbing in and out of sight on the grey, stormy horizon. Zak couldn't tell at this distance whether it was smaller or larger than the *Mercantile*. But he sensed one thing for sure: they were heading straight for it. Acosta's crew members had been expecting a rendezvous. It looked like this was it.

'Bind them!' Acosta instructed his men. 'And prepare the lifeboat.'

Zak heard Bea gasp. He turned to see her stepping nervously away. 'The . . . the lifeboat?' she stuttered. 'Surely you won't make us . . .' Her words petered out. Another good impression, Zak thought to himself, of a frightened kid. Or maybe it wasn't an impression at all. He didn't much relish getting into that tiny lifeboat himself. Not in high seas like this.

Karlovic and Eduardo approached. They were carrying cable ties – thin loops of plastic with a notch joining the ends. Eduardo forced Zak's hands behind his back, bound the wrists together and yanked one end of the loop. The smell of his body odour was still bad, even though the rain and the sea were giving him a more thorough shower than he'd probably had in ages. The cable tie closed around Zak's wrists, digging into the flesh and immediately making his hands feel swollen on account of the constricted blood supply. Karlovic did the same to Bea, who struggled and sobbed as she was being tied, but of course it did no good.

'Take them to the bow deck,' Acosta ordered once their wrists were tied. 'Alert me when we're close enough to board.' He stormed through the rain back along the deck and disappeared into the body of the ship.

'You heard him,' Karlovic shouted. 'Move!'

Zak and Bea walked side by side along the starboard deck, with Karlovic and Eduardo about three metres behind. The noise of the rain and the wind was enough to muffle their voices as they spoke.

'If Michael gave you any more intel about this RV,' Zak said from between gritted teeth, 'now would be a good time to tell me.'

'You know everything I do,' Bea replied, 'so you might as well stop asking. Whatever's going to happen, it's going to happen soon. Keep your mind on the job.'

'Thanks for the advice,' Zak muttered. He wasn't sure if Bea heard him above the elements, but she certainly acted as though she hadn't.

They passed the chest where Zak had found the bundle of netting, then the lifeboat. When they reached the bow deck, Karlovic forced them onto their knees. 'Guard them,' he shouted at Eduardo. 'I'll prepare the launching gear for the lifeboat.'

'Who's boarding with them?' Eduardo shouted back.

'Don't ask me. *El capitán* will decide who gets that pleasure.' He hurried away, leaving Zak, Bea and Eduardo alone on the bow deck. Zak caught the look of discontent on the bearded man's face.

At first Zak couldn't see the other vessel. The swell of the ocean had raised the level of the horizon and the air was thick with salt and spray. A wave crashed over the deck, knocking Zak and Bea from their kneeling position onto their backs. Bea screamed – Zak didn't know if it was for effect or if it was genuine. At a harsh bark from Eduardo, he struggled up to his knees again. This time, he caught sight of the ship in the distance. It appeared closer than when he'd seen it last, which had only been a couple of minutes ago. Despite the stormy weather and the high seas, the *Mercantile* was fast approaching the ship it was supposed to be meeting. And what then? Zak wondered.

What then?

Thunder. It boomed across the sky and was followed about ten seconds later by a flash of lightning. The sky grew darker, and the swell of the sea obscured the approaching vessel once more. When it reappeared a few minutes later, it was close enough for Zak to make out some of the detail on the main body of the ship – probably not more than 500 metres away, though he knew distances could be deceiving at sea. It was, he thought, smaller than the *Mercantile*. Because of this, it looked like the rough seas were buffeting it even more violently. It rocked and swayed, and when a wave crashed over its deck, the whole ship disappeared from sight for a few seconds. It didn't look, by any means, like somewhere Zak wanted to go.

He looked over his shoulder at Eduardo. The black bandanna round his neck was dripping wet and his beard looked bedraggled. 'Hey!' Zak shouted.

'Shut up, kid,' Eduardo replied.

'Anyone who gets in that lifeboat now, in these seas – they'd be an idiot, right?'

Eduardo's eyes darkened, but he didn't reply.

'You think you're going to get out of joining us? You think Karlovic and *el capitán* are going to put themselves in danger instead of you?'

'I said, shut up.'

'You *know* I'm right. You *know* how dangerous it is. If you don't want to board that ship, now's your chance.'

Eduardo gave him a puzzled look. 'What are you talking about, kid?'

'Untie us,' Zak yelled back. 'Untie us now. We can overpower Karlovic. We'll have the element of surprise. We can take the ship . . .'

'Jason, *no* . . .' Bea urged. 'The crew are armed . . .'

But Zak ignored her. All his attention was on the bearded man with the bandanna round his neck and the unfortunate odour surrounding him.

For a moment – just a brief moment – Zak thought Eduardo was going to agree. There was conspiracy in his eyes, and he looked over his shoulder as if he was seriously considering the proposition.

'Now's your only chance,' Zak pressed. 'Untie us. We can—'

He wasn't expecting the heavy kick in the guts that Eduardo delivered. Winded, he collapsed to the deck again. As he lay there trying to inhale, he felt Eduardo's hot, stinking breath against his face. 'You're a clever kid,' he hissed. 'But you don't know what you're talking about. You think we would cross Karlovic and *el capitán*? Maybe some of us would. But you don't know who's coming in that other ship. If *he* thought any of us had betrayed him, we wouldn't just be wishing for death – we'd be wishing we'd never even been born.'

'What's going on?' Karlovic had appeared. He was as drenched as the rest of them.

Eduardo stood up. 'Nothing,' he said. 'I've dealt with it.'

'Then get the prisoners to their feet. The lifeboat's ready. Load them up – I'll inform *el capitán*.'

Eduardo pulled Zak up onto his feet, then Bea. The approaching ship was closer, listing and lolling in the waves. With a sharp push, Eduardo pushed them along the port deck. 'Move!' he shouted. '*Move!*'

The canvas covering had been removed from the lifeboat and was crumpled in a heap by its side. Already the boat had a couple of inches of water in the bottom – a result of the intense rain and spray. As they approached, there was another crack of thunder and at the same time a wave hit the side of the boat. Zak was blinded by the sharp, salty spray, and when he looked back at the boat he reckoned there was another inch in the bottom.

'This is suicide!' he yelled. 'Think about it, Eduardo. Think what they're making you do!'

But Eduardo was having none of it. 'Get inside,' he instructed. 'And keep quiet.'

Climbing into the launch with their wrists bound was hard. Zak's shoes splashed in the water that had collected in the hull, but it made no difference – he was soaked anyway. When Karlovic reappeared, he had the skipper with him, along with seven other crew members Zak didn't recognize. They all looked nervous, and tried not to catch the eye of their captain.

Acosta looked around at them all. His face was un-impressed, as though he was staring at some very poor specimens of the human race. 'Cowards,' he hissed. 'All of you.'

His eyes fell on Eduardo. He looked as anxious as all the others and Acosta seemed to hold him in just as much contempt. 'You,' he announced. 'Get into the lifeboat.'

Eduardo looked crestfallen as he glanced out to sea, where the waves were rolling and crashing, and where the approaching ship was now only 100 metres away. '*El capitán*,' he muttered, 'please . . .'

Acosta wasted no time. From somewhere about his person, he pulled a wicked-looking knife – sharp and gleaming on one side and with jagged hooks pointing back towards the handle on the other. He pressed the point of the blade against the bandanna around Eduardo's neck.

'Do you have a problem following my instructions?' Acosta asked.

Eduardo backed away. 'N-no, señor,' he stuttered. 'No . . . no problem at all.' He scrambled into the lifeboat, giving Zak a dark look as he did so.

Acosta faced Karlovic. 'You stay here,' he said. A look of relief flickered across Karlovic's face. 'The *Mercantile* is to remain in sight at all times. If any of these . . .' He waved his knife in the direction of the other crew members. 'If any of these *women* become a problem, just kill them.'

'Yes, *Capitán*,' Karlovic replied. 'Are you sure you do not want to send one of them in your place?'

Zak saw Acosta's cheek twitch. 'No,' he replied. '*He* will expect to see me personally, not one of these dogs.'

'Who's "he"?' Zak shouted. 'Who are you talking about.'

Acosta didn't reply immediately. Clearly none of the others would dare to do so in his stead. 'You'll find out soon enough. When you do, I suggest you take some advice.'

'What?'

Acosta sneered. 'Fear him,' he said. 'If you know what's good for you, fear him.'

He climbed into the lifeboat, still brandishing the knife, and approached Zak and Bea, who were sitting together, their hands still tied behind their backs. With one strong arm, he grabbed Bea and lifted her to a standing position before spinning her round. With a swift swish of the blade, he cut the cable tie. The knife made short work of the plastic, but it also sliced the skin of her left hand. She drew a sharp intake of breath and immediately put pressure on the wound to stem the sudden flow of blood.

'Get to your feet, kid,' Acosta told Zak. He obeyed.

Seconds later he was rewarded with a cut of his own, but at least his hands were free. It crossed his mind to try and fight Acosta, but the knife was sharp and his enemy was vicious . . .

'Sit down. Hold on. Try anything stupid and I won't bother stabbing you, I'll just throw you over.' Acosta looked over at the others. 'Launch us,' he instructed as another cloud of spray blinded them and added an extra inch to the pool of water at the bottom of the boat. When Zak regained his vision, he saw that most of the crew had returned inside. Only three men remained. One of them was Karlovic, and he was inserting a key into the lifeboat's launching mechanism. He twisted it and hit the red button. Immediately, the arm connecting the launch to the main ship juddered into motion and they started to rise up into the air.

Zak felt his stomach go. He remembered a fairground ride he'd been on once. He had sat in a spinning capsule attached to an arm much like this one that raised him up and down as he went round. He had screamed with delight then, but any screaming he was likely to do now would be out of fear. When they were five metres above the deck, the ship lurched and he felt as though he was falling through space. The arm moved out and started to lower them down towards the sea. The way the water was ebbing and flowing, it was impossible to see where sea level was – the top of the bulge or the bottom of the trough. It was a bulge they hit first. Acosta pulled a lever in the centre of the launch and the boat separated from the arm. It spun round – like it had a mind of its own. Zak gripped the edge, ignoring the flow of blood that smeared his hands and the boat itself. He saw the others doing the same as they tumbled from the crest of the wave down into the trough. There was a booming sound. At first Zak thought it was thunder, but then he realized it was just the sound of the hull bouncing on the water.

Zak caught sight of Eduardo's face. He'd never seen such terror. Bea looked like she was concentrating hard on staying alive. As for Acosta, he appeared grimly determined as he manoeuvred himself to the enormous outboard motor at the back of the launch. Seconds later he had control of the lifeboat, and they were moving through the water, away from the *Mercantile* and towards the mysterious second ship that had come to meet them.

19

FEAR HIM

The lifeboat wasn't built for seas like this. It rocked and swayed like a toy. Zak realized as he gripped the side firmly that they could capsize at any moment. If that happened, death wasn't a probability. It was a certainty. Acosta, however, knew what he was doing. He directed the boat diagonally up the swell of the waves, avoiding the dangerous crests where the water turned white and curled over into the troughs. All the time, he kept his eyes firmly on the larger vessel up ahead. It was slow going through the wind and rain and battling against the ocean. Gradually, though, the distance between the two ships grew smaller. Within ten minutes, the battleship-grey hull of the new vessel was looming above them. Only when they were almost there did Zak remember the diamonds. Acosta was carrying nothing except his knife, which meant that handing the gemstones over was *not* the purpose of this RV. The thought chilled him even more than the elements.

Acosta manoeuvred the lifeboat alongside the larger ship. The two hulls crashed together, and the shock of the impact jarred against Zak's body. In a way he didn't mind the pain. At least it stopped him thinking about the fear. He looked up to see, about a metre from the stern of the lifeboat, a ladder fixed to the hull of the new vessel. The deck was about ten metres up, but the ladder followed the curved shape of the hull. Anyone using it would be leaning backwards over the ocean while they were climbing the bottom rungs.

Zak and Bea exchanged a nervous glance as the lifeboat bobbed and knocked against the bigger ship. It was Eduardo, however, who got the first instruction. 'Get up there!' Acosta barked. 'Quickly!'

Eduardo swallowed hard and he looked nervously upwards. He didn't move. Acosta, on the other hand, did. He shuffled along the boat and pressed his knife into the soft jelly just below Eduardo's right ear. 'You need me to sort out your hearing?'

'No, *Capitán*.' He edged away from his fierce-looking boss, past Zak and Bea towards the stern of the ship. Glancing back over his shoulder, he saw that Acosta was still glaring at him. And so he leaned over the side of the boat, stretched, and with one hand grabbed hold of the second rung up.

Zak found himself holding his breath as he watched Eduardo. It obviously took a great amount of courage for him to throw out his other hand and pull his body from the boat so that he was hanging from the ladder. Zak could almost feel the strain as he hauled himself upwards, feeling with his feet for the bottom rung and moving his arms up so his body was straight – even though it was leaning backwards at an angle of about twenty degrees.

He stopped. Despite everything, Zak was willing him on, but Eduardo appeared frozen with fear. It was difficult to tell with all the movement and rain, but Zak reckoned he could see him shaking. He raised his left leg onto the next rung, but then couldn't bring himself to continue and lowered it.

And it was just then that the wave hit.

It wasn't the biggest Zak had seen or felt over the last seventy-two hours, but it was big enough to crash over his head and against the hull of the larger vessel. Zak shouted in alarm as he was knocked down into the keel of the lifeboat. Water flooded up his nose and into the back of his throat. When the wave subsided, he was coughing and retching, so it was at least ten seconds before he looked back towards the ladder.

And saw that it was empty.

Zak rushed to the side again. Bea did the same.

They both looked into the stormy water, trying to see some sign of Eduardo. But there was none.

'*We've got to help him!*' Zak shouted. He turned to search the interior of the boat – surely there was rescue gear in here somewhere. All he saw, though, was Acosta. He had moved up towards Zak and Bea and was waving his cruel knife towards them.

'Forget about him,' he instructed. 'You next. Go!'

Zak looked at him in horror. 'He's drowning!'

'He's already dead. Get up the ladder now, otherwise I kill the girl.'

Zak knew he didn't have a choice. Acosta *would* kill Bea, and he'd probably enjoy it too.

He looked towards the ladder. The lifeboat had drifted slightly further away. He would have to jump to get at it. He looked at Bea. 'If I don't make it . . .' he started to say.

'You'll make it,' she replied, just a bit too quickly. Zak didn't know who she was trying to persuade: him or herself. 'Just be careful. I'll see you at the top.'

Right, Zak thought. *And then maybe we'll find out what this is all about.*

His hand was still bleeding as he stood up on the lifeboat, which wobbled and rocked. He put one foot up onto the very edge of the boat and got the ladder in his sights.

No point waiting, he told himself. It was waiting

that had been Eduardo's downfall. Either he was going to do this, or he wasn't.

He jumped.

The rungs of the ladder were wet and difficult to grip. His stinging, bleeding hand didn't help either. But the worst of it was the angle. He could feel the sway of the ship, lurching him backwards, closer to the water. His muscles burned with the effort of holding on, and it took all his strength and courage just to move up a single rung.

The wind was screaming around him. But suddenly there was another kind of screaming. Human. It was Bea. '*WAVE!*' she shrieked, and Zak knew he only had a split second before the ocean threw everything it had at him.

He gripped harder and clamped both his eyes and his mouth shut. Then he braced himself and tried not to think of Eduardo, struggling and drowning.

When the wave hit, it was like a sheet of rock, slamming Zak against the ladder. His feet slipped from the bottom rung and his left hand lost its hold. He was hanging on just by the fingertips of his right, desperately scrabbling to get a firmer grip as the water rushed around him, swinging and buffeting his body.

He felt like a feather in the wind.

He couldn't control his own limbs.

He was going to fall . . .

He was going to die . . .

The wave subsided just in time. Zak couldn't have held on with his right hand for a second longer, but now he could move his left and he gripped firmly with that. He looked over his shoulder to see both Bea and Acosta staring at him anxiously. It was no good concentrating on them. Zak knew he wouldn't survive another wave like that. He had to get to the top. Fast.

He was thankful for his training. Thankful for the punishing fitness regimes Raf had forced him through. Without them, he'd have been just another body at the bottom of the sea. He moved almost robotically. When the next wave hit, he was halfway up the hull, which was now vertical. Another eight rungs and his head emerged above the floor of the deck.

There were four people waiting for him here. They all wore wet-weather gear which included tight hoods, so he couldn't make out their faces. Two men grabbed his arms and hauled him onto the ship. That was as far as their consideration went, however. They hurled him to the hard, soaking deck. Three of them stood over him, while the fourth started frisking his body, looking for weapons or anything else of interest. They didn't seem very concerned about helping either Bea or Acosta onto the boat. Zak was the one they were interested in, but he didn't know why . . .

The man hadn't even finished frisking him when

Zak leaped to his feet and threw himself back towards the railings. He looked over the side. Bea was already on the ladder. She was moving quickly. Like a spider up a wall. Zak was impressed by her strength. If she was scared, she didn't show it. He could tell that both her body and her mind had received training for this kind of situation.

Hands, pulling him back. Zak shook them off and spun round to see himself hemmed in by the four men. He looked at them with contempt. 'If you think I'm not going to help her up,' he shouted, 'think again. What kind of men are you, anyway?'

They were the kind of men, it turned out, not to care if Bea lived or died. One of them stepped forward to grab Zak. It was a big mistake. As soon as he was close enough, Zak yanked his knee up into the man's groin. He doubled over in agony, which meant that when Zak raised his knee for a second time, he caught his assailant in the lower jaw. He fell backwards into a heap on the floor.

Zak looked at the others. They'd all taken a step back. 'I'll come quietly, but not till she's on board,' he shouted at them. 'Try and stop me and you'll get the same treatment as him.'

The remaining three men looked at each other and nodded. They still stayed close, but Zak was free to lean over the railings again. He thought that maybe he caught sight of an arm or a leg appearing above the surface of the water. Even if he was right, it disappeared as quickly as it had come. If it was Eduardo, he was a lost cause.

He turned his attention back down to Bea. She was still moving quickly up the ladder. Just a few more rungs now and he'd be able to help . . .

'NO!' he yelled suddenly.

Bea was almost at the top when she lost her footing. 'Hold on!' Zak shouted as he saw her slip down several rungs. '*Bea! Hold on!*'

There was no reply from the strange girl – or if there was, it was drowned out by the wind. She stopped her unintentional descent about halfway back down and looked up with an expression of fierce concentration. She only took a couple of seconds to catch her breath. Then she started climbing again.

Bea reached the top rung quickly this time, and Zak was there to help her over the railings and onto the deck.

She was out of breath. 'Acosta's following,' she told Zak.

He looked over the side. Sure enough, he saw the *Mercantile*'s skipper climbing up the ladder. He prepared to help Acosta up too, but Bea pulled him away. 'You know what?' she said. 'I reckon he can manage without our help, don't you?'

Zak's decision was made for him. The remaining three crew members were closing in. He didn't fancy taking them all on. He held up his hands. 'All right,' he shouted. 'Don't get excited. I take it someone's waiting for us.'

He felt Bea pulling at his arm. 'Over there,' she said. She pointed towards the stern of the ship. Zak looked.

All he saw was a single, solitary figure. He – or she, it was impossible to tell – wore black wet-weather gear which included a waterproof hood. It was large and the figure was wearing it pulled all the way over the front of his face. This obscured his features, as did the swirling cloud of grey rain and icy spray between them.

And yet, even though he could not see this figure's face, Zak felt a prickle of recognition.

Fear him . . .

Zak didn't know why, but for some reason he truly did.

Acosta appeared over the railings. He too had his eyes on the figure, and he looked reluctant to approach. He turned to the others. 'Stay where you are,' he told them. He jutted out his chin. It made him look like a man mustering his courage. Then he walked towards the figure. Zak couldn't help thinking that the man who had seemed so brutal on board the

Mercantile now looked rather pathetic. Like someone walking to his doom.

Zak, Bea and the crew members watched him silently. The man Zak had floored was on his feet again, but he didn't try to retaliate. He was too busy watching Acosta approach his boss. The *Mercantile*'s skipper stopped about a metre from the figure. He had his back to them, so Zak was unable to lip-read their conversation. Whatever they said, it was short. Thirty seconds, no longer, before Acosta started walking back along the deck towards them, the hooded figure following a metre behind.

The ship lurched again, forcing Zak, Bea and the others to grab the railings. By the time they could stand freely again, Acosta and his mysterious companion had joined them. Even close up, Zak couldn't make out the stranger's face through his hood. And when he spoke, Zak had to strain his ears to hear over the elements, because his voice was very soft.

'Acosta,' he said. He had an accent. There was something very familiar about it. 'Give me your knife.'

Acosta's eyes grew bright. He no longer looked scared, but eager. As if he was looking forward to something. He handed his vicious blade over to the stranger, who examined its sharpness and the jagged hooks on the underside from behind his hood. Zak noticed that his hand was very thin. He wore a signet ring on the fourth finger, and he was holding the knife forwards now. Like he was ready to strike.

Zak felt his muscles tensing. The crew members had surrounded him. He wondered if he could jump over the side of the ship and land in the lifeboat, but out of the corner of his eye he saw that the little boat had drifted out to sea.

Movement. Bea had stepped up next to him. He sensed that she was ready to fight . . .

Zak raised his voice over the wind. 'I don't know who you are,' he shouted. 'But you haven't brought me and Bea all this way just to kill us.'

The men surrounding them looked surprised that he'd dared to speak to the stranger in this way. Acosta just sneered.

It was the last thing he ever did.

The stranger wasn't even looking at the *Mercantile*'s skipper when he stabbed him. He just flicked out his right arm and slid the blade into the side of his abdomen. Acosta's eyes widened. He opened his mouth to speak but no words came. He stared at the hooded figure as he yanked the blade out again. Zak turned his head away in disgust. The hooks of the knife had pulled out several long, stringy gobbets of flesh – Acosta's insides, which the stranger flicked off the knife with irritation. Acosta hit the deck. He was holding both hands over the wound, but he couldn't stem the blood that was flowing out like a river.

'It should have been a simple thing,' the hooded figure announced over the noise of the storm as Acosta's life ebbed away, 'to find out the identity of our guest. A *very* simple thing. And if somebody who works for me cannot do a simple thing, they don't deserve to work for me any longer.'

Zak blinked. He'd placed the stranger's voice. *He knew who it was.*

'It's very important to have the right people around you,' the stranger continued. 'That's what my father always said, wasn't it, Jason Cole? Or should I say Harry Gold? Or Zak Darke? Or even Agent 21? Not that it's really very important, because the only name that's going to matter to you is the one they put on your tombstone once I've killed you. Your real tombstone, that is . . .'

Acosta was at the stranger's feet, surrounded by a pool of blood that mingled with the sea water on deck to produce a slippery, runny mess. Zak paid it no attention. He was too busy staring as the stranger removed his hood to reveal a face he recognized. A couple of years older than Zak himself. Black hair. Dark eyes. Tanned skin.

Cruz Martinez.

The boy who blamed Zak for the death of his father.

The boy Zak had befriended and betrayed.

The last person Zak had expected to see here in the middle of the Atlantic Ocean.

'Hello, Harry,' Cruz said in a voice that was almost devoid of emotion. 'It's so good of you to join us.' He looked over at the remaining crew members. 'Take them down below,' he instructed. 'We have a good deal to talk about before I finally sling his dead body overboard.'

20

POSITIVE ID

'Who is he?' Bea shouted.

'An old friend.'

'You want to choose your friends a bit more carefully in future.'

Yeah, Zak thought. Only the first time he'd met Cruz Martinez he had been an awkward, gangly teenager – a bit surly, sometimes, but not the kind of kid to stand up for himself. Certainly not the kind of kid to instil fear in anybody. He'd changed. Big time.

Zak realized that Bea was still shouting at him. 'He didn't *look* very friendly. You know, the way he stuck that knife into Acosta's guts and everything.'

They were in some kind of storage deck. It stank. A thick, greasy, petrol-station smell that made Zak feel nauseous. *Fuel*, he thought to himself. There were certainly a number of large red jerry cans stashed up against one far wall and held in place by a series of thick ropes. Aside from these jerry cans, there was nothing else. The ceiling was about three metres high and a single light bulb was suspended in the middle from a wire. The listing of the ship caused the bulb to swing, which made the shadows move around like they had a life of their own. The space was four times the size of Zak's cell on the *Mercantile*, but it was more than four times as terrifying. Here, in the bowels of the ship, they could hear the violent waves crashing against the metal hull. It boomed and echoed like a drum. The noise was constant and it vibrated through to Zak's core and made his ears numb. His throat was raw too – he felt like he'd done nothing but shout against the storm, and he had to yell even louder to be heard down here.

The entrance to the storage deck was via a big metal door. Zak was examining it as the ship listed and swayed. Just before Cruz's men had thrown them in here, he'd checked the bolt on the outside. Simple but heavy, and impossible to open from in here, even if he had tools, which he didn't. There was no way they'd be breaking out of this prison.

'Yeah,' he shouted back at Bea when he realized she was still waiting for an answer. 'When I say an old friend, I suppose what I really mean is . . . an old enemy.' He paused. Wasn't he too young to have enemies? And anyway, Zak had never thought of Cruz in that way before. He relived the moment his former friend had killed Acosta. Zak had no love for the brutal skipper of the *Mercantile*, but his death had been so sudden. So violent. And carried out with such lack of emotion. The memory made him shudder. That wasn't the Cruz he had known. But then, the death of a parent can change you. Zak knew that better than most.

He knew something else too. The two of them being together on a blank patch of sea, miles from land wasn't – *couldn't be* – a coincidence. Had Cruz been tracking him? Following him? Waiting for the moment to pounce? Or was there another explanation?

Suddenly the door opened. Cruz appeared. Zak noticed that he still had a smear of blood on the skin of his right hand. Acosta's blood, but *el capitán* wouldn't be needing it any more. Behind Cruz stood two heavily tooled-up crew members. Assault rifles. Pistols in their belts. Enough hardware to take out a platoon of soldiers, let alone two unarmed kids. Bea looked scared, and for the first time Zak didn't reckon she was faking it.

There was a silence. Zak broke it.

'Black Wolf?' he shouted.

'A sideline of mine,' replied Cruz. 'It pays to diversify. I admit, it would have been inconvenient if you had sunk the *Mercantile* and its little cargo. I can replace men, of course, but diamonds are a little more precious.'

'They told me I should fear you, Cruz,' he shouted.

'*Si*, Harry.' Cruz appeared very calm. 'They were right.'

Zak nodded in the direction of the two armed men. 'Maybe it's just the two guys with guns I should fear. Do you go everywhere with them? Or are you willing to talk man to man? Just the two of us.'

Cruz smiled. 'Like gentlemen, Harry? How very British. But it wasn't very gentleman-like, was it, how you deceived my father and me—'

'Your father,' Zak interrupted, feeling the anger flush to the surface of his skin, 'killed my parents. And he killed a lot more people besides. *You* don't have to be like him . . .'

Zak's words were like a spark, igniting Cruz's own fury. He stepped into the room. With a strength that Zak would never have expected of him – the last time he'd seen Cruz, he'd been anything but muscular – he grabbed Zak by the neck and pushed him against the back wall of the cabin. Zak hit the hard metal with a thud. He felt Cruz's fingers tighten around his throat.

'Don't tell me what I should be,' the Mexican hissed. 'Because whatever I am – *you* made me.'

With a flick of his arm, he threw Zak down onto

the ground. Zak scrambled to his feet again to see Cruz's dark eyes flashing as he inhaled deeply several times to regain his composure. The young Mexican strode back to his bodyguards and nodded curtly at one of them. The bodyguard handed over a thin sheaf of papers, which Cruz delivered to Zak with a dead-eyed look. 'Imagine how surprised I was when that animal Acosta sent me a photograph of the kid who was trying to blow up my ship, and I saw that it was *you*, Harry – the one person in the world I've been try-ing to find all these months. And imagine my delight when I realized I would be able to show you these. I'm sure you'll find them interesting.'

It was only when Zak had them in his hands that he realized the papers were in fact A4-sized photo-graphs. He examined the top one. It was in colour, but very grainy, as though it had been enlarged several times. That didn't stop Zak from recognizing what it was, however. And it didn't stop him from taking a sharp breath.

63 Acacia Drive was just as he remembered it. The front lawn was covered in a blanket of snow. Uncle Godfrey's Mondeo was parked on the driveway. It looked very bland. Very ordinary.

The front door was open and walking out of the house was a girl. She was wearing a dark winter coat and snow boots, and had a rucksack slung over her back. Her face was blurred, but not so blurred that Zak couldn't recognize it.

'Ellie,' he breathed.

He looked up at Cruz, who was staring at him with a satisfied expression.

Zak started thumbing through the rest of the photographs. Ellie featured in all of them. Walking down Camden Road. Outside the gates to the school Zak used to attend in what seemed like a different life. In some of the pictures he could make out her face; in others her features were indistinct but Zak could tell it was Ellie from the slope of her shoulders or the way she angled her head. He flipped through the images faster and faster. The more photos he viewed, the more panic rose in his chest.

The final picture, however, made his blood freeze.

It showed the inside of a fast-food joint. There were a couple of customers in the background, but Zak, of course, wasn't looking at them. He was looking at Ellie, sitting at a table with a polystyrene drinks cup in front of her. It had to be Diet Coke, because that was what she always ordered. But there was someone else sitting opposite her.

And Zak recognized him too.

The patch over Calaca's right eye did nothing to disguise him. Not from Zak, who had seen this monster close up; who had looked into his face as the one-eyed man prepared to kill him; who had only just escaped from him using a combination of training and good luck. He didn't really know if good luck was something with which Ellie was blessed; but she *hadn't* had Zak's training. Which meant that if Calaca was in her vicinity, she was in danger. Very grave danger indeed.

The sides of the hull boomed and echoed. Zak looked up slowly from the picture, his face as hard as the metal of the ship. 'What's he done to her, Cruz?' he asked flatly. He didn't shout this time, but Cruz appeared to hear every word perfectly. He stepped forward so they were no more than three paces apart.

'*Done* to her, Harry?' He was smiling slightly. 'So far, nothing. Not yet.' A look of pretend confusion crossed his face. 'Although I must say, I had expected news of her death even before I learned that you and I were to meet again. You see, Harry, I've been looking for you. And where better to start than with your family? Once Ellie had directed Calaca to your so-called grave, his instructions were to kill her. I told him it was so that she would not be able to identify him again, but I admit to feeling some satisfaction that you would probably hear of her death, wherever you were. But then you played straight into my hands. Such a happy coincidence! As you know, Calaca is extremely efficient. He knows how to contact me, and his instructions are to inform me the very moment he kills her. When that happens, it will be a moment we can share together, before I kill you too . . .'

Zak couldn't stop himself. He threw the full weight of his body against Cruz's. The two of them went flying, landing on the metal floor with a brutal thump. Before Cruz could even think about fighting back, Zak had one knee on his chest and his fist clenched above his face. 'You'd better get one thing straight, Cruz. Your men might fear you, but *I* don't. I *know* you. And if anything happens to Ellie, if she gets a single scratch on her knee because of you, I swear I'll—'

He didn't get to finish, because by then Cruz's bodyguards were on him. One of them kicked him in the stomach, knocking the wind from his lungs, while the other grabbed a clump of his hair and pulled him away from their boss. Cruz jumped to his feet. His face was angry. More than angry. There was madness in his eyes.

'You won't be a position to do *anything*, Agent 21.' He said these last two words almost as if they were poison in his mouth. 'I'd kill you now, but I want to see the look on your face when you learn that your cousin is dead. I want to see you suffer, like I suffered, before you die.' The mad look in his face grew even more insane. He turned to look at Bea. 'In the meantime,' he said, 'while we are waiting for word that Calaca has done his work, maybe I'll give you something else to think about.'

He didn't even look at his bodyguards as he gave the order.

'Kill her,' he said. 'Now!'

The bodyguards exchanged a glance.

'NOW!' Cruz roared.

'Get behind me!' Zak shouted at Bea. Cruz's guards were both raising their weapons. '*Get behind me!*'

Bea ignored him. Instead, she ran over to where the canisters of petrol were stashed by the wall. She pulled one past the rope that was keeping it in place and held it up in front of her chest and head. Zak could tell they must be very heavy.

'What are you doing?' he shouted. And then he realized. He turned back to Cruz. 'I hope you trust your guys not to miss her, Cruz. One bullet in the wrong place and that jerry can goes bang. Trust me, you really don't want a fire on board ship. There's nowhere to hide from it. We'll all go down together.'

He sensed Bea edging towards the back wall. Cruz's men hesitated; they were delaying. That was just what Zak wanted. His mind was turning over. Making connections. Why had Michael *really* sent him out to board the *Mercantile*? And why had he also sent Bea to sabotage his efforts? Suddenly the truth hit him. Cruz thought it was *coincidence* that Zak should turn up just when Ellie was in such danger, but it wasn't a coincidence at all. Michael had orchestrated the whole thing . . .

Suddenly he glanced down at the photograph in his hand. This time he didn't concentrate on Ellie, or on Calaca, but on something his unconscious was telling him he'd missed. There were other customers sitting in the fast-food joint behind Ellie, and Zak instantly saw that he recognized one of them. Shoulder-length grey hair. A slightly shabby overcoat.

Michael. Positive ID.

Zak was positive about something else too. The whole point of this operation was to bring Cruz out of hiding. He was nothing more than bait to catch a fish. And if Zak was bait, and Cruz was the fish, it meant there had to be a fisherman somewhere nearby.

He positioned himself between Bea and the two gunmen. But they were backing themselves into a corner. Zak knew it, and Cruz knew it too. All he had to do was instruct his men to pull the jerry can out of Bea's arms . . .

He didn't even bother to do that.

'Shoot her!' he commanded. It was as if he didn't even care if he died or not.

'Cruz, think about what you're doing!'

'SHOOT HER!'

'If that fuel explodes, the whole ship could go down.' He turned to the gunmen. 'I've seen the wreckage of a ship, guys,' he said. 'Trust me, it's not a nice way to go . . .'

The two gunmen glanced anxiously at each other. There was fear in their faces. But they must have been even more scared of Cruz than of the dangers involved in firing at Bea, because they raised their guns again, clearly preparing to take a shot.

Zak backed up again so that he was standing just a metre in front of Bea. 'You'll have to kill me first, Cruz,' he shouted.

Cruz gave him a thin smile. 'That's fine by me, Harry. That's absolutely fine by me.' He looked at the gunmen, who were now ready to fire, and nodded.

A deafening crack filled the air.

Zak tumbled to the ground. He sensed Bea doing the same, and heard the echo of the jerry can as it hit the metal floor. His first instinct was to check his body to see where he'd been shot. He knew that in the first moments, adrenalin could mask the pain of a bullet wound. He looked down his body. No blood. 'Bea!' he shouted. 'Are you hit?'

'I don't think so . . . I don't think they—'

Her words were hidden by the sound of a second

massive explosion, and it was only then that he looked over at Cruz and the two gunmen. They were on the floor too. Cruz was trying to push himself up to his feet, but a second later a shock wave hit the vessel and he fell over again.

Zak grabbed Bea's hand and pulled her up so they were both standing. 'Run!' he shouted. '*RUN!*'

Together they sprinted towards the door – between Cruz and the gunmen, who were still flat on the floor. Zak pulled the door shut behind him. 'It won't hold them for long,' he shouted. 'They've got weapons, they can shoot themselves out.'

'What was that explosion?' Bea asked as they ran along a long, narrow corridor away from the storage deck.

'Ever heard of the double camera trick?'

'What are you talking about?'

'You know the second device you hid on the *Mercantile*? I reckon it's just been detonated.'

Bea stopped and grabbed him by the arm. A frown had crossed her forehead but there was a look of hope in her eyes. 'If the device *has* been detonated,' she said, 'someone must have been around to detonate it.'

Zak winked at her. He held up the photograph that he was still clutching and pointed at the blurry picture of Michael in the background. 'Ring any bells?' he asked. Bea's eyes widened as she twigged what she was looking at. 'He's tracking us,' Zak told us. 'He has to be. Come on!'

Zak tried to run, but Bea held him back. 'That thing I said, about not seeing any sign of you being good.'

'You didn't mean it?'

Bea grinned. It was the first time he'd seen her smile and it completely changed her face. 'Oh no,' she said. 'I meant it. But I take it back now. I'm actually quite impressed.' Her eyes shone. 'Thank you for protecting me back there, Agent 21. I thought I was a goner.'

He returned her smile. 'You might as well call me Zak.'

'And you might as well call me Agent 20.'

Zak nodded. 'Agent 20,' he repeated quietly. It all made sense. 'You know that thing you said about *my* sticking my nose in where it's not wanted?'

'Did I say that?' she asked innocently.

'You bet. Well, I don't know where you learned it, Agent 20, but you do a very good impression of an interfering busybody yourself.'

Bea's grin became broader. 'Why, thank you, Zak,' she said, sounding flattered. As she spoke, however, they both heard the sound of bullets slamming into the door of the cabin they'd just left. No sign of any men yet, but it was just a matter of time.

'Come on,' Zak said. All hints of playfulness had left his face, and Bea's too. 'Unless I'm mistaken, we're going to see a few friendly faces pretty soon. Let's get up on deck. We don't want anyone to miss us, do we?

21

NOT BY STRENGTH, BY GUILE

Zak and Bea saw nobody as they headed up towards the deck, but it was still hard going. The ship was listing more than ever. They found it difficult to keep their footing in the narrow corridors. More than once, Zak found himself hurled against one side of a corridor or the other. His upper arms were bruised and sore by the time they emerged.

The first thing they saw was the rain. It was heavier than ever, like a grey curtain they couldn't see through, thundering down onto the deck with the noise of a thousand bullets. The second thing they saw was sea. It was grey too, and tempestuous. The waves rose over the side of the ship and their spray merged with the rain to create waterfalls of foam.

It was the third thing they saw, however, that commanded all their attention, and that was the MV *Mercantile*, about a hundred metres away.

Zak never knew a ship could sink so fast. In his

mind, they always slipped slowly below the water line. The *Mercantile*, however, was visibly disappearing. It was at a thirty-degree angle in the water and the stern end was already underwater. A thick plume of smoke was just visible rising up halfway between the centre of the boat and the sinking stern. Thirty seconds after Zak and Bea arrived on deck, however, the smoke disappeared as the sea extinguished the fire that was causing it. As the ship sank, it sent huge, powerful waves hurtling towards Cruz's vessel. They broke dangerously over the deck and tossed the ship around like a toy boat in the bath.

They stared. Through the mist of rain and sea water, Zak thought he could see something: figures, jumping from the side of the sinking ship. There was no way anybody could survive for long in these waters. Karlovic and his crew would soon be joining Eduardo on the sea bed. Either that or they would be washed up, bloated and rotten, on some distant shore. It gave Zak no pleasure to see this happening; but somehow it seemed like a fitting end.

And it was an end Zak and Bea would share if they didn't move quickly. They weren't the only ones staring at this dreadful sight. Further down the deck towards the bow, about twenty metres away, Zak could see six crew members clinging to the railings as they watched the *Mercantile* go down. One of them turned round and saw them. He shouted something – Zak couldn't hear what it was above the noise but he didn't need to. As one, the men turned. And then they started advancing – carefully on account of the movement of the ship and the impact of the waves, but steadily.

'*Run!*' Zak shouted at Bea, but she was already moving.

'If you're sure someone's going to rescue us,' she screamed, 'now would be a very good time for them to turn up.'

Zak couldn't disagree with that. He looked over his shoulder just as a wave hit, showering over them and blocking his view. When it subsided, the crew members were much closer than he expected. The men were gaining on them. They were only ten metres away, and Zak could see Cruz and his two bodyguards approaching ten metres behind that.

Another wave. Another loss of vision. It subsided, and Bea screamed. Zak looked beyond her.

More men up ahead, sandwiching them in.

They were trapped. Unable to move forward. Unable to move back.

Zak looked out to sea, desperately scanning the waves and the skies for something – anything – that would give him an inkling of hope that he was right about being rescued. All he saw was the fast-sinking

Mercantile, and the stormy, inhospitable ocean all around.

And two sets of enemy on the deck, closing in fast.

Another wave crashed over them. Zak and Bea were knocked back against the body of the ship. Zak shouted in pain. His arm had hit the hard, sharp corner of something attached to the wall. He looked to see what it was. A red metal case, with the words IN CASE OF EMERGENCY written on it. It was fastened with a metal clasp on one side. Ignoring the pain in his arm, Zak grabbed the clasp and opened it. The front of the case came away, to reveal what looked like a long-barrelled gun.

Only it wasn't a gun. It was an emergency flare. But Zak and Bea were in trouble. He was glad for any help he could get.

Zak pulled the flare from its housing. 'What are you doing?' Bea shouted at him.

'Stay close to me,' he replied. 'When I run, you run. Got it?'

'*What are you doing?*'

He examined the flare. It was intended as a distress call – a beacon to nearby vessels to come and help in the event of an emergency. If ever there was an emergency, this was it. But the flare consisted of only a single shot. Zak couldn't waste it by firing it up into the air. He had to use it more wisely than that.

He had to use it as a weapon.

He just hoped he was right, and that someone – *anyone* – knew where they were.

Zak looked left and right. To his left were the original four crew members. They'd been knocked over by the wave too and were just getting to their feet, so they were still ten metres away. Beyond them, Cruz and his two bodyguards. To his right, another five men. They were already standing. Already advancing. Three of them had rifles and they were holding them ready to engage.

Ready to shoot. Which meant Zak had to shoot first.

He raised the flare, took aim, and fired.

Firing a flare was nothing like firing one of the weapons back on the range at St Peter's Crag. It was unwieldy and inaccurate. Zak didn't mean to hit any of the approaching crew members; all he wanted to do was scare them. But the flare was difficult to control. It made a rushing sound as Zak fired, and brushed so close to one of the advancing crew members that it scorched his right arm, even through the man's wet clothes.

The crew member screamed, and the others were thrown into disarray, shocked because they'd come under fire when they didn't expect it. Zak grabbed Bea's hand. '*Run!*' he shouted. '*Now!*'

The two of them sprinted towards the surprised crew members. Zak kept the flare gun in his hand – not because he could use it, but because in the confusion the men might think it was a loaded weapon. They burst through them just as Zak heard a gunshot from behind. Even with the wind blowing strongly, he felt a rush of air as the round whizzed past his head.

'*They're firing!*' Bea yelled.

'I noticed,' Zak replied as they continued sprinting towards the stern of the ship, away from both sets of crew members. He didn't bother looking over his shoulder to see if they were giving chase. He knew they would be.

Another gunshot. Another rush of air. They had to get to cover. The stern of the ship was just ahead. If they could turn the corner it would give them a few seconds to regroup. A few seconds to . . .

'What's that?'

Bea pointed out to sea as they ran. Zak looked up. He saw something out there. A flash of grey, just a few shades darker than the sea itself. Close. Fifty metres, no more. It disappeared as the waves swelled – too quickly for Zak to be sure of what he'd just seen. But he had a pretty good idea.

They kept running. Seconds later they turned the corner, round to the stern of the boat and out of range of the shooters. Zak gave himself a moment to look out to sea again, and the next wave that crashed over him was one of relief.

Vessels approaching. Four that he could see, but unlike any vessels Zak had seen before. They were slender, long and pointed, like the nose of Concorde, and they seemed to pierce the rolling waves rather than float on the top of the sea. And they were fast. Bullet fast.

'*Looks like the cavalry's arrived!*' he shouted at Bea. '*My money's on the SBS . . .*'

But Bea wasn't looking. She was too busy grabbing a flotation ring from the body of the boat. Zak looked round. The crew members were turning the corner. The armed men led the pack. Zak couldn't see Cruz, but somehow he just knew his nemesis was in the mix.

Bea barged past him, clutching the flotation ring with both hands. She twisted her body round and, with a loud shout of effort, she hurled the ring towards the approaching men. It struck them full on, like a bowling ball making a strike, hitting three of them across the face. They fell back. One of them discharged his weapon accidentally, but the round shot harmlessly up into the air.

Zak and Bea started running again, round to the other side of the ship.

And it was as they ran that the gunfire started in earnest. A barrage of bullets and cracks.

'*Hit the ground!*' Zak shouted to Bea as he flung himself onto the hard metal floor of the deck. '*HIT THE GROUND!*'

Captain Frank Jackson had led SBS units through some choppy seas. None of them, though, had been as bad as this. Deep down, he reckoned he'd be lucky not to lose a couple of guys, but his OC had been adamant. Orders from on high. 'You can expect to find three teenage kids on board.'

Frank had given his OC a confused look. 'Kids?' he asked. 'What are these people, human traffickers?'

'Drug dealers.'

'Then what are kids doing on board?'

'Your job, soldier, is carry out orders, not question them. Two of the kids will be British nationals. Our intel suggests they can' – the OC had looked a bit dubious – 'that they can handle themselves. The third kid is older. Mexican. He needs to be captured or killed.'

Frank had blinked. Since when were the SBS in the business of taking out teenagers? The OC clearly caught the look of surprise on his face. 'Dead or alive, soldier. Those are your orders.'

'Roger that, boss.'

The OC had nodded. 'And, Frank?'

'Yes, boss?'

'Those British nationals. They're just kids. You get them home safe, come hell or high water.'

High water? Check. Hell? They'd have to wait and see.

They were travelling in a VT Halmatic VSV 16 – a 'very slender vessel'. Sixteen metres long, but only three metres wide at its broadest point. The exact composition of the hull – a mixture of carbon fibre and Kevlar, the same material from which their helmets were constructed – was classified information. But it was light and it was fast. Their target was approaching quickly.

He checked his weapon. MP5. It was already wet but that was OK. The sea water would just drain out of it. He looked around at his men. All dressed in the same way. Black helmets cut away around the ears. Skin-tight drysuits under their ops waistcoats. Sub-machine guns hanging from webbing fixed to their suits.

He felt the VSV slow down and looked to his men. 'Prepare to board!' he shouted into his patrol comms. 'Covering fire in three, two, *one—*'

Suddenly the howling of the wind and the rush of the waves was punctuated by a barrage of gunfire from one of the neighbouring VSVs. That was their signal to board. Their own vessel had drawn up alongside the ship now, and one of his men was extending a telescopic ladder with hooks at the end. He attached it to the railings of the listing ship in a matter of seconds. Frank looked at his men and shouted again. '*Go, go, go . . .*'

Standard operating procedure dictated that Frank, as unit commander, shouldn't be the first to climb. He didn't like not leading from the front, but those were the rules. He watched as two SBS troopers shimmied up the ladder in seconds while the covering fire from the other boat continued to keep them safe from enemy rounds.

Frank went third. The rope ladder swung and listed in the wind but he didn't let it slow him down. He'd trained for this, day in, day out, after all. As he emerged above the railings, he saw the two front-runners down on one knee, one of them aiming his MP5 to port, the other to starboard. To his right he saw a group of crew members. They'd hit the deck and had their hands over the back of their heads. Now that Frank and his men were spilling over onto the ship, the covering fire from the VSV below subsided. They could take care of themselves now.

To his left, Frank saw two figures. They too were lying on their fronts. He ran towards them. They were just kids. They'd be terrified. Knowing that his men were keeping him well covered, he knelt down where they were lying, ready to give them a few quick words of encouragement. He didn't want them freezing with fear in the middle of a rescue operation, after all.

He never got the chance.

The two kids – one boy and one girl – jumped to their feet the moment they saw him. They looked sharply left and right, taking in the situation with a few quick glances. Then the girl turned to Frank.

'Do me a favour,' she shouted. 'Next time you come to rescue us, don't leave it quite so long, would you?'

Cruz Martinez knew what anger – *real* anger – felt like. He'd experienced it enough times over the last few months. Before his father died, he'd been a mild-mannered teenager, not given to tantrums or loss of temper. Those days had gone. Now, on an almost daily basis, he tasted the bile in the back of his throat, the loss of control in his limbs. He saw the world through a tinge of red mist.

But he'd never felt anger like this. He'd been set up. He saw that now. Harry Gold – Zak Darke, or whatever his name really was – had set him up again. And now black-clad soldiers were swarming over his ship like ants. Ants that had arrived with one purpose in mind: to kill him and his men.

His two bodyguards had hunkered down on either side of him. Idiots. They were supposed to protecting him, not cowering at the first sign of danger. Cruz heard a voice shouting. He realized it was his. 'Shoot them! *Shoot them! Get up, you dogs, and SHOOT THEM!*'

It was the bodyguard on his left who was either the bravest, the stupidest or the most scared. He pushed himself up to his knees and fired a burst of rounds in the direction of the soldiers. As he fired, though, the ship swayed and the rounds fell harmlessly. He didn't get a chance to try again. One of the soldiers who was down on one knee and facing them fired a burst of his own. He was a lot more accurate. Bullets drilled into the bodyguard's skull, flinging him backwards and showering a spray of blood and gore over Cruz's back. He barely noticed it. The bodyguard on his right was still cowering uselessly, and the remainder of his men were also flat on the floor.

It looked to Cruz like he would have to deal with this situation himself.

'Give me your weapon,' he instructed the remaining bodyguard. The man shrank back from his boss, but it only took a severe look from Cruz and he did as he was told.

Cruz brandished the weapon and prepared to fight. The dead man's mistake, he realized, had been to stop firing. It wasn't a mistake Cruz intended to repeat. He squeezed the trigger of his weapon at the same time as he jumped to his feet. The automatic rifle sprayed bullets over the stern deck. Cruz stepped backwards, swinging his gun arm from left to right to left again. His men – the cowards – started crawling towards him. *They* should be protecting *him*, he raged. They would pay for it when the time came . . .

He saw one of the enemy soldiers go down. A round from Cruz's gun had hit him in the face. There was a flash of red – the last thing Cruz saw before he disappeared from the stern deck and started running along the starboard side of the ship, followed by what was left of his crew.

Cruz shouted over his shoulder: 'If I see any of you failing to fight, I'll kill you myself.'

And he meant it.

'Man down! We've got a man down!'

Frank was screaming at the top of his voice as he ran towards his fallen mate. He was aware of four of his colleagues advancing towards the starboard deck, another four heading to port. He crouched down by the body. His face was such a pulp Frank couldn't even be sure who it was. He went through the motions of checking for a pulse, but he knew it was pointless. This guy was going home in a box, if he made it home at all.

He jumped to his feet. The two kids were there, looking down at the dead man. Spray crashed over the deck. It washed some of the blood away from the face of the corpse. '*We need to get you off the ship!*' he shouted. '*Now!*'

'What about Cruz?' the boy shouted.

'Is he the kid who just killed my man?'

The boy nodded and Frank could feel his face turning severe. No need to tell these two what he intended to do to the kid who'd killed his man. 'We need to get you off the ship,' he repeated.

The boy gave him a dead-eyed look. 'We can't disembark until the crew is neutralized. It's too dangerous. If they start firing on us while we're trying to get off the ship, we'll be sitting ducks.' He bent down and grabbed the dead man's MP5.

'Hey, son – that's not a toy . . .' But Frank only had to see the way the boy held the weapon, and listen to the way he was talking, to realize he knew how to handle it.

'We'll stay here,' the kid shouted. 'I can protect us. You flush them out.'

Frank's eyes narrowed. He remembered what his OC had said, about the two British nationals being able to handle themselves. He nodded. 'Roger that. Whatever you do, don't move from this position. You see enemy targets, shoot on sight. Don't wait for them to fire first. We'll clear the ship and return when the targets are down.'

'Go!' the boy shouted. 'We'll be fine . . .'

Frank ran to join his men. He didn't like leaving those two by themselves, but it wasn't the first time he'd had to make a difficult call in the middle of an op. Wouldn't be the last, either. Still, brave kids, he thought as he sprinted round onto the starboard deck. Brave or stupid.

He couldn't help wondering how they'd managed to get themselves into a situation like this. And he didn't see the suspicious look the girl was giving the boy as Frank disappeared.

22

ENDGAME

'You're up to something. What is it?'

Zak could tell that Bea was doing her very best not to look at the pulped face of the corpse at their feet. 'You got rid of him for a reason,' she shouted. 'What was it?'

Bea was no fool. She'd seen through his plan even if the SBS man hadn't. He checked port and starboard, the forefinger of his right hand resting lightly on the trigger of his MP5. 'Cruz is clever,' he shouted back. 'He'll evade them.'

'How can you be sure?'

'Trust me. I know him.'

Bea's eyes narrowed. Zak could almost hear the wheels turning in her head. She started thinking out loud. 'Michael got you on board the *Mercantile* because he knew it would draw Cruz out of hiding. You're the one he wants. If we're alone here, you think he'll come and find us.' Her expression changed. She looked aghast at Zak, then at the MP5 in his hand. '*You want to kill him yourself . . .*'

Zak started prowling round the stern deck, looking left, right and even out to sea where the SBS's vessels were still circling. Bea shouted across the deck at him. 'Zak, it's too dangerous!'

He returned to her position by the corpse. 'Relax,' he told her. 'Nobody's killing anybody. Not if I have anything to do with it.'

'Then what . . . ?'

'My cousin's in danger,' Zak said, his voice grim. 'I know the man Cruz has sent after her. He tried to kill *me* once, and he's a monster. The only way I can save Ellie is by keeping Cruz alive.'

Bea looked at him like he was mad, her short wet hair clinging to her head. 'What? *Why?*'

Zak looked down at the corpse of the SBS man on the ground. 'Because,' he said quietly – so quietly that he knew Bea wouldn't be able to hear him over the wind and the waves. He strode across the deck towards the railings and looked out to sea again. 'Because he can't tell Calaca to stand down if he's dead.'

The wind screamed. It was shrill. Piercing.

Almost human . . .

It *was* human . . .

Zak spun round, and his heart almost stopped. It wasn't the wind screaming at all. It was Bea. And she had good reason. Cruz was standing behind her. In his left hand he had a clump of her short hair and he was twisting it hard. In his right hand was his knife – Acosta's knife, cruel and jagged. The smooth edge was pressed up against Bea's neck, and Cruz had a wild look of triumph in his eyes.

Zak raised his MP5. But as he did so, Cruz just pulled Bea's head further back, exposing more of her neck.

'Drop the gun, Harry,' he shouted. 'Over the side. You *know* I'll kill her if you don't.'

The two boys stared at each other through the rain. Slowly, Zak lowered his MP5.

'Over the side, Harry,' Cruz repeated. 'Now.'

Zak backed up to the railings. He knew he didn't have a choice. He hurled the MP5 into the billowing waves. Then he started walking back towards Cruz and Bea.

'Let her go, Cruz,' he shouted. 'This is nothing to do with her.'

'Chivalry, Harry? I didn't know you had it in you.'

'Let her go!'

The Mexican teenager grinned. 'Oh, I don't think so, Harry. I've gone to a great deal of trouble to see to it that your cousin is killed. And now fate puts another girl you have feelings for into my hands. I'd be foolish, wouldn't I, to pass up a chance like that . . .'

'If you let her go, Cruz,' Zak yelled, 'there's a chance you'll get off this ship alive. If you do anything stupid, I'll kill you myself.'

Cruz's grin grew wider. 'That's quite a threat, Harry Gold. But will you really? Will you really kill the one person who can save your cousin?'

They stared at each other. Zak could see the terror in Bea's face.

And the madness in Cruz's. He was going to do it. Bea had seconds to live . . .

Seconds to die . . .

Suddenly there was movement all around him. Round the corner, from the port and starboard decks, lines of SBS personnel appeared. Four from each side. They had their weapons aimed at Cruz. One man was shouting: *'Drop the knife! Drop the knife or we fire!'*

'FIRE, THEN!' Cruz screamed, his eyes now even wilder than the storm that raged all around them. 'FIRE, AND KILL US BOTH!'

'NO!' Zak shouted. He ran towards Cruz and Bea. He didn't even know what he hoped to achieve. Was he trying to stop Cruz slicing that knife into Bea's neck; or was he putting himself between the SBS unit and their target, in an effort to stop them opening fire.

Either way, he was unsuccessful.

The wave that crashed over the stern deck as Zak was running was the biggest yet. It totally engulfed them. Zak was knocked to the ground. He felt himself sliding along the deck, but he couldn't see anything for all the water in his eyes. The wave receded, sucking back into the ocean and dragging Zak with it. He tried to fight against it, to scramble up the deck, but it was impossible. He slid towards the railings, hitting them with such force that the wind was knocked from his lungs. But at least the railings had stopped him. He gripped them firmly with one hand, wiping the sea water from his eyes with the other. And then he looked round.

The wave had scattered everyone. The deck was littered with figures pushing themselves onto their feet. Zak's eyes quickly sought out Bea. She was holding onto the railings too, about five metres from Zak. She looked OK.

And a couple of metres beyond her, he saw Cruz. He looked bedraggled, but he still had his knife and he was advancing on Bea once again.

Zak sprinted towards him, past a shocked-looking Bea. Cruz looked shocked too as Zak threw himself against his former friend, sending them both hurtling towards the floor. Cruz tried to slash at him with the knife, but Zak was too fast. He grabbed Cruz's wrist and smashed it down on the deck. The knife fell out of his hand and slid a couple of metres from where they were fighting. Zak rolled away from

Cruz. Seconds later he had the knife in his hand.

Cruz scrambled to his feet. Zak did the same. The SBS men had recovered from the wave. Even now they were getting into position.

Ready to shoot . . .

'*HOLD YOUR FIRE!*' Zak roared. Brandishing the knife, he strode towards Cruz, positioning himself between his former friend and the gunmen who wanted to take him down. He heard shouting – '*Stand down! Stand down!*' – but he ignored it. All his attention was on Cruz, who had his back pressed up against the railings and whose eyes were flicking between Zak's face and the knife in his hand.

'Give it up, Cruz,' Zak shouted. 'They'll kill you if you don't.'

'They'll kill me,' Cruz yelled back, 'even if I do.'

Zak shook his head. 'I won't let them.'

'*Stand down! Stand down!*' The gunmen were advancing around him.

Cruz sneered. 'A guilty conscience, Harry?'

'No, Cruz. But my fight was never with you.'

The sneer became more pronounced. Cruz's hair blew in the wind. 'My father is dead because of you.'

'And my parents are dead because of your father. Give it up, Cruz. You can't win now. It's over.' Zak took a step towards him. '*It's over!*'

The sneer became a smile. An insane smile, but a

smile nevertheless. 'No, Harry,' Cruz said. He didn't shout this time, but Zak was close enough to hear. '*You* don't decide when it's over. *I* do.'

It happened so quickly.

Cruz suddenly pulled something from one of his pockets. At first, Zak thought it must be a gun. He quickly saw that it looked more like a mobile phone. Only *not* a mobile phone. Just a handheld device with a single switch.

A detonator.

'*STOP!*' Zak roared. He dropped the knife and dived forwards to stop Cruz flicking the switch. But too late.

There was a massive explosion. It came from the opposite end of the ship, but it sent shock waves all along the deck. Zak hit the ground just two metres from Cruz's position. The force of the blast had knocked Cruz sideways, but he was still standing. Zak crawled towards him, but as he crawled he saw Cruz leaning back over the railings. His hair blew in the wind; his eyes shone.

He was pushing himself back . . .

Zak stretched out to grab Cruz's nearest shoe. His fingertips touched the sole, but then slipped away as Cruz toppled backwards over the railings. Zak reached them just in time to see his body fall towards the boiling ocean.

He shouted again – '*NO . . .*' – and pushed himself to his feet just in time to see Cruz's body hit the water and sink into the ocean. '*Help him!*' he screamed. But he knew there was nothing anybody could do. Zak had already seen Eduardo fall into those treacherous seas. He knew Cruz's body could never reappear.

He knew his nemesis was dead.

'*Get down!*'

There was no time to mourn, even if he wanted to. Cruz had barely disappeared beneath the stormy water when a voice pierced the air. It was immediately followed by a shot. Zak hit the deck and looked back. It took a split second to process everything that was happening.

The ship's crew – seven of them – had reappeared. Clearly they didn't know their boss was dead, because they were coming at the SBS ready to fight, guns aimed. One of them had already fired a shot, and that shot had found its target.

Bea.

She was hit.

'*Stay down!*' The instruction from one of the SBS men rang through the air, but Zak ignored it and ran towards her. She had fallen to the floor. The bullet had squarely entered her left shoulder and blood was pouring out through her sodden clothes. Her face was white with shock and she was trembling. The wound was so bad that Zak barely noticed at first that the deck was at an angle. The bow of the ship was sinking. Cruz had scuttled it with his explosion . . .

Suddenly the air exploded with gunshots. The SBS personnel hadn't hesitated. They outnumbered the crew members, and they out-skilled them too.

Cruz's men didn't stand a chance.

Zak watched with a mixture of horror and relief as the SBS's shower of rounds hit them. There were no screams. No cries for help. Just a few seconds of fast, efficient killing. The men crumpled to the floor in a blur of blood and flesh. Another seven bodies to add to the day's death count.

But there was only one body Zak was interested in at that moment. Bea's. She was a mess. Her eyes were rolling. Her blood loss was heavy.

He looked up. The SBS unit leader was standing above him, his face as stormy as the sea. 'What were you doing?' he shouted angrily. 'You should have let us take the Mexican kid out—'

There was no time to explain. No time to tell the soldier that he'd been trying to save the life of an innocent girl thousands of miles away. Zak gritted his teeth. Nothing could now prevent Calaca catching up with Ellie. Anger and panic surged through him, but he put a lid on it.

He had to keep focused. Professional. The ship was

going down. They had to get off. Moreover, Bea needed medical attention. And if she didn't get it quickly, the body count was about to grow even higher.

19.00 hrs GMT

A white van was parked up in the vicinity of 63 Acacia Drive. Some of the residents had noticed it, but none of them thought it was suspicious. They just assumed it belonged to a builder or an electrician parking in the street while they carried out some work in one of their neighbour's houses.

Certainly nobody suspected it was the hideout of an assassin.

Calaca was not a naturally patient man. But he had been patient today. He had sat looking out of the tinted windows of his van all afternoon. At half-past four, he had watched Ellie Lewis return to the house with her parents after a trip to the local supermarket. And he watched her now, creeping furtively out of her house and walking quickly along the road. She had changed. Now she had on a fashionable pair of jeans, and a jumper interwoven with sparkling thread. She wore a colourful woollen hat, and Calaca thought she might even have applied a little lipstick and mascara, though these were not things he knew very much about.

He didn't know how to make faces beautiful. He knew how to make them dead.

He smiled thinly. Ellie Lewis had clearly made an effort for her secret rendezvous. He wondered who the lucky boy was, and if he too had chosen his best clothes. How sweet, he thought to himself, that they would both be shining and well-dressed for the moment of their death. Because he *would* have to kill them both. Just to be sure.

The girl turned the corner at the end of the street and disappeared. By then, however, Calaca was already getting ready. Laid out on the floor of the white van was his weapon. It was a Russian PP-93 sub-machine gun. Effective range, 100 metres. Very lightweight and easy to conceal, but deadly accurate in the hands of someone who knew how to handle it properly. Calaca was one such man. The barrel was silenced, so the retort of the gunshots would not echo around Hampstead Heath when the time came. The magazine contained thirty rounds. He would only be requiring two of them.

Even with one eye, Calaca never missed.

Next to the gun was a wig. It fitted his shaved head well, and suddenly he was no longer a bald one-eyed man; he had a thick head of brown hair, parted neatly at one side. He put on his glasses with the medical dressing on the blind side and checked his reflection in window of the van. Not exactly unremarkable, but the last person he looked like was himself.

Calaca secreted the weapon inside his coat before opening the back of the van and stepping outside. He locked the van and then looked up. The night sky was clear. It made a change after the terrible weather of the past few days. He would walk to Hampstead Heath, he decided. It was a crisp and pleasant evening for an assassination, and the fresh air would do him good.

23

LIFT OFF

Bea was slipping into unconsciousness. The ship was slipping into the water. Not as fast as the *Mercantile*, which was now almost completely submerged, but fast enough.

Zak's hands were bloodied from where he was putting pressure on Bea's wound. He was aware of shouts from the SBS personnel as they prepared to disembark over the side and into the waiting boats; and of the unit commander, screaming instructions into his patrol comms radio. Zak didn't know what he was saying, though. All his attention was on his friend.

The unit commander knelt down beside him.

'What's your name?' Zak shouted.

'Frank.'

'She's in a bad way,' Zak told him.

Frank nodded grimly. 'We can't get her into our boats. We need to airlift her out.'

'How?'

Frank looked out to sea. 'We've got a Sea King chopper on standby. It's heading in now. We've got a frigate waiting five nautical miles from here. If we can get her to the medics back there, she might have a chance.' He didn't look too convinced.

Bea shouted out suddenly – 'Don't leave me, Jay. *Please . . .*' A cry of pain. Then she slumped more heavily into Zak's arms.

The SBS were disappearing over the side, climbing down their rope ladders into the waiting VNVs. 'You need to go,' Frank shouted. 'My men will get you back to the ship. I'll stay with her till the chopper arrives.'

It only took Zak a couple of seconds to decide he wasn't going to do that.

'I'm staying,' he shouted. 'One of us needs to keep the pressure on that wound if she's going to make it.'

'No way! It's too dangerous, and my orders are to keep you safe. The ship's sinking. You need to get off while you can.'

Zak shook his head. 'Bea risked everything for this operation,' he shouted back. 'She deserves every chance now. And anyway, you'll need some help getting her into a harness when the chopper arrives. We haven't got time to argue about this, Frank – I'm needed here, and you might as well just accept that I'm not going anywhere till Bea's in that Sea King.'

Just like I might as well accept, Zak thought to himself, *that Calaca's going to kill Ellie. And if anyone thinks I'm going to leave Bea alone to die too, they've got another think coming . . .*

Frank frowned, but he didn't argue – what Zak was saying *did* make sense. Instead, he stood up and started barking instructions at his men and into the patrol comms. The ship suddenly shuddered and Zak felt it sinking. He saw some of the bodies of the dead crew members roll heavily along the deck on account of the angle of the boat. Bea cried out again. All the remaining SBS members had disappeared over the side.

'How long till the chopper gets here?' he screamed.

Frank pointed out to sea. Everything was grey – ocean, sky, the VSVs disappearing away from the ship – and a dot approaching from the horizon.

'That's it!' Frank shouted 'ETA three minutes. Maybe four in this weather. They wouldn't normally fly in these winds.' He crouched back down next to Bea. 'We need to keep her stable while we wait!' he yelled.

'Roger that,' Zak shouted. He pressed down on Bea's wound again and felt the warm, sticky blood seep between his fingers.

Frank handed him something from round his neck. It was a square tube of plastic, one end red.

'Morphine,' he shouted. 'For pain relief. Get it in her, now.'

Zak nodded. He raised the plastic shot casing and slammed it down on Bea's upper arm. He felt a slight resistance as the needle punctured her clothes and then her skin. Bea didn't respond. Zak wondered if she'd even felt the injection.

It was windy on Hampstead Heath. Calaca wasn't used to the sensation of his hair blowing around and he wondered how people put up with it. It was dark too. There were few people about. An occasional dog walker. A little crowd of young men sharing cigarettes and cans of beer. He was glad that he had recce'd the heath already in the dark. It meant he knew where he was going. He could almost have made his way blindfolded.

He checked his watch. 19.45. Fifteen minutes until eight o'clock. The lake, where Ellie Lewis had arranged her rendezvous, was just a hundred metres away. He'd be early, which was good. It meant he could find himself a suitable firing point, and check the wind direction to ensure that his shots were on target. By one minute past, his victims would be dead. Calcaca himself would be on his way to Heathrow, where he would catch that evening's flight to Mexico City. He was quite looking forward to telling the new Señor Martinez that he had been successful.

Everybody likes a little bit of praise, after all.

A dog barked in the distance. Calaca smiled and strode towards the water, his fingertips twitching and his mouth dry with anticipation.

The Sea King was a hundred metres away, and it was struggling. Zak could tell just by looking at it. It was being buffeted by the wind, and seemed to wobble in the air as it approached. Zak had seen enough helicopters in his time. They'd never looked so precarious in the air as this.

Lightning cracked in the air. Seconds later, a bellow of thunder. The sinking ship juddered as a wave crashed over the stern deck. 'Hold on!' screamed Frank. Zak just grabbed Bea's body and hunkered down until the wave had passed. He looked up again. The Sea King was closer. Maybe fifty metres. It seemed strange not to be able to hear the rotors, but the howling of the wind drowned them out. 'It's got to be Force Ten,' Frank shouted. 'We'd better hope the chopper makes it here – it's too rough for those VSVs to approach again now . . .'

Bea's lips had gone blue. Zak boxed away his panic and tried to check her pulse, but it was impossible because the ship was vibrating as it sank. The greasy smell of smoke wafted around him. 'Burning fuel!'

Frank shouted. 'We've got to get the hell out of here fast. The whole thing could blow at any minute . . .'

Thirty seconds passed. The Sea King had reached them. It was hovering twenty metres above the vessel and appeared to be swinging like the end of a pendulum. Zak supposed there was some down-draught, but he couldn't sense it because the wind was so strong anyway. He could see a black-clad figure at one of the open side doors. The figure threw out a rope, at the end of which was a harness. It swung all over the place as the Sea King's crew member lowered it down towards the three of them.

Frank turned to Zak. 'She needs to go up first,' he shouted. 'Will you be OK if I take her? We can't risk a three-man winch in these conditions. It could bring the chopper down.'

'Do what you need to do,' Zak replied. 'I'll be fine.' He said it with more confidence than he felt.

'Help me get her into the harness.'

The harness was hanging at their level now, but swinging violently because of the wind and the move-ment of the chopper. It took Frank twenty seconds to catch it, while Zak stayed crouched down by Bea. 'I don't know if you can hear me,' he said, his mouth close to her ear, 'but we're going to get you off this ship. You're going to be OK.'

Please, he thought to himself. *Let her be OK . . .*

Suddenly Frank was there again. He was holding the harness in one strong hand, and five or six metres of slack rope were coiled on the deck around him. 'Get her legs in,' he shouted. 'Like a pair of pants.'

Zak nodded and lifted Bea's legs. She shouted out in pain again, but gave no other sign of consciousness. Frank hurriedly pulled the harness up to her waist, then clipped the rope to the webbing around his dry-suit. He pulled his patrol comms radio out and handed it to Zak. 'This will keep you in touch with the chopper,' he shouted. 'We'll send the harness back down as soon as she's safely inside.'

Zak nodded. 'Go!' he shouted, before looking up towards the Sea King and giving a thumbs-up.

The slack rope started moving like a lazy snake. Then it suddenly became taut. Seconds later, Bea's body jolted and, like a corpse rising from a coffin, she started to stand upright. Frank grabbed her round the waist and slowly the two of them started to rise.

Zak found that he was holding his breath. Frank and Bea moved upwards so slowly, and yet they rocked to and fro like a feather in the wind. They were five metres up when he saw blood dripping from Bea's wound. It disappeared into the rain and the spray. And though every cell in his body wanted to see Bea safely up in the body of the chopper, he couldn't help feeling more and more alone the higher they rose. He grabbed the railings again, and another waft of greasy black smoke drifted in front of his nose. Half the vessel was underwater now. He didn't know how much longer he had before it submerged completely. Half an hour? Forty-five minutes? Certainly no more. He looked over at the *Mercantile*. Only a few metres of its tip was now visible. The gruesome image of the sailors' grave on the wreck of HMS *Vanguard* entered his mind, and with it the thought of Gabs and Raf.

What would he give to have his Guardian Angels with him now? Not that they could have done much to help, but as he was fast finding out, there are few places more lonely than a sinking ship in the middle of the ocean, surrounded by nothing but the body of the dead, and no guarantee that you aren't about to become one of their number.

19.53 hrs GMT

Calaca's position was in the shadow of an old oak tree trunk. There was a stump to its side, about twenty centimetres high. The perfect firing position. He could remain unobserved, but the stump was an ideal platform on which to rest his gun arm when he took the shots.

He removed his glasses. They made no difference, of course, to his aim, but he felt more comfortable with them off. Taking his PP-93 from the inside of his jacket, he lay down on the ground in the firing position and, with his good eye, looked through the scope. It had NV capability, and the edge of the lake was lit up in a green haze.

He saw a family of ducks congregating at the water's edge.

He saw an urban fox scamper down to take a drink. It quenched its thirst, then looked up and seemed to stare almost directly at Calaca before hurrying away again. Something had disturbed it. Seconds later, he saw what it was.

His targets. Two people, hand in hand, one male, one female. He recognized Ellie Lewis's colourful woollen hat, and he noticed that the male was wearing one too.

How sweet, he thought. His and hers.

They were looking around rather furtively, as if they weren't supposed to be there. They stopped at the water's edge. The male figure stood with his back to Calaca, camouflaging the female. All he could see was her hands wrapped round his back as they started to kiss.

Calaca smiled. '*Buenas noches, señor*,' he breathed. He aimed the crosshairs of his scope at the centre of the man's back.

And then he fired his first shot.

* * *

Zak's radio crackled. '*OK, son. Do you copy? Send.*'

'I got you,' Zak shouted. Frank and Bea had disappeared into the Sea King. 'How's she doing?'

The guy on the other end of the radio ignored the question. '*We're sending the harness down again. Make sure you clip yourself in safely. It's pretty choppy up here.*'

Zak watched the rope descending. It came down much more quickly than it went up, but it swung violently again as it came. He stretched out his left arm – holding onto the railings with his right – and the harness just brushed his fingertips before swinging out of his grasp again. The wind blew it up at an angle of thirty degrees from the vertical. When it swung back again, it missed Zak's position by at least six metres.

But it hit the railings.

Zak watched in horror as the rope curled round the top railing, then back onto itself, creating a messy, tangled knot. He hadn't been able to hear the chopper up till now, but suddenly he could – there was a high-pitched, whining sound above the noise of the wind. The rope strained and went taut; the chopper itself jolted into an alarming angle, firmly anchored to the sinking ship.

'*The rope!*' he screamed into the radio. '*It's—*'

He didn't finish. As quickly as it had become tangled, the rope suddenly fell from above, and the

Sea King juddered upwards, like a stone shot from a sling. Zak watched the cut end of the rope fall down over the side of the sinking ship.

Dead in the water. Just like his hopes of escaping.

Calaca's first shot was easy. Sometimes, he thought to himself, it was almost as if these people *wanted* to be assassinated. The round from his suppressed weapon made almost no noise as it left the barrel. Just a quiet knocking. It hit Ellie Lewis's secret boyfriend squarely between the shoulder blades.

He didn't fall to the ground immediately. There was a couple of seconds, during which his knees buckled. But when he did collapse, it was heavily. Calaca imagined his victim coughing up blood from his lungs as the life escaped from him, but he couldn't see his features to verify this. In any case, all his attention was focused on his main target.

Ellie had turned, ready to run. She hadn't screamed yet, but Calaca had done this enough to realize it was just a matter of time until she did.

He positioned the crosshairs of his PP-93 directly at the back of her head.

And then he fired his second shot.

It was not the rain or the wind that had turned Zak's blood to ice. It was hard, cold panic. The Sea

King was gaining height. He was marooned.

He shouted into the radio. 'The harness! *We've lost the harness!* You need to send down another—'

He didn't hear the reply, because the sinking ship suddenly pitched dramatically and a wave crashed over him. When it subsided, Zak looked over the side. At their lowest point, the waves were only four metres down. Three quarters of the ship was underwater.

'Say again!'

'*Negative,*' came the reply. '*The winch is damaged. We have to get the bird back to base.*'

'Send out another chopper . . .'

'*Negative. No more heli assets.*'

Zak felt nauseous. He didn't know what to say.

There was a horrible silence over the radio. The Sea King hovered in the air above Zak – immense and impressive, but useless for Zak.

'*This is Frank, do you copy? Send.*'

'How's Bea doing?' Zak shouted into the radio.

'*Not good. We have to get her back to the frigate now. The seas are too rough now for the VSVs to return. I can't risk more men.*'

A pause. Zak understood what he was saying.

'*You need to listen carefully. We're going to lower the chopper as close to your position as possible. I'm going to try and throw out a STARS extraction kit. Do you know what that is?*'

Zak swallowed hard. He remembered Raf's slightly scary description of the process . . . *We stick a harness on you that has a special inflatable balloon on a cord. The balloon rises up into the air and a Hercules flies along with a clamp at the front, grabs the cord and takes you with it . . .*

'Yeah. I think so.'

'*We're scrambling a Hercules from the RAF base on Ascension Island,*' Frank shouted. '*ETA, thirty-five minutes.*'

Zak looked over the side. He was sinking fast. Thirty-five minutes was pushing it.

'*I'm going to be honest with you.*' Frank's voice was grim. '*It's difficult and dangerous and we'll only get one shot at it. But it's our only option if we're going to get you off there safely. Do you think you're up to it?*'

'Do I have a choice?'

'*Not really, no. Hold onto your radio. You'll be able to use it to speak to the Hercules flight crew. They'll tell you what to do.*'

Zak gritted his teeth. 'OK,' he shouted. 'Send it down.'

Almost immediately the Sea King started to lose height. He saw Frank appear at the open doorway; seconds later, the SBS man started manually lowering a package on a rope. Zak wasn't going to let this one get away. He grabbed it the second it came within reach, then pulled the package towards him and held it tight as Frank dropped the rope.

The Sea King ascended again, then turned 180 degrees and sped off towards the horizon.

Zak didn't watch it go. He couldn't. All his attention was focused on the package in his arms and the pitching of the ship.

He prepared himself for what he knew would be the longest thirty-five minutes of his life.

Calaca fired his second shot.

He had aimed it not at Ellie Lewis's back, but at her head, the back of which was covered by her colourful woollen hat. The bullet found its target with deadly precision.

The impact of the shot flung her forwards. She landed on her front. Through the green haze of the scope, Calaca saw her left foot twitching. He was sure she was dead, but he was nothing if not thorough. He stood up from the firing position, secreted his weapon again and quickly, quietly, made his way towards the corpses.

There was nobody here to see him. The heath was quiet. As quiet as a grave. Funny that. With any luck, it would be morning by the time these bodies were discovered. By then, Calaca would be thousands of miles away.

The corpses were ten metres away. Five.

Strange, he thought to himself, how little blood there was. You never could tell how a body would react to the impact of a bullet. Sometimes the flesh collapsed in on itself; sometimes it exploded in a shower of blood and gore; other times there was just the smallest of entry wounds. It looked like this was one of those times.

Now, though, it was time to deliver the final safety shots.

He turned to the male figure first. Now that he was up close, Calaca could see his clothes in better detail. Black jeans. Black boots. Black leather jacket. Black woollen hat.

He blinked. There was something else under the hat. It looked like . . .

Head protection.

Calaca's eyes suddenly blazed as he plunged his hand into his jacket to remove the weapon.

But too late.

The figure moved quickly, turning onto its back. To the astonishment of the one-eyed man, the face wasn't male, but female. And very much alive.

'Hello, sweetie,' she said, but her voice didn't sound sweet. Before he could do anything else, she raised her right arm – which he now saw was carrying a weapon of some sort – and fired at him.

Adan 'Calaca' Ramirez took in so many things at once.

The tranquillizer dart that stuck into his leg just above the knee.

The numb feeling that spread around his body.

The lights – blindingly bright – that suddenly appeared all around him.

And Ellie Lewis, sitting up and removing her woollen hat to reveal a Kevlar helmet. Her face was pale and anxious, but she was not dead. Far from it.

People running towards him. Shouting. They were armed. Police? Soldiers? He couldn't tell. He tried to reach his gun, but the tranquillizer was doing its job and his body wouldn't obey the instructions of his brain.

Three seconds later he fell to the floor, and darkness engulfed him.

Zak was bruised and freezing cold. The ship was so low in the water now that even the smallest swells of the waves crashed over him.

The STARS harness would have been difficult to fit even under normal conditions. Here it was almost impossible. By the time he had the straps tightened round his legs and abdomen, fifteen minutes had passed and his muscles were exhausted from the effort. He tried not to think about Bea or Ellie. There was nothing he could do now to help either of them.

Activity on the radio. Noise. A voice, maybe? Zak couldn't tell. He was suddenly engulfed in spray. By the time it subsided, the radio was dead. He engaged the pressel and shouted into it. '*Can you hear me? Can you hear me?*'

Nothing.

And then . . .

'*Copy that.*'

Zak's voice was shrill, he realized, as he shouted into the radio. 'It's getting pretty hairy down here. How long till pick-up?'

'*We're ten minutes out, son. You're going to have to get into the water.*'

Zak looked over the fast-sinking side of the ship. He felt his muscles freeze. He'd been doing everything he could *not* to get into the water. The STARS harness had a built-in flotation aid, but this wasn't going to be like backstroke at the local swimming baths. He'd seen what happened to people who found themselves in these waters.

'*Do you copy, son?*'

'Yeah, I copy.'

'*When you're in the water, inflate the balloon. It'll take about three minutes to reach its full height. Make sure the wire that attaches it to your harness is let up smoothly.*'

'How will you know where I am?'

'*There's a white-light firefly inside the balloon. A beacon. We'll see it. Once you're in the water, you won't be able to maintain radio contact. Hopefully you'll hear us approach, but you need to be prepared for a sharp uptake. Once you're airborne, we'll start to reel you in towards the open tailgate. You might start to spin mid-air. If that happens, you'll be disorientated once you're on board. Don't try to stand. Last time someone did that, they walked straight out of the aircraft again.*'

'Thanks for the advice,' Zak muttered.

'*Say again?*'

'Nothing.'

He looked out to sea again. Huge peaks. Murky troughs. To jump in there felt like madness, but what choice did he have?

'I'm going in,' he shouted into the radio. 'Do me a favour and don't miss that balloon.'

'*Roger that. Good luck, son.*'

And the radio went dead.

Zak felt himself breathing hard. He was tiny among the waves. Insignificant. Like the forces of nature all around could crush him, if they wanted to, just as a human would swat a fly. Every cell in his body shrieked at him not to enter the water.

But the ship was sinking. He'd be entering the water anyway. It was just a matter of time.

He double-checked the straps on his harness. All tight. He made sure he could feel for the inflation toggle. Check.

And then he turned, faced out to sea and waited for a wave to swell so he wouldn't have so far to fall.

He didn't have long to wait.

The sea was high. The rain was heavy. The wind howled.

Zak filled his lungs with air and allowed himself to topple from the edge of the ship.

Two seconds later he hit the water.

He'd never known power like it. He immediately felt the currents sucking him down, like a hundred mermaids were pulling at his legs. He felt as if his whole body had filled with water, and the flotation aid that formed part of his harness didn't feel anything like up to the job of keeping him above sea level. Even though his eyes were open, he couldn't see anything in the murky water.

It was quiet under the water. He knew the storm was raging above him, but everything was eerily silent. Zak never thought he'd want to hear the sound of the storm again so much. His lungs started to burn. He didn't know if he was sinking because he didn't know which way was up. And he didn't know how long he'd been in the water. All he knew was that he needed oxygen.

Suddenly he was above the water again. His ears filled with the crashing, rushing sound of the waves as he gasped desperately for air. He was in the trough between two waves. Each of them was at least ten metres high, and he was unable to see the ship he'd just jumped from. He felt his body rising up with the swell of the sea. A moment later he could see the vessel. It was twenty metres away. Zak couldn't believe how quickly the currents had moved him.

He felt for the inflation toggle on his STARS harness and gave it a sharp tug. There was a sudden hissing as the balloon packed into the harness started to inflate. It took only a few seconds to reach its full size – a sphere a couple of metres in diameter. Zak lay on his back and allowed the balloon to rise up into the air, taking with it the thin, strong wire coiled round a pulley at the front of his harness. For a couple of seconds he could see the inside of the balloon flashing white. But then he was underwater again as the wave crested and currents knocked him around.

He was underwater for longer this time, or so it seemed. When he emerged again, coughing and spluttering, the ship was even further away and the balloon was thirty metres above him. It was being buffeted in the gale that howled all around, but it was still rising slowly.

Zak sank again. He tried to stay calm. This was the

third time the currents had pulled him down. He'd spent a lot of time in the water over the past few days, and he thought he knew what to expect. He thought he just had to hold his breath and wait until the flotation aid on his harness brought him to the surface again.

He was wrong.

Thirty seconds passed. His body started aching for oxygen. Surely he'd come to the surface any second now.

Forty-five seconds passed. He could sense his pulse slowing down; his lungs and abdomen shrieked with agony.

A minute. He was still underwater. The panic was subsiding. So was the pain. He felt woozy. Sleepy. Almost like he didn't care any more if he lived or died.

He felt his mouth opening. He was going to breathe in. Somewhere in the back of his mind he knew this meant his lungs would fill with water, but what did that matter? He was going to drown anyway . . .

When it came, it was like an electric shock. The harness tightened around him. Its straps dug into the flesh on his legs and arms. Suddenly he was moving faster than he'd ever moved before. The water rushed past him and in an instant he was out in the open air.

He inhaled noisily and felt the life surge back into him. Only then did he have the presence of mind to be scared.

Zak looked up. The Hercules was there. He could just make out the large V-shaped clip at the front of the aircraft that had grabbed hold of his STARS wire. He was rising fast. One moment the sea was just five metres below him as he skimmed at immense speed along the waves; the next it was twenty. Thirty . . .

The gale-force wind meant nothing to him now as he surged through the sky, praying that the wire would hold. He felt the plane swerve. From this new angle he could see a frigate in the distance. The SBS base. Had Bea made it? Was she getting the treatment she needed? Was she even still alive?

He rose higher and higher. And as he rose, he started to spin. Slowly at first, so the sea around him looked like a rotating disc. But it soon became a blur as he spun faster and faster, still screaming through the air and still ascending.

Zak closed his eyes. He had to, otherwise the nausea would overcome him. He tried to take deep breaths, but somehow it was difficult at this speed and this altitude. He was feeling weaker again. Woozier.

A new sound. Different from the rushing of the wind. Engines. Above him. Zak opened his eyes and instantly wished he hadn't because the whole earth seemed to be spinning. He clenched them shut again as the noise of engines grew louder.

Louder.

Louder.

All of a sudden he felt hands on his body and the sharp scraping of his skin against metal. He was being gripped and pulled. The sound of engines was screaming in his ears. He could do nothing except let it happen.

He was lying down, but still everything felt like it was spinning.

Zak dared to open his eyes. He saw three men looking over him, anxious frowns on their foreheads. Beyond them, the cavernous interior of the Hercules – all webbing straps and khaki-painted metal. The greasy stench of aviation gas. The throb and vibration of the engines.

Safety.

'*He's conscious*,' one of the men shouted.

'*Hold him down*,' yelled another. '*Don't let him get up and walk – not till the tailgate's closed.*'

Get up and walk? Zak was so exhausted he wondered if he'd ever get up and walk again.

'You OK, kid?' one of the men shouted. Zak saw now that he was wearing olive overalls and a large pair of earphones connected to the side of the plane by a long wire. He was screaming loudly to be heard, holding two thumbs up and wearing a quizzical look.

He nodded weakly, and tapped the flat of his hand against the solid floor of the Hercules – just to be sure he really was safe.

'Yeah, I think so,' Zak shouted back. 'Oh, and by the way . . .'

'What? *What?*'

'Thanks for the lift,' he said.

24

REVENGE

There had been several minutes of confusion on Hampstead Heath. Lights. Shouting. Ellie had seen the tranquillized form of her would-be assassin being carried away by armed police. Nobody seemed to pay her any attention. Suddenly they were all gone. All except Raf and Gabs.

Gabs helped Ellie up from the ground. 'Well done, sweetie. That took some courage. Our friend Calaca was caught red-handed. He won't be seeing anything with that one eye of his except the inside of a prison cell for a very long time to come.'

Ellie removed her woollen hat and the helmet it had been concealing. It was made from the same sturdy material as the body armour she was wearing underneath her clothes. She shook her hair out, not quite able to believe what she'd just done.

'Why were *you* pretending to be my boyfriend?' she asked Gabs. 'Why not Raf?'

'He's a little stocky for a fourteen-year-old boy, wouldn't you say?'

'He's also,' said Raf, holding up a Browning semi-automatic, 'a better shot for backup.'

Gabs grinned at Ellie. 'Harsh,' she said, 'but true.'

'You should get home,' Raf said. 'Your folks will be wondering where you are.'

'Will they find out about this?' Ellie asked. 'I mean, surely I'll be questioned and . . .'

'Don't worry, sweetie,' said Gabs as they walked away from the lake and towards the road. 'We have ways of sorting it. Nobody's going to know a thing. You can just get on with your life. Pretend it never happened.'

'Will I . . .' She chewed for a moment on her thumbnail. 'Will I see you again?'

'I really hope not.' Ellie felt herself blushing. 'Don't get me wrong, sweetie. It's just that we only tend to crop up when things are going badly.' Gabs smiled at her. 'With a bit of luck, everything will go right for you from now on. We'll just get you home safely first.'

She held out her hand, but Ellie didn't take it. Not yet. She had one more question to ask, but she wasn't sure she wanted to know the answer.

'That picture Calaca showed me. The first day I saw him in Burger King. It was of Zak. I just . . . I can't help thinking . . . I was just wondering . . .' She closed her eyes and took a deep breath. 'This is something to do with him. So does that mean he's still alive? Have you seen him? Do you *know* him?'

Ellie kept her eyes closed and felt herself wincing. She wanted Gabs to say yes. To tell her that her cousin was alive and well. But deep down she knew it was impossible. And the longer Gabs remained silent, the more she realized that she was clutching at straws.

'I'm sorry,' she said. 'It was a stupid question.' And she opened her eyes.

Ellie drew a sharp in breath. She spun round. 'Gabs?' she breathed. 'Raf? Where are you?' She peered into the darkness, and listened hard for the sound of footsteps.

But there were none. She spun round on the road by the heath, but her mysterious acquaintances had disappeared.

'Ellie Lewis?' There was a police car waiting, and a policewoman opened a door. 'We're to take you home,' she said. Ellie groaned. What would her parents say if they saw a police officer walking up to their front door *again*?

Having spent so much time in the water, Zak now felt as though he was living in the air. The Hercules to Ascension Island; a UN flight to Brize Norton; a chopper back to St Peter's Crag. He'd heard busy people say that their feet barely touched the ground. For Zak, it was true.

He slept wherever there was somewhere to rest his head. But his sleep, like so often, was filled with horrors. He saw water everywhere, and sinking ships. He saw corpses and jagged, bloodied knives. He saw Cruz: the look of madness on his face as he toppled into the sea. But these were not the greatest of the horrors that haunted him. Far worse were the faces.

There were three of them. The first was a girl with short red hair. Her skin was deathly white, her lips blue. In his dreams, Zak would look at Bea's shoulder to see the gun wound. The blood had started to clot, leaving a dark, wobbly jelly. Her body didn't move.

The second face was Ellie's. It was twisted into an expression of terror and she was screaming. The scream of someone who knew she was about to die.

And the third face? It was just as familiar. The sight of Calaca's one eye made dread seep into Zak's sleeping bones.

He woke with a start. For a moment he didn't know where he was. He didn't even know *when* he was. Then he vaguely remembered stumbling from the chopper that had set him down on the windswept heath in front of St Peter's House. Michael had been there, and Gabs and Raf; but Zak had been too exhausted even to speak to them. He'd gone straight to his room and slept, and dreamed.

Now, though, for the first time since he'd left Angola, he felt refreshed. Refreshed and full of questions. He pulled on a pair of jeans and a hooded top and touched his fingers to the doorknob of his room. The door recognized his fingerprint and opened. Zak hurried downstairs. Less than a minute later he was rapping on the door of Michael's impressive oak-panelled office. He didn't wait for an answer before striding in.

Nobody looked surprised to see him. Michael was sitting behind his large, old-fashioned desk; Raf and Gabs were side by side next to the fire. Only Gabs looked wary, as though she was unsure how Zak was going to react.

A silence in the room.

'Well?' Zak asked. He had one eyebrow raised.

'A necessary deception,' Michael said mildly.

'Necessary for who?'

'Just necessary.'

'Are there any more lies you want to tell me about? I mean, now would be a good time, wouldn't it? To get things out in the open?'

Michael said nothing. He just stared.

Zak lowered his head. He had questions to ask, but he wasn't sure he was ready for the answers.

'Bea?'

'Recovering nicely. I'm sure she'll be delighted that you asked.'

Zak closed his eyes. He couldn't allow himself to feel relieved just yet. 'And Ellie?' he whispered.

A pause.

'A little shaken up, I believe. Señor Ramirez is, as you know, a ruthless opponent. Happily Raphael and Gabriella were on hand to give her a little ... guidance.'

Zak looked up sharply. Both Raf and Gabs had mysterious smiles on their faces. He turned to Michael, whose green eyes twinkled. 'You knew,' he breathed. 'You knew Calaca was targeting Ellie. That's what this has all been about?'

'I've been keeping my eye on Messrs Martinez and Ramirez, if that's what you mean. The day I realized Ellie was in danger, I decided it was time to act. I mean, I wouldn't be much of a guardian angel,' Michael replied, 'if I didn't keep one eye on the things I know are important to you. I think you'll find, Zak, that Calaca won't be bothering your cousin any longer.'

'Is he dead?'

Michael smiled. 'Not dead, no. But imprisoned in the UK and awaiting trial. We'll see to it that his sentence is ... appropriate to his crimes. Tell me, Zak, are you familiar with the Greek myth of the hydra?'

Zak gave him a confused look. What did the hydra have to do with anything? 'Yeah, it was a snake or something. Loads of heads. Cut one off and another grew, right?'

'Quite right, Zak. Calaca was like one of the heads of the hydra. It was necessary to chop it off, but if Ellie was ever going to be truly safe, the hydra itself had to be dealt with.'

'You mean Cruz?'

'Very good, Zak. But Cruz Martinez was hard to get to. If we were to neutralize him, we needed to get *him* to come to *us*. That was why I needed you on the MV *Mercantile*.'

'I was bait,' Zak challenged.

'Really, Zak, you do have a knack for choosing the most unpalatable words to describe these things.'

'Why couldn't you just tell me all this in the first place?'

'Because I knew you would be captured and possibly tortured. If you told your captors your true identity, that would be one thing. But if you had told them you were really on board to draw Cruz out from hiding, he would never have ventured out of Mexico. So you see, it really was necessary, if we were to prevent another hydra's head threatening Ellie's life. I had to make a call, Zak. I had to decide whether, if you were in full possession of the facts, you would have embarked upon such a dangerous mission in order to save the life of your cousin. I decided, on balance, that you would.'

'So you did all that just for Ellie?' he demanded.

'Honestly?'

'Honestly.'

'No. I did it because I knew Ellie's death would hit you hard. Maybe even make you think twice about what you are doing here. For my superiors, that would be . . . unacceptable.'

'And that's it?'

Michael inclined his head. 'Cruz has been on our hit list ever since you saw him last,' he said.

Zak was quiet for a moment. There was, after all, not much he could say to that. When he spoke, he could hear a dark tone to his voice. 'He won't be threatening anyone ever again. He's dead. I saw him fall overboard. I think he committed suicide.'

'I'd like to say I'm sorry about that,' Michael observed, and suddenly the twinkle left his eyes and his face hardened. 'But it would be a lie. The world is better off without murderers in it.'

Zak remembered one of the last things Cruz had said to him. *Whatever I am – you made me.* 'He wasn't always a murderer,' he said quietly.

'Nobody was *always* a murderer, Zak. Every man chooses his own path.'

He thought of the madness in the eyes of his former friend. 'But some people have help,' he murmured. 'What about Black Wolf?'

Michael shrugged. 'With Cruz no longer around to mastermind it, I expect it will fade away. The *Mercantile* did sink, along with the diamonds. That would have hit the organization hard.' Michael sounded satisfied about that.

Zak looked towards Raf and Gabs. 'Does Ellie know?' he asked. 'About me? That I'm still alive?'

'She had her suspicions, sweetie,' Gabs said. 'She's a bright girl. Brave too.' She glanced meaningfully towards Michael. 'She'd make a good agent.' Michael didn't look like he'd even heard her. 'But it's better that she thinks you're dead. Safer. You understand, don't you?'

Zak nodded. He walked across the room and looked out through the tall windows to the sea beyond. It was overcast and choppy, but compared to what he was used to, it was practically still.

'Bea told me she was Agent 20.'

Raf and Gabs glanced towards Michael again. He stayed silent.

'Will I see her again?'

Again, nothing.

'I have something you might like to see, Zak,' said Michael finally. He held up what looked like a photograph. Zak stepped forward to take it. It was an aerial photograph of a town by the sea. He could make out a series of jetties on the beach, and a long road leading up from the water in the main town.

'It's Lobambo,' he said.

'One of our spy satellites took this image yesterday. And this one.' He handed Zak a second photograph, more close-up than the first. It took a while to work out what it showed, but after a few seconds something clicked in Zak's brain.

'The school,' he said. Already he could see that the walls had been half built. 'Marcus and the others, they've made a start!'

'I was rather disappointed, Zak, when I heard that you'd been interfering in local affairs. I thought we discussed that before you left. And I hear that your friend Malek was somewhat displeased too.'

Zak felt a twinge of embarrassment at the memory of his friend's anger.

But Michael smiled. If he truly was disappointed, he didn't show it. 'Ntole and his men have left the village,' he said. 'It appears your little game rather embarrassed them. The building work is making good progress. I understand, for what it's worth, that Malek has been trying to track you down to apologize. He won't succeed, of course, but . . .'

'Thank you, Michael,' Zak said quietly. 'It's worth

a lot.' He turned to Raf and Gabs. 'And thanks for looking after Ellie,' he said. 'If anything had happened to her because of me, I'd . . .'

He didn't finish his sentence. The truth was, he didn't know *what* he'd do.

Gabs stepped towards him and put a reassuring arm on his shoulder. 'Hey,' she said. 'Don't mention it. We're all family now, after all. And you did more than any of us to keep her safe. No more Cruz, no more danger.'

Zak smiled. 'Oh yeah?' he asked.

'Well' – Gabs grinned – 'maybe for a while. But you know, I can't help thinking life would get a bit boring if we didn't have a bit of mortal peril, just to keep us on our toes. Don't you think?'

Her grin grew even broader and she suddenly started to laugh. It was infectious. Zak couldn't help but join in.

The spy satellite that had taken the imagery of Lobambo was capable of circling the Earth seven times a day. From high up in the atmosphere, it could covertly take pictures of minute detail. It could track cars. Ships. It could even, if the conditions were right, identify individuals.

If, at that moment, it had directed its attention to a small patch of sea two nautical miles from Ascension

REVENGE

Island in the Atlantic, at a bearing of thirteen degrees, it might have picked up several bodies. They were fat and bloated with death. The wild sea had knocked several limbs out of place, which were now pointing out at crooked, irregular angles. Flesh had already started to rot from the faces. It meant that Eduardo, if the spy satellite had focused in on him, would have been quite unrecognizable. The same went for Karlovic, and for *el capitán*, who looked more frightening in death than he ever had in life. Maybe these bodies would eventually be washed up on some distant shore. Maybe they would eaten by creatures of the deep. Maybe they were destined just to travel the oceans until they rotted down into nothingness.

But the spy satellite was not trained on these gruesome corpses. It was somewhere else entirely. There was no shortage of surveillance targets, after all. And so it did not see the shingle beach on the north-east coast of Ascension Island. It did not see a figure emerge from the water, stagger onto dry land and collapse when the young man's knees could no longer carry him. It did not see his dark skin or dark hair, or his lean body, as he lay unconscious on the beach.

And of course it did not see his dreams. Dreams that were filled with just two things: the face of Agent 21, and Cruz's own thoughts of revenge.

IS STILL ON DUTY.

Look out for him in the thrilling book three, coming soon . . .

Some authors just write about it. Chris Ryan has been there, done it – and here is the gripping real-life tale . . .

Read on for an extract from *The One That Got Away*

Now available for younger readers for the first time, adapted from the huge, best-selling personal account.

It was a tough decision. My last friend had disappeared . . .
I checked my compass and started walking north. Alone.

During the Gulf War in 1991, Chris Ryan became separated from the other members of the SAS patrol, Bravo Two Zero.

Alone, he beat off an Iraqi attack and set out for Syria. Over the next seven days he walked almost 200 miles, his life constantly in danger.

Of the eight SAS members involved in this famous mission, only one escaped capture. This is his story . . .

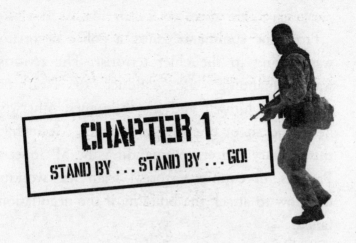

CHAPTER 1
STAND BY ... STAND BY ... GO!

Our target was a disused mental hospital.

Five terrorists were inside, holding nine hostages captive. After a three-day siege, matters were moving swiftly to a head.

As commander of the SAS eight-man sniper team of 'B' Squadron, I was in charge of seven other men. We were positioned with our rifles at observation points in outhouses, trees and on the ground. Two men were watching each face of the hospital and sending back running commentaries over their throat-mike radios to the command centre. This had been set up in a separate building 200 metres from the front door. Each face of the hospital had been given a special code so that everyone knew which bit they were talking about.

From the command centre a police negotiator was talking to the chief terrorist. The terrorist was demanding safe conduct to Heathrow airport for himself and his colleagues; otherwise he would shoot one of the hostages. Meanwhile, the military officer commanding the SP (Special Projects, or counter-terrorist) team was working out how to attack the building if the negotiations failed.

Suddenly a shot cracked out from within the hospital. A hostage had been executed. The terrorists called for a stretcher party to take the body away. The front door opened briefly, and a limp figure was bundled out. A four-man team ran over to collect it. Then the chief terrorist threatened to kill another hostage in half an hour if his demands were not met.

The moment had come for the police to hand over to the military. The police chief signed a written order passing command to the OC (Officer Commanding) of 'B' Squadron, the senior SAS officer present. The OC then gave the three eight-man assault teams their orders. The moment he had finished, the men moved to their entry points.

Now it was just a question of waiting for my snipers to get as many terrorists in their sights as possible. Listening to our commentaries on the radio, the OC suddenly called out the order we'd all been waiting for:

'I have control. STAND BY . . . STAND BY . . . GO!'

For the past two days the grounds of the old hospital had been eerily silent. Now the whole place erupted into action. Two vehicles screamed up to the building and a swarm of black-clad assaulters jumped out. Explosive charges blew in the windows. Within seconds, a Chinook helicopter was poised above the roof and more black figures were fast-roping out of it, abseiling down to the windows or entering through the skylights. Stun grenades blasted off; smoke poured out. The radio carried a babble of shots, shouts, explosions and orders.

In a matter of minutes the building had been cleared, the five terrorists killed and the remaining eight hostages rescued. The assault commander reported that he had control, and command was formally handed back to the police.

* * *

On this occasion, this had all been just an exercise – but as always, the assault had been realistic in every detail, and had been excellent training. Just another day for the Regiment, as members of the SAS refer to themselves. And exactly the kind of task we could at any time be called upon to perform, efficiently and explosively. Practice was essential.

'Well done, everybody,' the OC told us. 'That was pretty good.'

We packed our kit into the vehicles and set out for SAS headquarters in Hereford. But on the way events took an unexpected turn.

It was 2 August 1990, and on the news we heard that Saddam Hussein, the tyrannical leader of Iraq, had just invaded Kuwait, a small country on his southern border.

'So what?' said one of the guys scornfully. 'Saddam's an idiot.'

'Don't be too sure of it,' said someone else. 'It'll make big trouble, and we'll probably find ourselves out there.'

He was right. Saddam's invasion of Kuwait was the opening salvo of the 1990–1991 Gulf War. I don't think any of us realized just how this news would change our lives.

* * *

For the next two months, nobody knew what was going to happen. The leaders of different governments around the world got together to discuss the situation and the UN Security Council called for Iraq to withdraw from Kuwait – and gave them a deadline. When the Iraqis did not leave Kuwait, a war was inevitable. In total thirty-four countries joined together in a coalition to oppose Saddam Hussein. These countries included not only the USA and Great Britain but also Arab countries in the Middle East region, like Egypt and Syria.

'A' and 'D' Squadron went out to the Gulf for build-up training; but me and my mates in 'B' Squadron were told we wouldn't be going, as it was our turn to take over what are known in the SAS as team tasks – assignments for which small teams of men are needed in various parts of the world.

The SAS is made up of four squadrons – A, B, D and G. Each squadron is made up of four troops – Air Troop, Mountain Troop, Boat Troop and Mobility Troop. There should be sixteen men in each troop, but because it is so difficult to get into the SAS, there are often as few as eight.

Rumours started to fly. Some people said we might become sky-marshals on civilian flights to the Middle East. It would mean pretending to be normal passengers, but in fact carrying weapons to deal with any terrorist who might attempt a hijack. The idea seemed quite likely – on the SP team we'd done lots of assaults on and inside aircraft, so we knew what to do.

But then, a week before Christmas, we were dragged into the briefing room at Hereford and told that half of 'B' Squadron was going to deploy to the Middle East after all.

That meant me.